The Tome of Blighted Horrors

for use with The Blight: Richard Pett's Crooked City

`I0611106`

Credits

Authors
John Ling, Richard Pett, Pete Pollard,
Alistair Rigg, Jeff Swank,
and Greg A. Vaughan

Based on original material by
Richard Pett

Developers
Alistair Rigg and Greg A. Vaughan

Producer
Bill Webb

Editor
Jeff Harkness

5E Rules Conversion
Steve Winter

Layout and Graphic Design
Charles A. Wright

Cover Design
Charles A. Wright

Interior Art
Terry Pavlet, Peter Fairfax, and Felipe Gaona

FROG GOD GAMES IS

CEO
Bill Webb

**Creative Director:
Swords & Wizardry**
Matthew J. Finch

**Creative Director:
Pathfinder Roleplaying Game**
Greg A. Vaughan

Art Director
Charles A. Wright

Lead Developer
John Ling

Marketing Manager
Chris Haskins

Customer Service Manager
Krista Webb

Zach of All Trades
Zach Glazar

Espieglerie
Skeeter Green

**5TH EDITION RULES,
1ST EDITION FEEL**

**FROG
GOD
GAMES**

5th Edition Fantasy

Other Products from Frog God Games

You can find these product lines and more at our website, **froggodgames.com**, and on the shelves of many retail game stores. Superscripts indicate the available game systems: "PF" means the Pathfinder Roleplaying Game, "5e" means Fifth Edition, and "S&W" means *Swords & Wizardry*. If there is no superscript it means that it is not specific to a single rule system.

GENERAL RESOURCES

Swords & Wizardry Complete [S&W]
The Tome of Horrors Complete [PF, S&W]
Tome of Horrors 4 [PF, S&W]
Tome of Adventure Design
Monstrosities [S&W]
Bill Webb's Book of Dirty Tricks
Razor Coast: Fire as She Bears [PF]
Book of Lost Spells [5e, PF]
Fifth Edition Foes [5e]
The Tome of Blighted Horrors [5e, PF, S&W]
Book of Alchemy* [5e, PF, S&W]

THE LOST LANDS

Rappan Athuk [PF, S&W]
Rappan Athuk Expansions Vol. I [PF, S&W]
The Slumbering Tsar Saga [PF, S&W]
The Black Monastery [PF, S&W]
Cyclopean Deeps Vol. I [PF, S&W]
Cyclopean Deeps Vol. II [PF, S&W]
Razor Coast [PF, S&W]
Razor Coast: Heart of the Razor [PF, S&W]
Razor Coast: Freebooter's Guide to the Razor Coast [PF, S&W]
LL0: The Lost Lands Campaign Setting* [5e, PF, S&W]
LL1: Stoneheart Valley [PF, S&W]

LL2: The Lost City of Barakus [PF, S&W]
LL3: Sword of Air [PF, S&W]
LL4: Cults of the Sundered Kingdoms [PF, S&W]
LL5: Borderland Provinces [5e, PF, S&W]
LL6: The Northlands Saga Complete [PF, S&W]
LL7: The Blight [5e, PF, S&W]
LL8: Bard's Gate [5e, PF, S&W]
LL9: Adventures in the Borderland Provinces [5e, PF, S&W]

QUESTS OF DOOM

Quests of Doom (Vol. 1) [5e]
Quests of Doom (Vol. 2) [5e]
Quests of Doom (includes the 5e Vol. 1 and 2, but for PF and S&W only) [PF, S&W]
Quests of Doom 2 [5e]
Quests of Doom 3 [5e, S&W]
Quests of Doom 4* [5e, PF, S&W]

PERILOUS VISTAS

Dead Man's Chest (pdf only) [PF]
Dunes of Desolation [PF]
Fields of Blood [PF]
Mountains of Madness [PF]
Marshes of Malice [PF]

* (forthcoming from **Frog God Games**)

Table of Contents

Introduction

Let's be honest with ourselves for a moment: I think we all kind of already knew that Richard Pett is a little messed up, right? I mean, **Frog God Games** agreeing to publish *The Blight* didn't bring about the book's inception — it was something Richard had already written … years before … for his players at home! (God rest their sanity-blasted souls.) So when we decided that he had created a sufficient number of new monsters for the book to justify an entire *Tome of Horrors* — a *Tome of* Blighted *Horrors*, if you will — I don't think anyone was surprised by the disturbing segments of brain-matter-given-life that tumbled out of Richard's skull. But when we asked a handful of other writers, veteran and novice alike, to contribute to this compilation of congealed madness, the horrors that tumbled from their own mental palettes, well … there's where the surprise — the kind of surprise that begins as a startle and then slowly transforms into numbing horror — really began.

I have only myself to blame really. When Richard and I were first spit balling this project (originally intended to be a release for Sinister Adventures) years ago, I sat down to write an additional adventure set in Rich's diabolically twisted playground. I read through Richard's material, permitted myself a cruel chuckle at its depravity, read as many forbidden, sanity-destroying tomes as I could get my hands on through Amazon (who knew they had Ludwig Prinn's *De Vermis Mysteriis* in paperback!!), and then sat down at my keyboard deciding to channel my inner Pett. I thought I'd delve a little into the body horror for which Richard has such an affinity and … babies! … nothing's scarier than larval humans, right? So this little descent into madness brought about the introduction of the insidious spite-waif. "Heh, heh," I thought, "that'll scare 'em." Fast forward to 2016 when I began to get turnovers in from the various other authors hired to contribute to the new ***Tome of Blighted Horrors***.

Some things I learned:

1. Yes, babies are truly scary. Having spawned three of the little monsters myself, I should have already known this, but the proof came in the form of how many of the authors dipped into the same well (without prompting). And how much their creations frightened me. From Richard's own totally-unnecessary-why-did-he-do-it-for-the-love-of-God-why? caul cuckoo and caul cuckoo syre, I soon realized I was in trouble. The true shock, however, didn't come until I laid eyes on the work from freshman designer Jeff Swank, when he sent in his totally original monster design of the gravid ghoul. Jeff is a doctor, I must add. I think, perhaps, I should reflect a bit on my own career choice after this …

2. Artists aren't always quite as on board with the insanity. Terry Pavlet (bless his heart) took on the task of illustrating about 99% of this beast. I don't know Terry well, but I don't think his background is specifically in dark fantasy art because of how many times he asked me for an example of what I was trying to describe in my art orders. No, Terry, there is no example I can give you for which we can thank God, natural selection, and a merciful universe. There are no examples because these things weren't meant to exist in a universe governed by scientific laws. I can't blame him though. Trying to illustrate the interior of Richard's brain is like trying to illustrate a Lovecraft story. It's tough to come up with a concept sketch off the description, "the terrible thing is indescribable." I did my best. I can't tell you how many email replies I received from Terry that started with, "Hahahahahahahaha!" Kudos to you, Terry. You're a real trooper. We are deeply indebted to your patience and creative skills. In reward for this, you shall be the last to be eaten.

3. I believe Friedrich Nietzsche said, "[I]f you gaze long into an abyss, the abyss also gazes into you." Yeah, that sounds about right.

Now if you'll excuse me, I can hear them thumping around in the basement again. Mustn't let anyone get free before the big ceremony.

Iä! Iä! The Beautiful fhtagn!

— Greg A. Vaughan
July 19th
(1973 – 2016)

Foreword

The first time I met Richard Pett, an exuberant Nicolas Logue—no doubt channeling a scene from the Grast Farm in his infamous *Hook Mountain Massacre*—was holding him down on a leather couch while attempting to wear him like a glove puppet. I was pretty drunk, granted, but I'm fairly certain that Nick failed in his anatomic insertion attempt, and thus Rich's identity as the true author of *The Skinsaw Murders* was defended…much to Nick's chagrin.

The second time I met Richard Pett, I was far less drunk and Nick was nowhere in sight, so we talked about adventure and setting design. Rich, as you're surely aware, is a master of both. His work for Paizo may be among his best known, having written—to date, because there are no signs of him stopping—twelve parts of Pathfinder adventure paths—from the aforementioned chapter of *Rise of the Runelords* to *The Whisper Out of Time* in the imminent *Strange Aeons*—and five Pathfinder modules, including *Carrion Hill* and the popular *We Be Goblins* series.

However, I'd been a fan since his earliest publications in *Dungeon Magazine* where he, along with Nick, first established his design credentials and rose to prominence. And so we talked a little about *The Devil Box* and of his contributions to the 'proto-paths,' including *The Prince of Redhand* and the Midnight's Muddle and Alhaster backdrops for *Age of Worms*, along with *The Sea-Wyvern's Wake* and *Serpents of Scuttlecove* for *Savage Tide*. But we spent the most time discussing what are perhaps now regarded as his seminal works: *The Styes* and *The Weavers*. These were the inventive, gritty, stylish scenarios that first distinguished him and I wanted to know all about their evocative setting and any other adventures within it that I may have missed.

That's when I learned of his long-running home campaign and its vast body of unpublished works based in those shadowed and sleazy docklands. And not only that, but that he was organizing and updating it all in preparation for future publication through Frog God Games. I immediately offered my help and, a few weeks later, the manuscript of *The Crucible* arrived in my inbox, ready for conversion, development, and editing, and my descent into what would become *The Blight* began. That was over three years ago.

What you now hold in your hands—this nexus of nightmare—is a distillation of the spiritual abuse that Mr Pett has inflicted upon Greg, Jeff, John, Dave, Pete, or I at some point over that time. For while Rich himself has personally detailed only a handful of the monstrosities herein, you'll notice that almost all are inspired by something he'd already described in *The Blight*. Crones whose emetic, morbidly obese bodies can barely withstand the intake of each of their five heads' prodigious appetites for flesh. Insane reincarnations of the devolved bodies of plague victims that morph through aberrant physicalities to further spread death and disease. Emaciated fey who float up from the depths of the Lyme to flood the lungs of their hypnotized victims through a kiss. Small slimy humanoids who compress their cartilaginous skeletons to live in the wall and floor spaces of other peoples' homes and watch their intimacies.

"Based on material by Richard Pett."

It's not a credit, it's a mental health warning. For herein, you'll also find fiendish entities of flame that grow in size and power as they incinerate people; 'machines' of reanimated muscle and tissue which sometimes manifest an emergent consciousness that reflects the thoughts, fears, and desires of those who operate them; incarnations of arachnophobia whose young eat their way out of their victims' stomachs; and the freakish hybrids that result from the amoral application of obscene fertility magic.

So that's nice. As he proved to Nick, Rich is no other designer's meat puppet. But the truth is, some of us may now be his.

— Alistair J. Rigg
September 9th, 2016
Sydney, Australia

Bileborn

This revolting creature appears to be formed of a tangle of limbs and pieces of rotting corpses that splay in all directions like some kind of demented sea urchin. The many appendages flail spastically as it moves with a disturbing, rolling motion. Barely discernible amid this tangle are a number of severed, rotting heads, their eyes open and watching, their lips wordlessly mouthing unheard imprecations.

Bileborn

Large undead, chaotic evil

Armor Class 14 (natural armor)
Hit Points 110 (13d10 + 39)
Speed 30 ft.

STR	DEX	CON	INT	WIS	CHA
19 (+4)	10 (+0)	17 (+3)	6 (-2)	10 (+0)	10 (+0)

Skills Perception +3
Damage Resistances bludgeoning, piercing, and slashing from nonmagical weapons
Damage Immunities poison
Condition Immunities exhaustion, frightened, poisoned, prone, unconscious
Senses darkvision 60 ft., passive Perception 13
Languages Common
Challenge 6 (2,300 XP)

Coordinated Burst (1/day). As a bonus action, the bileborn synchronizes its flailing motion. Its speed increases to 60 feet, and it can make 8 slam attacks on its turn. This effect lasts until the end of the bileborn's current turn.
Many Arms. Creatures have disadvantage on attempts to escape from the bileborn's grapple.

ACTIONS
Multiattack. The bileborn makes four melee attacks, using any combination of Slam and Absorb. It can use its Babbling Scream in place of two melee attacks.
Slam. *Melee Weapon Attack:* +7 to hit (reach 5 ft.; one creature). *Hit:* 1d8 + 4 bludgeoning damage. If two or more slam attacks hit the same creature in the bileborn's turn, the creature is grappled (escape DC 14).
Absorb. *Melee Weapon Attack:* +7 to hit (reach 5 ft.; one creature already grappled by the bileborn). *Hit:* 2d6 + 4 piercing damage, and the creature is pulled into the bileborn's space and absorbed into the monster's body. An absorbed creature is blinded and restrained, and it takes 2d6 + 4 piercing damage at the start of the bileborn's turn. One Medium creature or two Small creatures can be inside the bileborn at one time. An absorbed creature is unaffected by anything happening outside the bileborn or by attacks from outside it. An absorbed creature can escape from the bileborn's body by using an action to make a successful DC 14 Strength (Athletics) check, or it can get out after the bileborn's death by using 5 feet of movement.
Babbling Scream (recharge 5-6). The bileborn screams in incoherent babbles. All creatures within 60 feet that hear it must make a successful DC 13 Wisdom saving throw or be confused (as the *confusion* spell) for 1 minute. At the end of each of its turns, an affected target can make a Wisdom saving throw. If it succeeds, this effect ends for that target.

ECOLOGY
Environment any land
Organization solitary

The bileborn is an undead creature born of alchemical and necromantic experimentation. Its purpose and the identity of its creator are unknown, but the mistakes of this master have long since been paid for, as the original bileborn ultimately escaped and slew its creator, incorporating his body among the rest.

A bileborn seeks to increase its mass by absorbing creatures into its body. This does not increase the creature's size or change it in any fundamental way, but the crowd of body parts grows denser at its center. Then at some indeterminate point, the creature reproduces by fission. The fused conglomeration of rotten body parts splits down the middle, forming two bileborns of equal size and power. These instinctively avoid each other as they go their own ways in search of victims to absorb.

These creatures are little more than horrid masses of dismembered and absorbed victims that somehow work in necromantic coordination and demonstrate considerable stealth and surprising speed for their size and composition. Despite their chaotic and jumbled appearances, their fleshy mass is physically tough, quickly using the dismembered parts of its interior to switch out damaged limbs on it exterior. The bulk of its absorbed brain tissue resides within the severed heads of the central mass of the creature, allowing it to function in a rational manner, though its purpose and goals are likely to be inscrutable to living, sane creatures.

Body Snatcher

A massive lump of shadow, like a gargantuan hillock, shifts in the darkness and reveals itself to be a living creature. Its body is mostly torso and is roughly barrel shaped, with four elephantine legs and two long arms ending in three-fingered hands. A massive mouthlike opening dominates the top of its frame, from which extends a long, prehensile tongue studded with spiky growths at its tip. The entire beast appears to be covered in — or perhaps made of — a lumpy, lichenlike substance of tiny, leafy growths.

Body Snatcher

Gargantuan plant (fungus), neutral evil

Armor Class 19 (natural armor)
Hit Points 264 (16d20 + 96)
Speed 40 ft., climb 30 ft., swim 30 ft.

STR	DEX	CON	INT	WIS	CHA
24 (+7)	12 (+1)	22 (+6)	13 (+1)	10 (+0)	10 (+0)

Saving Throws Dex +6, Wis +5, Cha +5
Skills Perception +5
Damage Resistances cold; bludgeoning, piercing, and slashing from nonmagical weapons
Damage Immunities psychic
Condition Immunities charmed, frightened, prone, stunned, unconscious
Senses blindsight 60 ft., passive Perception 15
Languages understands all spoken languages, but can't speak
Challenge 15 (13,000 XP)

Absorb Cadaver. A creature slain by the body snatcher is immediately absorbed into its body as a bonus action. If the body snatcher is still alive at the end of its next turn, the cadaver is irrevocably destroyed. If the slain creature was Large, then its body takes 2 rounds to destroy, and a Huge creature takes 3 rounds. Creatures larger than Huge can't be absorbed. If the body snatcher is killed before an absorbed cadaver is fully destroyed, then the body (or parts of it) it can be recovered from among the mounds of blight lichen.

Hive Mind. The body snatcher can't be surprised. In addition, the body snatcher is aware of all growths of blight within 50 miles. It can see everything within visual range of these patches at all times. It can direct the direction and speed of a patch's growth (no action required) as long as that patch is in darkness, but it can control only one patch per round. A patch of blight that's in complete darkness and under a body snatcher's control can increase its size by 100 square feet per round.

Light Somnolence. When exposed to bright light, the body snatcher becomes slow and lethargic; the effect is equivalent to a *slow* spell, and it lasts for as long as at least half of the body snatcher is in bright light.

Regeneration. The body snatcher heals 10 hit points at the start of its turn. This ability doesn't function if any part of it was exposed to bright or dim light since its previous turn.

Swallow. A swallowed creature is blinded and restrained. It must hold its breath or begin suffocating. Two Large, four Medium, or eight Small creatures can be inside the body snatcher at one time. A swallowed creature is unaffected by anything happening outside the body snatcher or by attacks from outside it. A swallowed creature can get out of the body snatcher by using 5 feet of movement, but only after the monster is dead.

ACTIONS

Multiattack. The body snatcher spits out a spore globule, slams twice, and makes either a tongue attack or a bite attack.

Slam. *Melee Weapon Attack:* +12 to hit (reach 5 ft.; one

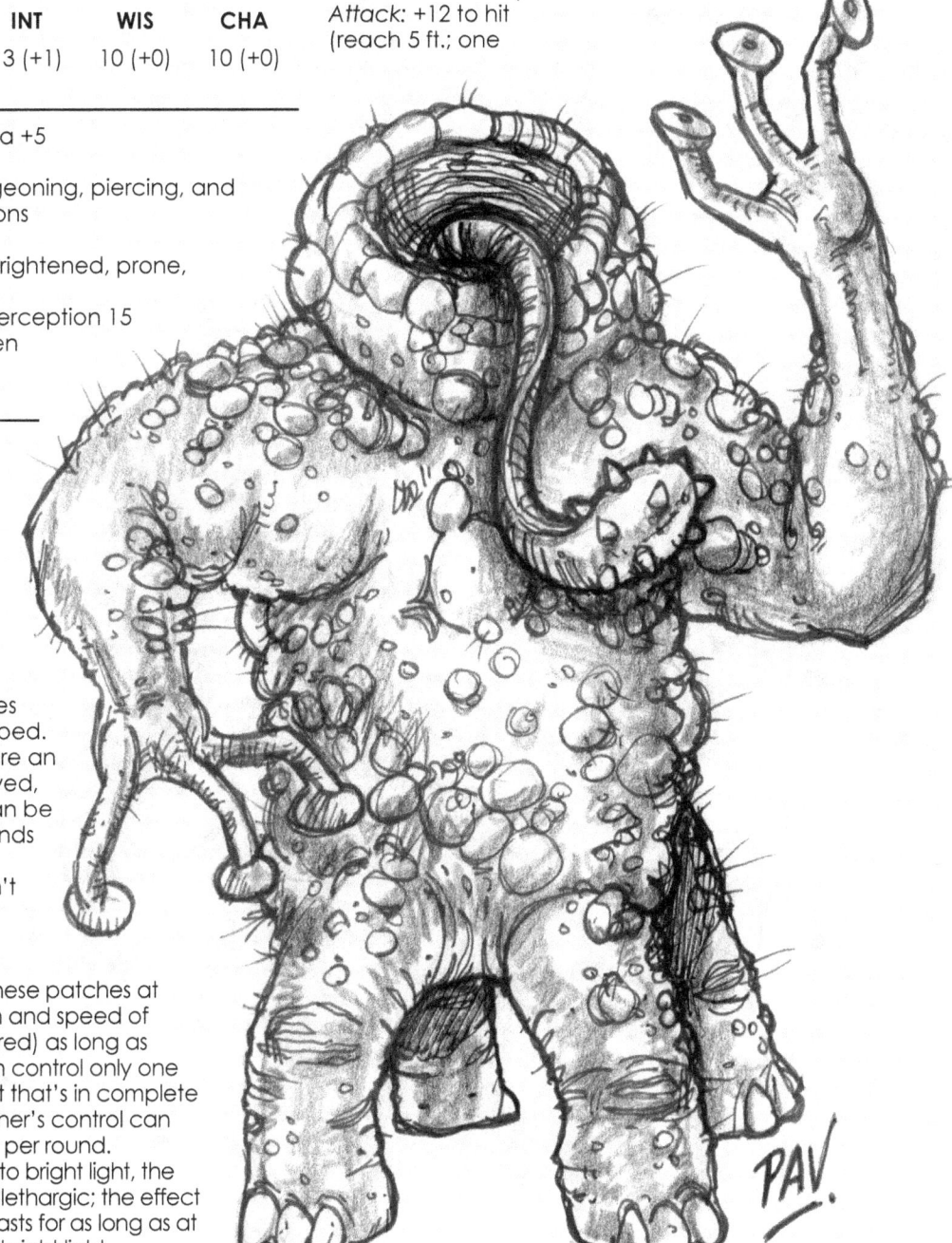

creature). *Hit:* 4d8 + 7 bludgeoning damage.

Tongue. *Melee Weapon Attack:* +12 to hit (reach 10 ft.; one creature). *Hit:* 3d6 + 7 slashing damage, and the creature must make a successful DC 20 Strength saving throw or be grappled (escape DC 17). The body snatcher can grapple one creature at a time and can't use its tongue attack while it has a creature grappled.

Bite. *Melee Weapon Attack:* +12 to hit (reach 10 ft; one creature already grappled by the body snatcher's tongue). *Hit:* the creature is pulled into the body snatcher's space and swallowed (see above).

Spore Globule. *Ranged Weapon Attack:* +6 to hit (range 40 ft.; one creature). *Hit:* 6d6 + 1 bludgeoning damage.

Create Blight. The body snatcher exudes a 10-foot-by-10-foot patch of blight (see Appendix C) in an area adjacent to itself. This patch is immediately eligible to be grown and directed as part of the body snatcher's Hive Mind ability.

ECOLOGY

Environment underground (the Blight)
Organization solitary

Known only as the Body Snatcher by the dwarves of the Underneath, this massive overgrowth of ambulatory blight lichen lurks in the deepest caverns where the boundaries between the mundane world and Between are thinnest. The creature somehow possesses sentience — likely from its long exposure to the strange influence of that other-realm — and shares some traits of Between creatures. The conglomeration of lichen growths has taken on the form of a massive quadruped, but it shares no special affinity with that form and, in truth, its body possesses no internal organs or structures other than the undifferentiated blight of which is it composed.

The Body Snatcher, like the blight that makes up its body, is at its strongest in absolute darkness and is debilitated by the presence of bright light. Its hive mind gives it a mental connection to and the ability to see through all growths of blight within 50 miles, and it is with this ability that it has managed to maintain observation of the lands above and its inhabitants since before the city existed. Through this observation, it has learned much of the ways of humanoids and has come to understand many of their languages. And it desires nothing more than to consume their bodies upon their deaths, directing its remote blight growths to do that whenever possible. The nutrients obtained from the consumed corpses help feed the growth of these blight patches, but something about these feedings is somehow transmitted telepathically back through the hive mind and serves some mysterious purpose for the Body Snatcher. It is for this reason that the dwarves gave the Body Snatcher its name, though none understand the full significance of the creature's impulse to consume these corpses. Whatever the reason, most speculate it has something to do with the creature's proximity to Between and that it is unlikely to have any benign purpose.

The Body Snatcher stands 25 feet tall. Even though it is made only of tiny lichen growths, these conglomerate quite densely so the creature weighs more than 30,000 pounds. It is well over a thousand years old and is probably much older, and it may well be immortal.

Copyright Notice
Author Greg A. Vaughan, based on material by Richard Pett.

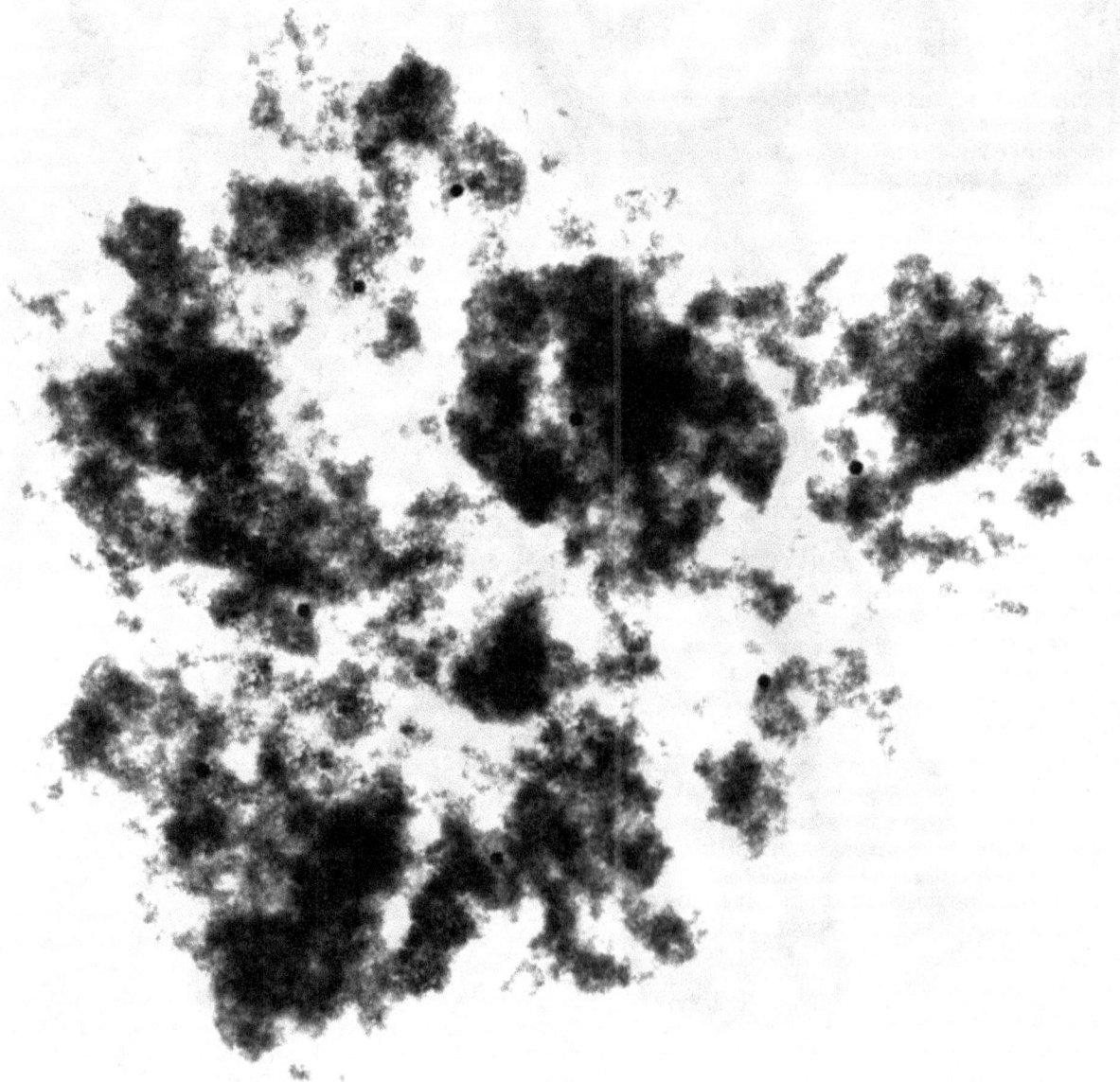

Bog Lantern

A ball of pale yellow light bobs and floats in the distance, its flickering pattern beckoning.

Bog Lantern
Small undead, neutral evil

Armor Class 15
Hit Points 68 (8d6 + 40)
Speed fly 50 ft. (hover)

STR	DEX	CON	INT	WIS	CHA
1 (-5)	20 (+5)	10 (+0)	9 (-1)	18 (+4)	8 (-1)

Saving Throws Con +3, Cha +2
Skills Deception +5, Perception +7, Stealth +8
Damage Resistances all damage types except force
Damage Immunities poison
Condition Immunities exhaustion, frightened, grappled, poisoned, prone, restrained, unconscious
Senses darkvision 60 ft., passive Perception 17
Languages understands Common, but can't speak
Challenge 5 (1,800 XP)

Out of Phase.
Bog lanterns exist partially in the Ethereal Plane and partially in the Material Plane. This accounts for their resistance to most damage. Weapons, spells, and other attacks that are capable of striking into the Ethereal Plane or that come from ethereal attackers aren't affected by this resistance.

ACTIONS
Mind Bend. *Melee Spell Attack:* +8 to hit (reach 5 ft.; one creature). *Hit:* 1d10 + 4 psychic damage plus 1 level of exhaustion, and the creature must make a successful DC 15 Wisdom saving throw or lose 2 points from Intelligence and Wisdom. The target dies if this reduces its Intelligence or Wisdom to 0. Otherwise, the reduction lasts until the target finishes a short or long rest.

ECOLOGY
Environment swamp
Organization solitary

Whether the bog lantern is simply an undead will-o'-wisp raised by some odd negative energy current within the Great Lyme River or a separate creature that is superficially similar is unknown. The only traits the bog lantern seems to share with its potential cousin are its appearance and a desire to lure passers-by off the relative safety of the roads and paths meandering through the boglands that surround the Lyme.

A typical bog lantern is about 3 feet in diameter. Most of the time, they opt to float 4 to 5 feet off the ground, though they can move around in three-dimensional space adroitly.

On closer inspection, a bog lantern is observed to resemble a glowing skull etched with hundreds of mysterious runes that appear to penetrate completely through the glowing bone into its dark, inscrutable interior. A pair of glowing points of light hover within its dark eye sockets.

Unlike the will-o'-wisp, a bog lantern cannot alter its color, brightness, or pattern of illumination. It is an "always on" glowing ball shedding yellow light equal to a torch. To simulate flickering patterns, bog lanterns move in and out of brush and other foliage, or cause their eye socket lights to roam around within the dark interior to cause light to shine intermittently through the dark runes that cover its surface. In this way, it can appear to be several flickering lights — perhaps a large colony of fireflies, for example.

Bog lanterns feed directly on the damage they inflict to their target's mental abilities. They prefer to feed on mental energy from humanoids — they simply find the "taste" to be a delicacy — and in particular, young humanoids. However, many a trapper has found the desiccated remains of an alligator, panther, or other beast unfortunate enough to cross paths with a hungry bog lantern. A bog lantern attacks by lashing at adjacent foes with psychic energy. The attack appears to be a flash of light (sometimes confused with an electrical discharge because of the bog lantern's similarities to a will-o'-wisp), but it's actually the bog lantern forming a tendril-like appendage and touching its prey.

BookTown Panther

This black-furred panther would not seem noteworthy were it not for its exceptional size and six legs, one of which has a twisted and mangled paw from some past hunter's trap. The beast seems to bear a perpetual snarl as one side of its face is badly scarred, pulling its mouth up and its eye into a puckered squint.

BookTown Panther
Large monstrosity, neutral evil

Armor Class 13 (16 with *barkskin*)
Hit Points 55 (10d10)
Speed 30 ft., climb 20 ft.
<RULE>

STR	DEX	CON	INT	WIS	CHA
14 (+2)	16 (+3)	10 (+0)	8 (-1)	15 (+2)	7 (-2)

Saving Throws Cha +1
Skills Athletics +5, Perception +5, Stealth +6
Senses darkvision 60 ft., passive Perception 15
Languages Common, Sylvan; telepathy with giant wasp companion
Challenge 4 (1,100 XP)

Innate Spellcasting. The BookTown panther can use the following spell-like abilities, using Wisdom as its casting ability (DC 13, attack +5). The panther needs only vocal components in its casting.
At will: *poison spray, resistance, create or destroy water, jump, speak with animals*
1/day each: *barkskin, darkness, fog cloud, pass without trace*

ACTIONS
Multiattack. The BookTown panther bites once and claws three times.
Bite. *Melee Weapon Attack:* +6 to hit (reach 5 ft.; one creature). *Hit:* 1d10 + 3 piercing damage.
Claw. *Melee Weapon Attack:* +6 to hit (reach 5 ft.; one creature); *Hit:* 2d6 + 3 slashing damage. If all three claw attacks hit the same creature on the panther's turn, the creature takes an additional 2d6 slashing damage.

ECOLOGY
Environment urban (the Blight)
Organization solitary

This creature is a legend in BookTown. Allegedly, a panther of great size originally imported from the distant swamps of southern Akados for the private gardens of a dabbler in the arcane arts, it is said that this arcanist worked magic beyond his abilities, causing the panther to mutate, grow additional limbs, and ultimately, develop a malign intelligence of its own. Each tale of the BookTown panther describes tortures visited on the creature at the hands of its demented master, each more horrible than the previous.

The truth of these tales remains in question, but what is not in question is that a black panther of prodigious proportions does stalk the unwary among the roofs and gables of BookTown. Eyewitnesses report that it indeed has an extra set of limbs, though one has been badly injured at some point in the past.

Efforts to hunt the beast have failed, as it proves to be incredibly elusive, and it seems to have a great knowledge of where the many nests of wasps, centipedes, and other vermin can be found among the gables. The few times hunters have even gotten close to it, they have run afoul of swarms of such insects while the beast made its escape.

The truth of the matter is that a demented urban druid of BookTown indeed tortured and experimented upon the panther. The druid raised the panther's IQ to the point of sentience and self-awareness, but his magic wasn't entirely successful — the newly aware creature was not inclined to friendliness toward him. At first feigning obedience, the panther merely awaited an opportunity when the druid's guard was down and its cage left unsecured before striking and messily devouring the fool. The panther did not escape unscathed. Traps left as contingencies by the druid severely injured the beast and crippled one of its legs as it disappeared into the night.

Rather than try to flee the city where it knew that it would be hunted, the BookTown panther chose instead to lair among the dangers of the city's rooftops where few dared to venture. Its great size and strength provided it with some protection from the myriad dangers to be found there, allowing it to turn its newfound sentience toward its survival and revenge against all humanoids as it pursued the path of the hunter. In doing so, it learned to harness the ubiquitous vermin that continually swarmed among the spires and rooftops of the city, eventually even gaining a giant wasp as an animal companion.

The panther has shed the name given to it by its former master as a mark of its past shame and captivity, and instead prefers to remain nameless. It has heard the moniker of BookTown panther given to it, and doesn't care one way of the other. It simply sees the soft, fleshy humanoids as prey to sate its hunger for revenge. It likewise doesn't name the giant wasp that always accompanies it, seeing it as nothing more than an expendable resource to be used for assistance and protection, and indeed is already on its seventh giant wasp companion, the prior six all having fallen in the panther's wake as it abandoned them to effect its own escape. The BookTown panther is a remorseless killer, but it is careful and cunning. It has lived many years atop the tenements of BookTown and has no intention of meeting its end anytime soon. It is patient and cautious in its hunts, willing to stalk a chosen victim for days, maybe even harassing it with swarms of vermin before moving in to make its kill.

The city of Castorhage has offered a 15,000-gp reward if this creature is captured or killed.

Crathog

This creature draws its leech-like body along by great barbed spindly tentacles that glisten with fluid. Somewhere inside its cluster of spines and sharp bones lurks a great maw that distends itself outward.

Crathog
Huge aberration, neutral evil

Armor Class 16 (natural armor)
Hit Points 123 (13d12 + 39)
Speed 30 ft., swim 30 ft.

STR	DEX	CON	INT	WIS	CHA
20 (+5)	13 (+1)	17 (+3)	10 (+0)	13 (+1)	9 (-1)

Saving Throws Dex +4, Wis +4, Cha +3
Skills Perception +4, Stealth +4
Damage Immunities acid
Condition Immunities prone
Senses darkvision 60 ft., tremorsense 30 ft., passive Perception 14
Languages Aquan, Deep Speech
Challenge 8 (3,900 XP)

Acidic Trail. The crathog's skin exudes a layer of acid. This coating leaves a slimy trail behind the crathog similar to a slug's trail. All spaces that the crathog occupied since its last turn retain this acidic coating; any creature that enters or starts its turn in such a space takes 1d6 acid damage. At the start of the crathog's turn, all previously acidic spaces become safe.

Blending Skin. When at rest, a crathog shifts the color of its flesh to blend perfectly with the surrounding terrain. While motionless, the crathog is invisible.

ACTIONS
Multiattack. The crathog attacks twice with tentacles, then either bites twice or uses distended bite once.

Tentacle. *Melee Weapon Attack:* +8 to hit (reach 10 ft.; one creature). *Hit:* 2d8 + 5 bludgeoning damage plus 1d10 acid damage. If both tentacle attacks hit the same creature on the crathog's turn, the creature is grappled (escape DC 15). The crathog can have up to two creatures grappled and still use tentacle attacks.

Bite. *Melee Weapon Attack:* +8 to hit (reach 10 ft.; one creature). *Hit:* 1d8 + 5 piercing damage plus 1d10 acid damage.

Distended Bite. *Melee Weapon Attack:* +8 to hit (reach 20 ft.; one creature); *Hit:* 1d12 + 5 piercing damage plus 1d10 acid damage.

ECOLOGY
Environment coast
Organization solitary

The crathog are octopod horrors that had their origins in the exits of large cities' sewers emptying into the sea. The mixture of alchemical fluids, waste products, and other toxins caused mutations within the sea life that grew in the area until a new species spawned and bred true. The crathog began to gain an incessant drive to reproduce, a deeper understanding of their surroundings, and a greater intelligence.

A crathog seeps a corrosive acid from its porous flesh. Its tentacles move with eerie quickness to grasp its prey and pull it toward its distended jaw. These jaws are hinged on a flexible tendon that allows the crathog to contract a coiled muscle and launch this set of jaws outward to burst from its clustered mouth. The creature is able to blend into its surroundings like a chameleon. It moves almost totally silently, but leaves a slimy trail which in itself is acidic and dangerous. A crathog is incredibly strong and stealthy, known to climb onto ships to feed on unsuspecting sailors, dissolving their flesh with its acid.

Their intelligence allows them the insight to use their special abilities as ambush hunters. They tend to hide in crooks of old harbors and lie in wait until a fisherman ventures past. Crathog are not only cunning, they are incredibly cruel; they delight in mutilating or tormenting prey, and disfiguring their opponents with their acids. Why they do this is open to conjecture, but many scholars believe that crathog are somehow spawned by the influence of Between and that they seethe with the inherent injustice of those who have died in the river, particularly those who have suffered from its acidic toxins.

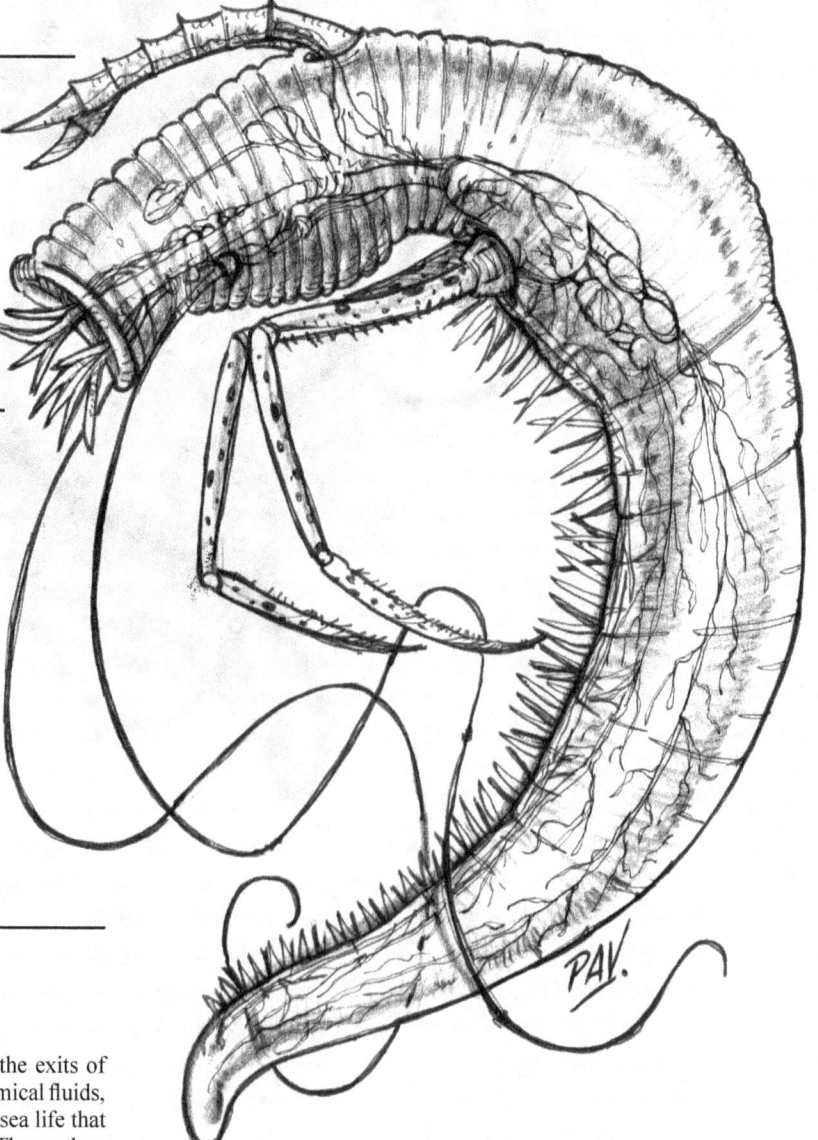

Dog, Fighting

Dogs are ubiquitous throughout human lands. Most other humanoids don't have the same attachment to canines that humans have.

Blight-Bull (Light Fighting Dog)

This small but nasty-looking dog is scarred from many battles.

Blight-Bull

Small beast, unaligned

Armor Class 14 (studded leather)
Hit Points 9 (2d6 + 2)
Speed 40 ft.

STR	DEX	CON	INT	WIS	CHA
9 (-1)	15 (+2)	10 (+1)	3 (-4)	12 (+1)	6 (-2)

Skills Perception +3, Stealth +4
Senses darkvision 60 ft., passive Perception 13
Languages none
Challenge 1/8 (25 XP)

Ferocity. When the Blight-bull drops to 0 hit points, it immediately makes one attack against a creature within 5 feet as a reaction before dying.

ACTIONS
Bite. *Melee Weapon Attack:* +4 to hit (reach 5 ft.; one creature). *Hit:* 1d4 + 2 piercing damage, and a Small or smaller creature is grappled (escape DC 9). A grappled creature takes 1d4 + 2 piercing damage at the end of its turn.

ECOLOGY
Environment urban
Organization solitary, pair, or pack (3-12)

Pit Mastiff (Heavy Fighting Dog)

This vicious-looking dog is heavily muscled and glares threateningly at everyone who gets near.

Pit Mastiff

Medium beast, unaligned

Armor Class 14 (studded leather)
Hit Points 22 (4d8 + 4)
Speed 40 ft.

STR	DEX	CON	INT	WIS	CHA
14 (+2)	14 (+2)	13 (+1)	3 (-4)	12 (+1)	7 (-2)

Skills Perception +3, Stealth +4

Senses darkvision 60 ft., passive Perception 13
Languages none
Challenge 1/2 (100 XP)

Ferocity. When the pit mastiff drops to 0 hit points, it immediately makes one attack against a creature within 5 feet as a reaction before dying.

ACTIONS
Bite. *Melee Weapon Attack:* +4 to hit (reach 5 ft.; one creature). *Hit:* 1d8 + 2 piercing damage, and a Medium or smaller creature is grappled (escape DC 12). A grappled creature takes 1d8 + 2 piercing damage at the end of its turn.

ECOLOGY
Environment urban
Organization solitary, pair, or pack (3–12)

Dogs bred and trained specifically to fight are tougher than normal breeds. They are typically garbed in light barding and have been taught to lock their jaws to bring opponents down. Their training has suppressed some of their natural instincts and rendered them quite specialized; consequently, they aren't of much use for other activities, such as tracking, but continue to fight past the point when other dogs would no longer be able to continue.

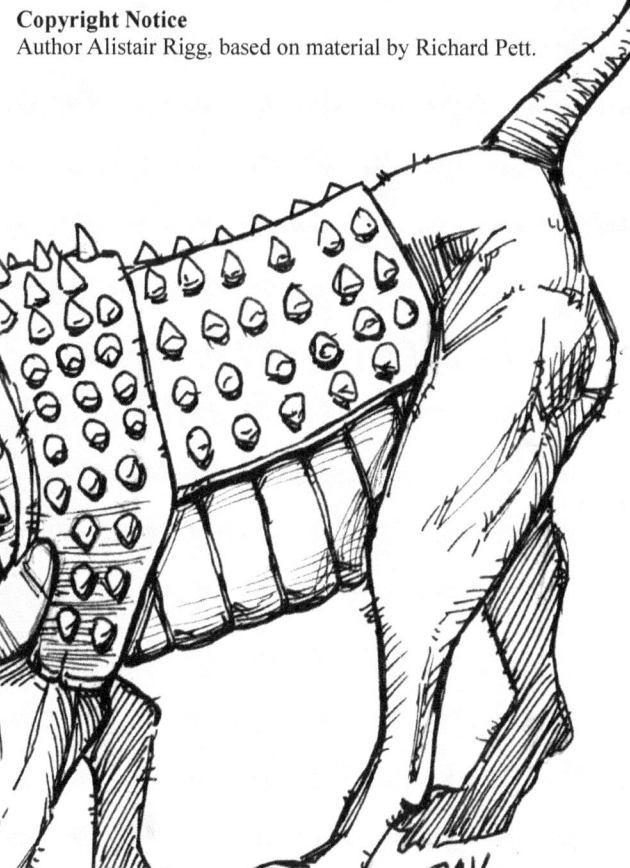

Terrier

This small dog's legs are long for its size, and its coat is shaggy and rough. It has a short muzzle and small ears that flop forward.

Terrier

Tiny beast, unaligned

Armor Class 12
Hit Points 2 (1d4)
Speed 40 ft.

STR	DEX	CON	INT	WIS	CHA
4 (-3)	15 (+2)	10 (+0)	3 (-4)	12 (+1)	7 (-2)

Skills Perception +3, Stealth +4
Languages none
Challenge 0 (XP 10)

Keen Senses. The terrier has advantage on Wisdom (Perception) checks that depend on hearing or smell.

ACTIONS
Bite. *Melee Weapon Attack:* +4 to hit (reach 5 ft.; one creature). *Hit:* 1 piercing plus 3 (1d6) bludgeoning.

ECOLOGY
Environment any land
Organization solitary, pair, or pack (3–12)

Frequently kept as pets by both the impoverished and well-to-do of Castorhage, these small dogs were originally bred to hunt the rats and other vermin so commonly found in the Blight. They are intelligent and extremely loyal, working well as both trained hunters and family pets. They stand up to 16 inches tall and usually weigh around 14 pounds.

Elemental, Ragefire

The rage and hatred that emanate with the white-hot heat from this demonic fire are palpable.

Ragefire Elemental

The rage and hatred that emanate with the white-hot heat from this demonic fire are palpable.

The ragefire elemental is a type of fire elemental that grows as it consumes fuel. All ragefire elementals start out as Tiny sparks, called ragefire spawn. As they burn their way through their surroundings, they steadily increase in size until they become gargantuan infernos.

Every size of ragefire elemental has stats identical to a standard fire elemental, except as noted on the table below. The table lists the hit points, melee attack bonus, melee damage, ongoing damage to flammable objects ("Burn"), and challenge rating of every size of ragefire elemental. Burn damage also applies as the damage done by the elemental's Fire Form ability.

Besides the differences noted above, Tiny through Large ragefire elementals also have the trait **Intensify:** As an action, a Tiny, Small, Medium, or Large ragefire elemental incinerates the corpse of a humanoid it killed within the last minute and whose space the elemental occupies. The elemental heals 5 hit points and, if it is Tiny, it becomes a Small ragefire elemental with full hit points minus its current amount of damage. Likewise, a Small, Medium, or Large ragefire elemental grows to the next size after incinerating a number of humanoid corpses equal to its current challenge rating.

Huge and Gargantuan ragefire elementals don't have the Intensify trait. Instead, they have the trait **Spawn Ragefire:** As an action, a Huge or Gargantuan ragefire elemental incinerates the corpse of a humanoid that it killed within the last minute and whose space the elemental occupies. A newly-created ragefire spawn (a Tiny ragefire elemental) appears in an empty space within 5 feet of the spawning elemental.

Ragefire elementals embody the chaos and evil of their Abyssal heritage, manifesting in demonic forms of living flame, smoke, ash, and cinders. They exist to incinerate life and, in so doing, grow stronger and more destructive.

A ragefire elemental cannot enter water or any other nonflammable liquid. A body of water is an impassible barrier unless the ragefire elemental can step or jump over it or the water is covered with a layer of something flammable, such as oil.

Ragefire Elemental

Size	HP	Attack	Damage	Burn	CR
Tiny	33	+3	1d4+3	1d4	1
Small	52	+4	1d6+3	1d6	2
Medium	75	+5	1d10+3	1d8	3
Large	102	+6	2d6+3	1d10	5
Huge	124	+7	3d10+3	1d12	8
Gargantuan	189	+8	4d10+3	1d20	11

Familiar

Presented here are the base statistics for a number of types of familiars commonly found in and around the city of Castorhage. These statistics can also be used for normal animals of these types. Small animals like these use Dexterity in place of Strength when making most Athletics checks.

Blight Albatross

This seabird has an expansive wingspan of pure white plumage, a long hooked beak, and tail feathers tipped in black.

Blight Albatross
Small beast, unaligned

Armor Class 11
Hit Points 2 (1d6 - 1)
Speed 10 ft., fly 40 ft.

STR	DEX	CON	INT	WIS	CHA
3 (-4)	13 (+1)	8 (-1)	2 (-4)	11 (+0)	6 (-2)

Damage Immunities poison
Condition Immunities disease; poisoned
Skills Perception +2
Languages none
Challenge 1/8 (25 XP)

Cursed Fate. Any creature that kills a Blight albatross must make a successful DC 11 Wisdom saving throw or receive a curse. A cursed creature treats all d20 rolls of natural 20s as 1s instead. A cursed creature repeats the saving throw every time it completes a long rest, ending the effect on a success.

ACTIONS
Beak. *Melee Weapon Attack:* +3 to hit (reach 5 ft.; one creature). *Hit:* 1 piercing damage.

ECOLOGY
Environment coast
Organization solitary, family (2–3), flock (4–12), or colony (13–24)

Sometimes known as a gooey bird or a muckmawk, the Blight albatross is common along the shores of the sea around the city of Castorhage. They gained these nicknames for the feeding technique of the bird, where they dive into the muck-laden waters and emerge with fish and feathers coated with the filmy sludge that covers the Lyme River on most days.

The Blight albatross's diet is predominantly fish, crustaceans, and offal, although they also scavenge carrion when necessary. Due to the nature of the pollution found in the river and its inhabitants, the Blight albatross has developed considerable resistance to diseases and poisons. The folk of Castorhage are reluctant to kill one of these birds, for it is considered bad luck. Those that have slain one of these creatures soon finds the legends are very true, and for a period of time find their luck changed for the worse.

The adult plumage of most of the Blight albatrosses is usually some variation of dark upper-wing and back with white undersides. A Blight albatross stands 3 feet tall with a wingspan of up to 12 feet and weighs 20 pounds.

Blight Cockerel

Lanky and bedraggled, with thin feathers other than a wide tuft around the neck, this rooster is particularly ugly for its kind. Its wattle and comb are both shredded and torn from past battles, and razor-sharp spurs have been tied to the backs of its legs.

Blight Cockerel
Small beast, unaligned

Armor Class 11
Hit Points 2 (1d6 - 1)
Speed 10 ft., fly 50 ft.

STR	DEX	CON	INT	WIS	CHA
2 (-4)	13 (+1)	8 (-1)	2 (-4)	11 (+0)	6 (-2)

Skills Perception +2
Languages none
Challenge 0 (10 XP)

Ferocity. When the Blight cockerel drops to 0 hit points, it immediately makes one attack against a creature within 5 feet as a reaction before dying.
Fighting Fury. When a Blight cockerel sees another member of its species or other similar-sized bird (other than a chicken), it instinctively triggers its fight response. It spends 1 round attempting to intimidate its opponent, then attacks, gaining a +1 bonus to attacks and damage. A Blight cockerel in a fighting fury fights until it or its opponent is dead.

ACTIONS
Beak. *Melee Weapon Attack:* +3 to hit (reach 5 ft.; one creature). *Hit:* 1 piercing damage.

ECOLOGY
Environment any land (the Blight)
Organization solitary

Cockfighting is a common pastime among the coarser citizens of the Blight (and secretly many of the upper crust as well) and the gamecocks have been bred for centuries in the city just for these contests. The resulting breed of Blight cockerel is a distempered gamecock known for its viciousness in fights and its instinct to continue fighting even after having taken a mortal wound. Many runners of cockfights no longer allow Blight cockerels in their venues because of the likelihood that neither bird will survive and their investment in training a prized gamecock will be lost even in victory. Blight cockerels are bred with normal chickens and always attack another Blight cockerel on sight unless restrained.

Before fighting matches that involve betting, some Blight cockerels are outfitted with fighting spurs: razor-sharp blades tied to their legs. Fighting spurs replace the bird's beak attack with a spur attack, which has the same attack bonus and reach but does 1d4 slashing damage.

A Blight cockerel stands 2 feet tall and weighs 10–15 pounds.

Blindingcrow

This glossy black crow has fleshy pustules and sores growing out from under its plumage. This bird is has a thick, heavy bill and even more surprisingly has a central third leg that ends in an array of sharpened talons.

Blindingcrow

Tiny monstrosity, unaligned

Armor Class 12
Hit Points 1 (1d4 - 1)
Speed 10 ft., fly 50 ft.

STR	DEX	CON	INT	WIS	CHA
2 (-4)	14 (+2)	8 (-1)	2 (-4)	12 (+1)	6 (-2)

Condition Immunities Blindness
Skills Perception +3
Languages none
Senses darkvision 30 ft., passive Perception 13
Challenge 1/8 (25 XP)

Blinding Sickness. A creature infected with blinding sickness must make a DC 9 Constitution saving throw after completing each long rest. On a failure, the infected creature gains 1 level of exhaustion; on a success, it loses 1 level of exhaustion. The disease is cured when the creature has 0 levels of exhaustion, or through *lesser restoration* or comparable magic. *The real danger from the disease, however, is blindness. When a creature reaches 3 levels of exhaustion caused by blinding sickness, or when it has taken 3 or more necrotic damage in less than 10 minutes from blindingcrows that carry the disease, the creature is permanently blinded. Greater restoration or comparable magic is needed to cure this blindness.*

ACTIONS

Beak. *Melee Weapon Attack:* +3 to hit (reach 5 ft.; one creature). *Hit:* 1 piercing damage, and the creature must make a successful DC 9 Constitution saving throw or take 1 necrotic damage and contract blinding sickness (see above).

ECOLOGY

Environment non-arctic land
Organization solitary, pair, flock (3–12), or murder (13–100)

Blindingcrows are fairly intelligent carrion birds known for their problem-solving skills and ability to adapt within the city environment. Despite past attempts to exterminate them, blindingcrows are more common than ever in the city's trash dumps and are known for their distinctive screeching caw. Sociable, especially when not nesting, blindingcrows may gather in communal roosts on winter nights, sometimes with thousands or even tens of thousands roosting at one location.

When large groups of these bird gather, they sometimes form a huge swarming flock and chase predators in a behavior called mobbing. Loud noises are the most common cause for a murder of blindingcrows to attack an individual.

As foragers, these birds also clean up dead animals and garbage. In fact, blindingcrows are often blamed for overturning garbage cans when the real culprits are usually raccoons or dogs. From prolonged exposure to the toxins and wastes in their urban environments where the blindingcrows live and feed, they have developed an ironic affinity for a particular disease. Blinding sickness has festered within these birds, and they pass it from one to another during mating and while feeding. The feathers of these birds, although a glossy black, are marred by oozing, sores that drain diseased fluid and that dry and become encrusted. When the birds preen themselves, this diseased fluid transfers to their beaks where it

infects their bite attacks. Despite their third claw and sinister reputation, blindingcrows are no more effective with claw attacks than a normal crow. Only when blindingcrows swarm do their claw attacks really present a threat and live up to their name.

Canary

This tiny songbird has feathers of pale yellow with a slight greenish tinge and is streaked with gray and brown on its back and wings.

Canary

Tiny beast, unaligned

Armor Class 11
Hit Points 1 (1d4 – 1)
Speed 5 ft., fly 40 ft.

STR	DEX	CON	INT	WIS	CHA
1 (-5)	12 (+1)	8 (-1)	2 (-4)	12 (+1)	8 (-1)

Skills Perception +4
Languages none
Challenge 0 (XP 10)

Gas Vulnerability. Canaries are particularly vulnerable to the effects of inhaled poisons and fouled air. They have disadvantage on saving throws against any effect caused by an inhaled gas or substance.

ACTIONS
Bite. *Melee Weapon Attack:* +3 to hit (reach 0 ft.; one creature). *Hit:* 1 piercing damage.

ECOLOGY
Environment forest (any land in captivity)
Organization solitary, pair, or flock (3–12)

These tiny birds were originally discovered among the subtropical islands of the south and were brought to the mainland to be bred as songbirds. Their numbers have flourished in captivity over the years, and it was eventually determined that they were useful in detecting dangerous gases in mines and caverns. Since that time, they have been widely employed by miners as sentinel animals to detect the presence of otherwise undetectable gas hazards before the miners are overcome by them.

Fleshgine

Fleshgines are constructs of flesh combined with other materials designed for a specific purpose. They might pump water from a city's reservoirs into rooftop cisterns to supply the inhabitants with running water, or they may lift or pull — anything a humanoid body can do. But fleshgines are built to improve upon a humanoid's ability through modification and vast strength. While they are not uncommon in Castorhage, they often operate out of sight; their disturbing appearance being something the civilized locals choose not to acknowledge. They can be heard though — their steady stormy breathing, the asthmatic wheeze behind a grate, the slithering of flaccid limbs between floors. They also have a strong odor — a sort of organic sweatiness that can smell of the many other odors from the things they work in and around, which they absorb and amplify.

Fleshgines come in all shapes and sizes, and while no two are ever alike, they often fall into a set pattern. Each is very strong, and many — an uncannily large number — are weakly sentient creatures in their own right. Different fleshgines tend to have different abilities; some are simple brutes that occasionally go mad, some are more cunning, lurking and growing behind plaster and wainscoting and brooding their dark, strange dreams and wants.

All fleshgines have the trait **Berserk:** Every time a fleshgine is injured in combat, roll d100. If the result is less than or equal to the total number of hit points the fleshgine has lost so far in this combat, its elemental spirit breaks free and the fleshgine goes berserk. The berserk fleshgine attacks the nearest living creature; if no creature is close enough for the fleshgine to attack with a single move, it attacks an object instead. The fleshgine's controller can try to reestablish control, provided the fleshgine is within 60 feet. The controller must use an action to speak firmly and authoritatively to the construct and make a successful DC 15 Charisma check. A damaged fleshgine that spends at least 1 minute outside combat has its chance to go berserk reset to 0 percent.

Sentient Fleshgines: While most fleshgines are simple, mindless servitors made of flesh stitched and grown to inorganic parts and contraptions, some grow into something altogether different. Sentient fleshgines take on aspects of their humanoid neighbors that seep in from their close proximity on a daily basis. These aspects include tics, habits, language, and even some of their vices. These creatures are often bloated by the desires and madness of Between and become enraptured by it, seeking new directions and becoming fixated in disturbing ways. These constructs often form complex alliances with those who dwell behind the veneer of the Blight, particularly with the ghouls of the Fetch (who have enough inert humanity to understand and fear the construct). Some say the thoughts of the Crooked Promethean violate their dreams and awaken them; others say that it is a simple accident of nature. These sentient constructs lurk in plain sight and are driven by whatever twisted needs or goals have grown within their warped consciousness.

As more complex fleshgines are grafted from darker sources of flesh and bone, so too the risk of disaster becomes greater. Philosophers within the city-state already worry what fleshgines might do if they rebelled en masse. They point to the curious whale-song that occasionally haunts certain nights, and which seems to come from the fleshgines calling to each other across the city. What are they saying or planning, they wonder? The golem-stitchers and homuncule wives laugh at such suggestions; their creations are simple flesh-and-blood machines after all. What maliciousness could possibly lurk within this humble framework?

All sentient fleshgines that have gone berserk at least once in the past develop an urge toward murderous abduction called "take" or "taking." Occasionally the fleshgine's habits and needs drive it to seize a victim at least one size category smaller than the fleshgine. The fleshgine is always cunning in this action and manipulates its manifold parts and surroundings to camouflage its action. If the fleshgine's Stealth check beats the victim's passive Perception, the victim doesn't see the attack coming and the fleshgine gets to make a grappling attack with advantage. If the victim notices the attack coming, then it's just a normal attack by the fleshgine. While the victim is grappled by the fleshgine, it's also restrained, muffled (unable to cry out or speak), and suffocating. After a number of rounds equal to its Con modifier (minimum of 1), it becomes unconscious. At that point, the fleshgine hides the victim in some convenient location around or within its body. The victim remains unconscious until it dies or it's rescued.

Casual observers notice the hidden victim if their passive Perception exceeds (10 + the fleshgine's Stealth bonus). Anyone specifically looking for a victim taken by the fleshgine must win a contest of their Perception against the fleshgine's Stealth or Deception (fleshgine's choice). A taken victim is found automatically if the fleshgine is destroyed, but also might be injured, depending on the type of attacks used against the fleshgine and the size difference between them; GMs can apply their own judgment in these cases.

If a victim escapes the fleshgine's grapple, the fleshgine might attack or flee, depending on the situation.

A taken victim takes damage equal to any one of the fleshgine's melee attacks after every 24 hours. The taken victims are used to vent the leeched needs of the fleshgine — whether they be simple hunger, torment, or sexual — before their dead and broken remains are cast away.

A sentient fleshgine is always torn between its urges to seize a victim and the knowledge that discovery means certain punishment and death. It therefore carefully watches its chosen victim, often for weeks or months before striking.

The following entries describe three sample types of fleshgines. Many more are possible.

Dungier's Buggy

The rumble of a coach's wheels upon the cobbles comes out of the misty night, but it is not accompanied by the clip-clop of hooves. Rather, there is a soft slapping of skin upon the hard stones. Emerging from the fog is a hansom cab drawn not by a team of horses but rather by the upper torso of an ogre melded to the front of the conveyance. It walks on its massive hands, and its head stares forward, the eyes alert but vacant.

Dungier's Buggy (Fleshgine)
Huge construct, unaligned

Armor Class 10
Hit Points 51 (6d10 + 18)
Speed 40 ft.

STR	DEX	CON	INT	WIS	CHA
19 (+4)	10 (+0)	16 (+3)	2 (-4)	7 (-2)	3 (-4)

Damage Resistances cold; bludgeoning, piercing, and slashing from nonmagical, nonadamantine weapons
Damage Immunities necrotic, poison, psychic
Condition Immunities disease; charmed, frightened, paralyzed, poisoned, prone, stunned, unconscious
Senses darkvision 60 ft., passive Perception 8
Languages understands Common and Giant but speaks only programmed phrases
Challenge 3 (700 XP)

Berserk. Every time the fleshgine is injured in combat, roll d100. If the result is less than or equal to the total number of hit points the fleshgine has lost so far in this combat, its elemental spirit breaks free and the fleshgine goes berserk.

The berserk fleshgine attacks the nearest living creature; if no creature is close enough to attack with a single move, it attacks an object instead. The fleshgine's controller can try to reestablish control, provided the fleshgine is within 60 feet. The controller must use an action to speak firmly and authoritatively to the construct and make a successful DC 15 Charisma check. A damaged fleshgine that spends at least 1 minute outside combat has its chance to go berserk reset to 0 percent.

Cover. The coach portion of a Dungier's buggy provides three-quarters cover to occupants. The coach is built from iron and wood. It has AC 8, 80 hit points, and is immune to necrotic, poison, psychic, and radiant damage. If the coach is destroyed, the fleshgine becomes a Large creature and loses its Cover, Facing, and Trample traits.

Facing. Because the legless ogre is permanently melded to a wagon, it can only move forward and backward, or turn. Its speed is halved when it moves backward. Its slam and bite attacks can be made only against targets in front of it. It can trample while moving forward or backward. behind it as normal. Once a Dungier's buggy's front side has been determined, it requires a move action to turn its facing greater than 90 degrees. A Dungier's buggy is aware of attackers behind it but cannot see them, though it can accurately estimate what space they are in if within 20 feet.

Narrow. Though a Dungier's buggy is Huge, it can move through areas only 10 feet wide without penalty. It can't, however, squeeze through spaces narrower than 10 feet.

Trample. As the Dungier's buggy moves, it can enter spaces occupied by enemies but can't stop there. Creatures in spaces the Dungier's buggy enters can attempt DC 13 Dexterity saving throws. On a failed save, the creature takes 2d10 + 4 bludgeoning damage and is knocked prone; on a successful save, the creature moves 5 feet out of the buggy's path and can make an opportunity attack if it's allowed to react. A Dungier's buggy can trample any number of creatures during its move, but it can't trample the same creature more than once per round.

ACTIONS

Multiattack. The Dungier's buggy slams once and bites once.

Slam. *Melee Weapon Attack:* +6 to hit (reach 5 ft.; one creature). *Hit:* 2d6 + 4 bludgeoning damage.

Bite. *Melee Weapon Attack:* +6 to hit (reach 5 ft.; one creature). *Hit:* 2d4 + 4 piercing damage.

ECOLOGY

Environment urban (the Blight)
Organization solitary

Perhaps the most successful of Castorhage's many fleshgines are the hired coaches of the golem-stitcher Dunaven Dungier. His method of crafting a hansom cab with the animated upper torso of an ogre (occasionally a hill giant) fused to its front in place of a team of horses proved both practical and popular in a city as vast and populous as the Blight. Soon Dungier's buggies were traveling throughout the city providing swift, reliable transportation for the noble and common alike and for only a modest fare. Dungier's popularity with the other cab drivers and owners of hacks proved to be less than stellar, though, and only three years after the introduction of his ingenious cab, portions of his body were found floating in the Great Canal. It is assumed that sough eels or some other denizen devoured the rest. Fortunately for his legacy, Dungier's methods were fairly easy to reproduce, and now hundreds of these coaches — still known colloquially as Dungier's buggies — travel the streets of the city.

Hobbreth's Mighty Pump No. 87

The stench of sweat and the distant sounds of heavy breathing engulf you — whatever it is, you are catching the merest glimpse of the whole. In the oily dark you can see sickly appendages gulping, a horrible sense of brooding vastness, and a glowering cluster of eyes filled with misery just below a vast, idiot, crooked mouth.

Hobbreth's Mighty Pump No. 87 (Fleshgine)

Gargantuan construct, unaligned

Armor Class 10
Hit Points 205 (10d20 + 100)
Speed 20 ft., climb 20 ft.

STR	DEX	CON	INT	WIS	CHA
30 (+10)	10 (+0)	30 (+10)	4 (-3)	4 (-3)	1 (-5)

Damage Resistances cold; bludgeoning, piercing, and slashing from nonmagical, nonadamantine weapons
Damage Immunities necrotic, poison, psychic
Condition Immunities disease; charmed, frightened, paralyzed, poisoned, prone, stunned, unconscious
Senses blindsense 60 ft., passive Perception 7
Languages understands Common but can't speak
Challenge 12 (8,400 XP)

Berserk. Every time the fleshgine is injured in combat, roll d100. If the result is less than or equal to the total number of hit points the fleshgine has lost so far in this combat, its elemental spirit breaks free and the fleshgine goes berserk. The berserk fleshgine attacks the nearest living creature; if no creature is close enough to attack with a single move, it attacks an object instead. The fleshgine's controller can try to reestablish control, provided the fleshgine is within 60 feet. The controller must use an action to speak firmly and authoritatively to the construct and make a successful DC 15 Charisma check. A damaged fleshgine that spends at least 1 minute outside combat has its chance to go berserk reset to 0 percent.

ACTIONS
Multiattack. The fleshgine bites once and makes three tentacle attacks in any combination.
Bite. *Melee Weapon Attack:* +14 to hit (reach 5 ft.; one creature). *Hit:* 1d10 + 10 piercing damage.
Tentacle Slam. *Melee Weapon Attack:* +14 to hit (reach 20 ft.; one creature). Hit: 4d6 + 10 bludgeoning damage.
Tentacle Grab. *Melee Weapon Attack:* +14 to hit (reach 15 ft.; one creature). *Hit:* creature is grappled (escape DC 20).
Tentacle Crush. *Melee Weapon Attack:* automatic hit (one creature already grappled by the fleshgine). *Hit:* 4d10 + 10 bludgeoning damage, and the creature is restrained.

ECOLOGY
Environment urban (the Blight)
Organization solitary

"You can't see her all, of course, even I never did when I was stitching her and moulding her, making her flesh and breathing life into my baby.

I recall her formation though, her crisp newness — the endless flesh, and the stench of pigs — for it was pig-flesh I grew and nurtured, and spread across her carcass like a great sail on a vast living sailing vessel.

In her base she is all purpose — her many sucking mouths, which in truth I suppose you'd call tentacles (if such a crude word could be used for such grace), with so many eyes clustered together so she can see from her sweaty groin below that pointless mouth — she must have a mouth, of course. Her flesh engorges above, like some vast flaccid organ that could fill a great hall, bloated, booming, pumping. Veins cross her every inch — you can see the swelling blood pumping as she draws her harvest upward through her cathedral mass far, far above.

She rises then, reaching high into the city, her pumping limbs extending endlessly upward with surprising — some have said alarming — strength to the digits that grasp her farthest reach. Some have likened the digits to fleshy spiders, but I think that's simple scare-mongering to frighten children; they simply grip the vessel they spend her harvest into. And here her harvest is drawn, the life-giving water that sustains those in the streets high above pumped from sphincter mouths between each cluster of thin many-jointed hands.

It may taste a little of her sweat — her feral porcine nature — but it is water, saving the lower city from drowning and keeping the upper city drinking.

How many have I made? Oh, hundreds, no two quite alike. The stories about them going berserk? Rubbish put about by those with a grievance — anarchists would say anything to cause discontent amongst the ignorant.

I do sometimes wonder if they have a soul, though, my fleshy babies lurking between walls and dreaming. What do they dream of, I wonder?"

— Emilia Hobbreth, Homuncule Wife

Macabre Lift

The dark shaft of the vertical tunnel appears to be empty until its wooden floor suddenly lurches and rises from where it rested. Beneath the planking of the floor, you can see that a great fleshy organism has grown like a distended bladder that covers the entirety of its underside. From this sweaty, rugose sac extend four muscular limbs that grasp the walls of the shaft with their multi-fingered appendages and begin to climb, carrying the cargo of its wooden flooring smoothly up the shaft.

Macabre Lift (Fleshgine)

Large construct, unaligned

Armor Class 7 (15 from above)
Hit Points 90 (12d10 + 24)
Speed 10 ft., climb 30 ft.

STR	DEX	CON	INT	WIS	CHA
22 (+6)	5 (-3)	14 (+2)	1 (-5)	4 (-3)	1 (-5)

Skills Athletics +8
Damage Resistances cold; bludgeoning, piercing, and slashing from nonmagical, nonadamantine weapons
Damage Immunities necrotic, poison, psychic
Condition Immunities disease; charmed, frightened, paralyzed, poisoned, prone, stunned, unconscious
Senses darkvision 30 ft., passive Perception 7
Languages none
Challenge 3 (700 XP)

Berserk. Every time the fleshgine is injured in combat, roll d100. If the result is less than or equal to the total number of hit points the fleshgine has lost so far in this combat, its elemental spirit breaks free and the fleshgine goes berserk. The berserk fleshgine attacks the nearest living creature; if no creature is close enough to attack with a single move, it attacks an object instead. The fleshgine's controller can try to reestablish control, provided the fleshgine is within 60 feet. The controller must use an action to speak firmly and authoritatively to the construct and make a successful DC 15 Charisma check. A damaged fleshgine that spends at least 1 minute outside combat has its chance to go berserk reset to 0 percent.

Crush. A macabre lift can fall on foes beneath it as its move. Every creature under the lift takes 1d8 bludgeoning damage per 10 feet the lift fell, or half damage with a successful DC 13 Dexterity saving throw. Creatures that fail the saving throw are restrained under the lift; a restrained creature can escape by using an action and making a successful DC 16 Strength (Athletics) check. Restrained creatures take 2d8 bludgeoning damage at the start of the lift's turn.

Heavy Floor. The floor of a macabre lift is built from heavy wooden planks. Attacks against the macabre lift from creatures above it (such as passengers that were being raised or lowered in the lift) are made against AC 15, not AC 7.

ACTIONS

Multiattack. The fleshgine slams twice.

Slam. *Melee Weapon Attack:* +8 to hit (reach 5 ft.; one creature). *Hit:* 2d8 + 6 bludgeoning damage.

ECOLOGY

Environment urban (the Blight)
Organization solitary

One of the first fleshgines envisioned by the golem-stitchers of Castorhage, the macabre lift has found widespread usage among government buildings and other large, multilevel structures with the budget to install such amenities. These constructs are rather simple in design, with a fleshy, leathery hide grown on the underside of a 10-foot-by-10-foot deck of heavy wooden planks. Four stocky limbs extend from the underside of the creature at its four corners and end with club-like pseudopods surrounded by a fringe of grasping fingers with thick, coarse nails. The entire fleshgine is no more than 2 feet thick but weighs 1,500 pounds or more (3,500 pounds if constructed with an iron deck).

Macabre lifts are designed to be placed in vertical shafts whose dimensions match those of the fleshgine. The fleshgine then lies flat at the base of the shaft and allows passengers to step upon its decking. Upon a signal —usually the ringing of a small bell set into the side of the shaft — the macabre lift begins to climb the shaft while keeping its deck level and stable. Handholds are often built into the walls of the shaft to make the climb easier for the fleshgine, but its climbing pseudopods are so adept that it rarely needs any sort of assistance. The number of times that the bell is rung indicates to what floor the lift is supposed to carry its passengers. Likewise, bells set into the shaft at floors above summon it from below to pick up passengers. The rise and fall of the climbing fleshgine is so smooth that most passengers easily forget that they are riding upon the back of an animated construct.

If a macabre lift goes berserk, its usual tactic is to tip itself over to try to dump any passengers to the floor of the shaft below. Anyone riding the lift when it does this must make a successful DC 13 Dex saving throw to grab hold of the fleshgine's deck and not fall.

Gable Hate-Owl

This sinister-looking owl has pitch-black plumage and a pallid face with yellow eyes. The V-shaped pattern of feathers on its brow gives the appearance of a perpetual scowl of utter scorn.

Gable Hate-Owl

Small monstrosity, neutral evil

Armor Class 12
Hit Points 14 (4d6)
Speed 10 ft., fly 60 ft.

STR	DEX	CON	INT	WIS	CHA
5 (-3)	15 (+2)	10 (+0)	3 (-4)	15 (+2)	16 (+3)

Skills Perception +4, Stealth +4
Senses darkvision 60 ft., passive Perception 14
Languages none
Challenge 1/2 (100 XP)

Flurry of Wings. If the hate-owl's bite and claws attacks both hit the same target on the hate-owl's turn, the target takes an additional 1d8 + 2 bludgeoning damage.

ACTIONS
Multiattack. The hate-owl bites once and attacks once with its claws.
Bite. *Melee Weapon Attack:* +4 to hit (reach 5 ft.; one creature). *Hit:* 1d4 + 2 piercing damage.
Claws. *Melee Weapon Attack:* +4 to hit (reach 5 ft.; one creature). Hit: 2d6 + 2 slashing damage.
Spiteful Glare. A creature within 60 feet that can see the gable hate-owl's eyes must make a DC 13 Charisma saving throw. If it fails, the creature drops one item it's holding (roll randomly if more than one item is held) and has disadvantage on attacks, ability checks, and saving throws until the end of its next turn, and the hate-owl can immediately move up to 60 feet (if it hasn't moved yet) and use Multiattack against the creature.

ECOLOGY
Environment urban (the Blight)
Organization solitary

The gable hate-owl is a shadow among the homes and buildings in the Blight. Viewed as a thing of ill omen, the presence of the owl roosting is feared by the common man. Spiteful, petty birds, the gable hate-owl got its name from the hateful scowl its natural plumage creates. They have been known to kill or torture for sport, attacking dogs and other small animals as they flense off flesh and fur and then leave the poor victims to limp away.

These great owls are large, although most of their bulk comes from fluffy feathers and large heads, with plumage that gives that appearance of wearing a high-collared cloak. Great horned owls have wingspans of up to 5 feet and weigh up to 4 pounds. Gable hate-owls primarily hunt at night, locating prey through their excellent hearing and sight. Their diet consists of rodents supplemented by smaller birds and rabbits.

Their gaze particularly unsettles the folk of the Blight, as the piercing black eyes that seem dead peer out from under the sharp contrasting pale facial feathers. This sinister-looking visage creates ill fate to any that the owl wishes, typically casting its hateful look upon those that startle or interrupt the bird. A gable hate-owl's wickedly sharp beak lets it easily rip open hard shells or strip the flesh from its meals.

Gargoyle, Scrimshaw

The eerie humanoid-shaped creature is perched precariously on the edge of the building. The light from the full moon glints off its alabaster-colored body, revealing intricate etchings along the surface. As it surveys the land, the creature throws back its head and emits a piercing howl into the night.

Scrimshaw Gargoyle

Medium construct, chaotic evil

Armor Class 13
Hit Points 58 (9d8 + 18)
Speed 30 ft., fly 60 ft.

STR	DEX	CON	INT	WIS	CHA
12 (+1)	16 (+3)	14 (+2)	6 (-2)	11 (+0)	7 (-2)

Skills Stealth +5
Damage Resistances bludgeoning, piercing, and slashing from nonmagical weapons
Damage Immunities thunder
Condition Immunities paralyzed, petrified, poisoned
Senses darkvision 60 ft., passive Perception 10
Languages Common, Terran
Challenge 3 (700 XP)

Stony Appearance. The gargoyle is indistinguishable from a statue and can't be detected as alive by any means while it remains motionless.

ACTIONS
Multiattack. The scrimshaw gargoyle bites once and attacks once with its claws.
Bite. *Melee Weapon Attack:* +5 to hit (reach 5 ft.; one creature). *Hit:* 1d4 + 2 piercing damage.
Claws. *Melee Weapon Attack:* +5 to hit (reach 5 ft.; one creature). *Hit:* 2d6 + 2 slashing damage.
Shrieking Howl. By tilting its head up and forcing air through its weathered bones, a scrimshaw gargoyle emits a high-pitched shriek. Creatures within 150 feet who hear the shriek must make a successful DC 12 Wisdom saving throw or become frightened for up to 1 minute. An affected target can make another saving throw at the end of their turn. A successful save results in the target not being affected by the effect of the Shrieking Howl for 24 hours.

ECOLOGY
Environment urban (the Blight)
Organization solitary, pair, or wing (3–12)

The origin of these strangely carven sculptures in the city of Castorhage is shrouded in the mystery of the past, but their existence is now well known through its entirety. Originally created as mere constructs lacking the status of truly living creatures, their exposure to eddies and currents of malevolent energy among the city's high places, over the years somehow granted the missing spark of life.

A scrimshaw gargoyle is meticulously crafted from painstakingly carved whale bones joined together at the joint articulations. However, these craftings were all completed centuries ago, and no new ones have been constructed in the long years since. The existing scrimshaw gargoyles are, therefore, all old, their whale bones weathered and discolored by time and climate. Though it is thought that thousands of these creatures existed upon the city's rooftops in the distant past, it has been estimated that fewer than 50 of them are now

in existence, each of them recognizably distinct with their individual unique markings. However, the thinking on this is beginning to change as in recent months several new specimens have been spotted upon the rooftops. These new gargoyles are clearly composed of parts cannibalized from previously destroyed gargoyles. Most believe the scrimshaw gargoyles, taken as a whole, are too dimwitted to produce new members of the species. Some contemplate a secret cabal of magical practitioners as responsible for this change; others theorize that certain scrimshaw gargoyles have advanced much farther in their power and understanding of magic and are somehow responsible. Whatever the cause, it appears that the scrimshaw gargoyle population is on the rise for the first time in living memory.

It is thought that the scrimshaw gargoyles' original progenitors built the creatures to serve as guardians. To this end, the horrific shriek the gargoyle emits probably originally served as an alarm. The gargoyle generates the sound through careful fluting of the bones around its mouth, and a supernatural means of passing air — even on still nights — through the narrow structure. As the gargoyle evolved from a simple guardian to a menace, however, its shriek also evolved. No longer a loud noise to alert those nearby, now the shrieking howl is capable of striking fear into the heart of the bravest man.

A scrimshaw gargoyle stands just over 5 feet tall and weighs a mere 80 pounds.

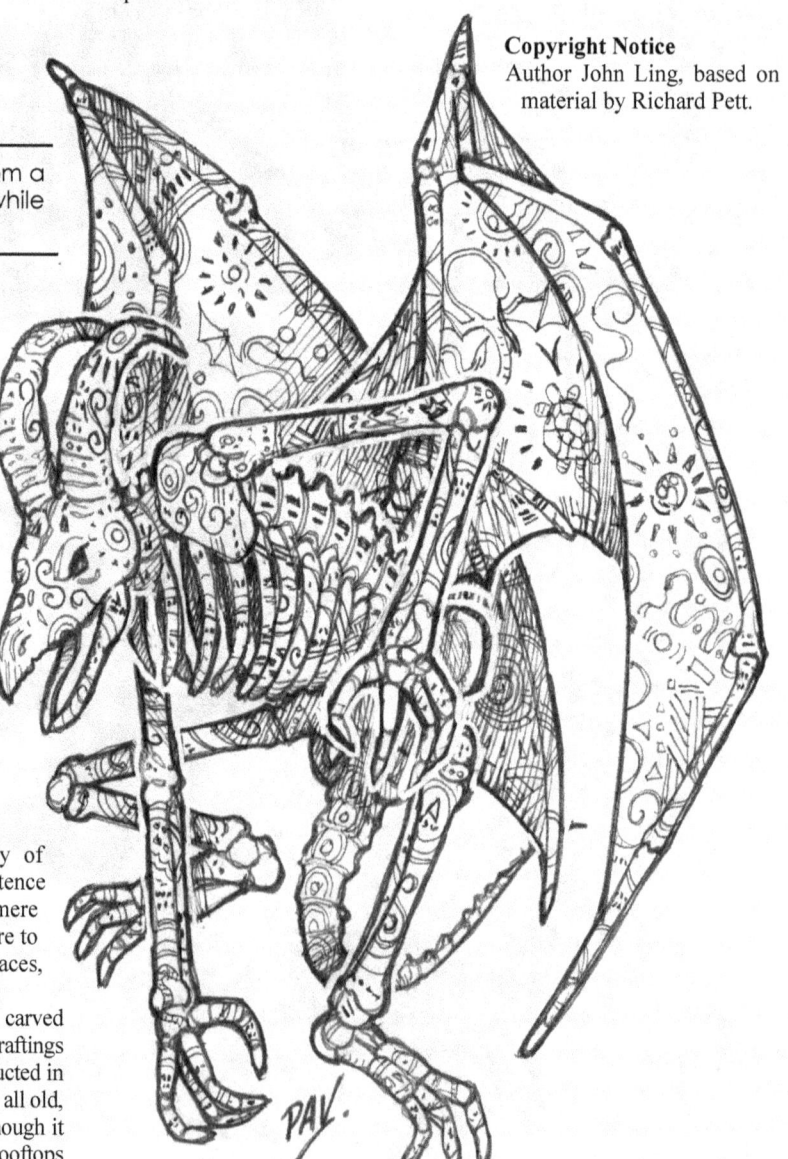

Ghoul, Gravid

This horrid creature walks upon the hands and legs of a female humanoid body bent over backward, its spine painfully creased at an acute angle. Protruding from its flaccid, torn abdomen sits an infant-sized creature with a two-foot-long, bright-red tongue that constantly bathes its gaunt, pallid flesh in sanguine fluids scooped from the cavity in which it sits.

Gravid Ghoul

Medium undead, chaotic evil

Armor Class 11
Hit Points 60 (11d8 + 11)
Speed 30 ft., climb 20 ft.

STR	DEX	CON	INT	WIS	CHA
16 (+3)	12 (+1)	12 (+1)	7 (-2)	12 (+1)	16 (+3)

Saving Throws Dex +3, Wis +3
Skills Perception +3, Survival +3
Damage Immunities poison
Condition Immunities exhaustion, frightened, poisoned, unconscious
Senses darkvision 60 ft., passive Perception 13
Languages Common
Challenge 3 (700 XP)

Blood Frenzy. A gravid ghoul that drops a foe to 0 hit points gains 10 temporary hit points and continues attacking the dying creature until that foe is dead. Until its foe is dead, the gravid ghoul's AC is reduced by 2.

Diseased Exudate. The flesh of a gravid ghoul constantly seeps disease-ridden fluid. Any creature that strikes the gravid ghoul from a range of 5 feet or less, or comes into physical contact with the gravid ghoul, must make a successful DC 11 Constitution saving throw or contract ghoul fever (see below).

Ghoul Fever. A creature that contracts ghoul fever must make a DC 11 Constitution saving throw every time it completes a long rest. If the saving throw fails, the creature gains 1 level of exhaustion; if it succeeds, there is no effect. A creature can't recover from exhaustion by resting while it has ghoul fever; the disease must be cured with *lesser restoration or comparable magic* first. A humanoid that dies from ghoul fever transforms into a ghoul moments after its death.

Smell Blood. The gravid ghoul has advantage on Perception checks to detect injured creatures and on Survival checks to track injured creatures.

Stress Mind. The very sight of a gravid ghoul instills a sense of anxiety in living creatures. Upon seeing a gravid ghoul within 60 feet, a creature with Intelligence 3 or higher must make a successful DC 13 Wisdom saving throw or be frightened for 1 minute. A creature can repeat the saving throw at the end of each its turns, ending the effect on a success. If the creature's saving throw is successful or the effect ends, it is immune to the gravid ghoul's Stress Mind for the next 24 hours.

ACTIONS

Multiattack. The gravid ghoul bites twice and attacks once with its tongue.

Bite. *Melee Weapon Attack:* +5 to hit (reach 5 ft.; one creature). *Hit:* 1d6 + 3 piercing damage, and the creature must make a successful DC 11 Constitution saving throw or contract ghoul fever (see above).

Tongue. *Melee Weapon Attack:* +5 to hit (reach 10 ft.; one creature). *Hit:* 1d4 + 3 piercing damage plus 2d6 psychic damage, and the creature must make a successful DC 11 Constitution saving throw or contract ghoul fever (see above).

ECOLOGY

Environment any land
Organization solitary or gang (2–4)

The gravid ghoul is an undead creature of the foulest nature. In the darkest alleys of inner cities, there are humanoids who will pay for the touch and bed of an undead creature. Whether out of fascination, fetish, or illness of the mind, these couplings on occasion have been known to develop into a gravid ghoul. The ghoul harlot typically is unaware of its pregnancy until it is far too late. The fetal ghoul that grows inside the undead mother awakens with blood lust and the hunger of a newborn. The only warning the ghoul mother receives is an increase in its own feeding instinct and a slight swelling of the midsection before the small ghoul-thing bursts from the mother's abdomen. The newborn creature sits within the gaping cavity of the mother's broken body, which is folded in half in a backbend to serve as a perch and means of mobility for the offspring. Despite its appearance as vehicle and driver of a sort, the offspring and mother are a single creature and cannot be separated without destroying both.

The new gravid ghoul awakens not only with a terrible hunger, but with a terrible intelligence as well. Through the umbilical attachment, it can access its mother's husk and what's left of her mind, devouring her memories and controlling her body's movements. It perches atop the ruined remains of the body and makes use of her arms and legs in spider-like movements to walk and climb. The rigors of its indelicate control often fracture the bones of the mother's limbs, creating joint articulations that were never meant to be, but the controlling offspring cares little and finds its movements unimpeded by these injuries. The controlling offspring and the lolling, idiot head of the mother sport the same terrible grin of razor-sharp teeth. The gravid ghoul's fetal skin tissue is dry and cracked. It uses its tremendously long, bright-red tongue to bathe itself in its mother's bloody, rotting fluids.

The flesh of the fetal portion of a gravid ghoul is fragile and requires constant bathing in the moisture of its womb-perch to avoid drying out. However, in a dry environment, this is insufficient to maintain the tissue's requirements, causing it to desiccate and crack. If a gravid ghoul does not have access to a moist environment for more than 1 hour (a place that is foggy or has open puddles of water is sufficient to meet its needs), it begins drying out painfully. More than an hour of drying out shuts down the ghoul's Diseased Exudate ability until it reaches another source of moisture.

A gravid ghoul stalks the night looking for prey. They tend to venture into sewer networks, better to keep out of sight and in the shadows. The wet nature of sewer systems helps the gravid ghoul to keep its fetal-self moist.

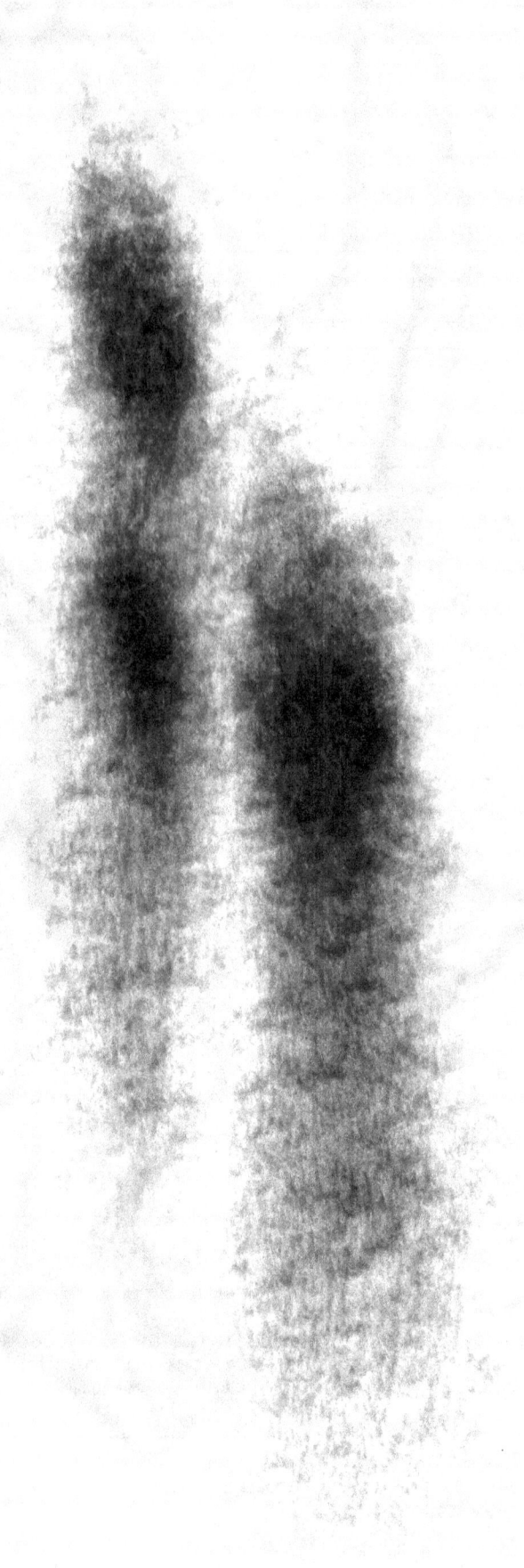

Golem, Lesser Flesh

A creature staggers into view, a construct that is pieces of flesh carved and assembled into a vaguely humanoid whole.

Lesser Flesh Golem
Medium construct, neutral

Armor Class 9
Hit Points 60 (8d8 + 24)
Damage Immunities Lightning, poison; nonmagical, non-adamantine weapons; charm, exhaustion, fright, paralysis, petrification, poison
Speed 30 ft.

STR	DEX	CON	INT	WIS	CHA
17 (+3)	9 (-1)	16 (+3)	4 (-3)	10 (+0)	5 (-3)

Senses darkvision 60 ft., passive Perception 10
Languages understands the language of its creator but can't speak
Challenge 3 (700 XP)

Berserk. When a lesser flesh golem starts its turn with 26 or fewer hit points, it has a 1-in-6 chance of going berserk. A berserk golem attacks the nearest living creature it can reach. The construct's creator can regain control over the golem, if he's within 60 feet, by using an action and making a successful DC 15 Charisma (Persuasion) check.
Fear of Fire. If the golem takes fire damage, it has disadvantage on attack rolls and ability checks until the end of its next turn.
Lightning Absorption. Each point of lightning damage that hits the golem heals 1 hit point.
Magic Resistance. A lesser flesh golem has advantage on saving throws against magic. It is immune to effects that would alter its form.

ACTIONS
Multiattack. The golem slams twice.
Slam. *Melee Weapon Attack:* +5 to hit (reach 5 ft.; one creature). *Hit:* 2d6 + 3 bludgeoning damage.

ECOLOGY
Environment any land
Organization solitary or pair

A lesser flesh golem is constructed from a whole cadaver or a number of humanoid body parts stitched together into a single composite form. It moves with a stiff-jointed gait as if not in complete control of its body. A lesser flesh golem typically stands 6 feet tall and weighs 300 pounds.

While most lesser flesh golems are mindless, some reanimate with a sliver of sentience, and with that spark comes memories of a previous life. The head and brain of such a lesser flesh golem must be just the right combination of fresh enough and (in its previous life) strong-willed, and even then luck and chance during the lesser flesh golem's creation seem just as important in retaining the creature's mind. These sentient flesh golems have the same stats as other lesser flesh golems, but can have Intelligence 6–16.

Lesser flesh golems cannot normally speak, but sentient lesser flesh golems retain the knowledge of one language they knew in life (usually Common). They have a difficult time expressing themselves in anything more than simple terms, but, in most cases, a sense of horror at their newfound state is easy to discern. With patient reeducation, they might be able to regain much of their former intellect.

Great Canal Python

A serpentine behemoth glides silently through the still water. Large fishing hooks protrude from its hide where they have snagged in past attempts to capture the creature, and the jagged blade of a broken harpoon is embedded in one side of its jaw.

Great Canal Python

Huge beast, unaligned

Armor Class 13
Hit Points 93 (11d12 + 22)
Speed 30 ft., swim 30 ft.

STR	DEX	CON	INT	WIS	CHA
20 (+5)	14 (+2)	14 (+2)	1 (-5)	10 (+0)	4 (-3)

Saving Throws Dex +5, Con +5, Wis +3
Skills Perception +3, Stealth +5
Damage Immunities poison
Condition Immunities prone
Senses blindsight 60 ft. (in water), passive Perception 13
Languages none
Challenge 5 (1,800 XP)

Lockjaw. Every creature that took slashing damage from the python must make a DC 13 Constitution saving throw at the end of their next long rest after the combat. If the saving throw fails, the creature contracts lockjaw from the rusty harpoon blade embedded through the python's jaw. An affected creature is unable to speak until the disease is cured with *lesser restoration* or *comparable magic.*

ACTIONS
Bite. *Melee Weapon Attack:* +8 to hit (reach 10 ft.; one creature). *Hit:* 2d6 + 5 piercing damage.
Constrict. *Melee Weapon Attack:* +8 to hit (reach 5 ft.; one creature). *Hit:* 2d8 + 5 bludgeoning damage plus 3d6 slashing damage, and the creature is grappled (escape DC 15) and restrained. A grappled creature takes 2d8 + 5 bludgeoning plus 3d6 slashing damage at the start of the python's turn. The python can constrict only one creature at a time. Creatures that take slashing damage may contract Lockjaw (see above).

ECOLOGY
Environment urban waterway (the Blight)
Organization solitary

This amazing specimen of serpentkind was brought at considerable risk and expense all the way from the Razor Coast for a Castorhage menagerie, only to promptly break free from its inadequate containment and escape into the murky water of the Great Canal. Already a beast of incredible strength and endurance, its years spent among the deadly denizens of the city's water has honed it into a truly apex predator. It spends most of its time sleeping in the shallows of the canal during the day, looking like nothing more than the normal detritus that lines the canal bottom. At night it swims silently just beneath the surface in search of prey — whether it be some creature of the canal itself or some boatman or dockworker unlucky enough to have caught its attention. The massive serpent feeds nightly, so there are always disappearances near the water that can likely be attributed it, and the occasional finding of a massive molted skin beneath a dock or in a canal-side alley keeps the presence of the creature fresh on everyone's mind. Many fishermen, hunters, and guardsmen have died in attempts to destroy the creature when it has been spotted, and its thickly gnarled hide bears many scars and marks of these hunts. So far, however, it has always proven to be the superior hunter in these contests.

The city of Castorhage has offered a 10,000-gp reward if this beast is captured or killed.

Hollow and Broken Hills Crocodile

A large crocodile floats in a pool of swampy water, completely still. Its eyes have been replaced by large multifaceted green jewels.

Hollow and Broken Hills Crocodile
Huge monstrosity, chaotic neutral

Armor Class 16 (natural armor)
Hit Points 126 (12d12 + 48)
Speed 30 ft., swim 50 ft.

STR	DEX	CON	INT	WIS	CHA
22 (+6)	10 (+0)	18 (+4)	13 (+1)	13 (+1)	14 (+2)

Skills Insight +9, Perception +9, Stealth +4
Damage Resistances bludgeoning, piercing, and slashing from nonmagical weapons
Damage Immunities blindness
Senses truesight 60 ft., passive Perception 19
Languages Common, Deep Speech, telepathy 60 ft.
Challenge 9 (5,000 XP)

Charming Gemstone. A creature that starts its turn within 30 feet of the crocodile, or that moves to within 30 feet on its turn, must make a successful DC 14 Charisma saving throw or be charmed by the crocodile for 1 minute or until it takes damage. A charmed creature repeats the saving throw when it takes damage.
Hold Breath. The crocodile can hold its breath for 30 minutes.
Lunging Bite (recharge 6). The crocodile extends the reach of its bite attack by 5 feet until the start of its next turn (no action required).
Innate Spellcasting. The crocodile's green gemstone eyes enable it to use the following spell-like abilities, using Charisma as its casting ability (DC 14). The crocodile needs no components to use these abilities.

    2/day each: *fear, hypnotic pattern, suggestion*
    1/day: *modify memory*

Water Camouflage. The crocodile has advantage on Stealth checks while in water.

ACTIONS
Multiattack. The Hollow and Broken Hills crocodile can use one spell-like ability and make both a bite attack and a tail swipe.
Bite. *Melee Weapon Attack:* +10 to hit (reach 5 ft.; one creature). *Hit:* 3d10 + 6 piercing damage, and the target is grappled (escape DC 16) and restrained. A restrained creature takes 3d10 + 6 piercing damage at the start of the crocodile's turn. The crocodile can't bite another creature while it has a creature grappled, and it can grapple only one creature at a time.
Tail Swipe. *Melee Weapon Attack:* +10 to hit (reach 10 ft.; one creature not grappled by the crocodile). *Hit:* 2d8 + 6 bludgeoning damage, and the creature must make a successful DC 18 Strength saving throw or be knocked prone.

ECOLOGY
Environment sea (the Blight)
Organization solitary

The aged clergyman Neberiah Scrum was renowned for the fine herpetarium that he kept behind his modest church. If it made any of his parishioners nervous with its proximity, he never bothered to notice. His prized specimen was his saltwater crocodile "Nellie" that he had obtained at considerable expense. Feeding it live gulls in its pen every Prayerday after services was a hobby that he particularly relished. But apparently the Good Reverend Scrum had other hobbies as well, and these occurred at night behind the closed doors of the church and involved strange rituals. On one occasion, he decided to combine his two favorite pastimes and brought Nellie into the church on a chain leash for one of these late-night ceremonies. The next day, the church was found locked. Upon forcing the door, the constables found the Reverend Scrum lying dead upon the floor, along with the corpses of four other, unidentifiable men. Their bodies lay roughly in a circle with the fragments of a shattered mirror lying between them next to a chain leash. Of Nellie, there was no sign. The herpetarium was torn down, its occupants sold or released, and the church was repurposed as a storage building for uncertified relics — the bones, grave shrouds, and assorted organs and body parts dried or stored in jars of brine and ascribed to belong to saints for whom the church has been unable to confirm provenance.

In that last fateful ritual performed in the church, somehow Reverend Scrum's beloved pet slipped into Between. She remained there for 8 hours before finding her way back to the city, and, upon her return, she was no longer the same. Nellie had become the Hollow and Broken Hills

Crocodile. The effects upon Nellie's body were remarkable: her eyes replaced by two large jewels of unidentifiable stone, her body infused with the very essence of that realm. But the effects upon her mind were far more profound. The Hollow and Broken Hills Crocodile had gained a new awareness, an awareness above and beyond that of the mundane world and its hairless monkey masters. The Hollow and Broken Hills Crocodile was given the ability to "see" in a way that normal minds cannot comprehend.

The crocodile now haunts the waterways and brackish pools that make up the lower reaches of the Broken and Hollow Hills, occasionally glimpsed by some passer-by. It is not a hunter like other creatures that stalk the city, or at least not in the same way. The crocodile lurks in the dark, wet places of the district, remaining almost motionless for days on end. When it feels hunger, it merely opens its great maw and some river trout or gull inevitably ventures inward of its own volition, disappearing into the maw as it slowly closes — never a squawk or a splash to disturb the silence. At times, every few weeks or months the crocodile springs into motion, suddenly needing to be somewhere or do some task that only its mind comprehends. But there are no warning signs of when it's about to make these sudden violent movements, so more than one fisherman has been crippled or killed when what he thought was a log floating nearby suddenly became a flurry of motion with its 2,000-pound frame bull rushing on its way, heedless of its surroundings. Also, after reports of the crocodile's sudden thrashing appearances and subsequent disappearances, inevitably a citizen or two of the district will go missing. No one knows for sure if these disappearances are connected to the activities of the crocodile, but the missing are never found and speculation tends to run in that vein.

The green gemstone eyes of the Hollow and Broken Hills Crocodile are of no known mineral and are an organic part of the creature's body, rather than just being inset like jewelry. Most of its supernatural abilities seem to arise from the gemstones. The gemstone eyes no longer function if removed from the crocodile, though they may still be of value to some scholars.

What the Hollow and Broken Hills Crocodile sees with its gemstone eyes remains a mystery to all, but those who study things esoteric speculate as to the nature of the secrets that they might reveal. That the creature has been to Between and back, beginning as an ordinary animal and returning as something else entirely further fuels interest among those who practice strange, arcane arts. Because the Hollow and Broken Hills Crocodile does not seem to actively prey upon the folk of Castorhage, the city has taken a more ambivalent approach toward its existence. There is only a 1,000-gp reward for its capture or death, but the Illuminati have discreetly offered 10,000 gp to anyone who can bring it to them alive and intact.

The Hollow and Broken Hills Crocodile is 23 feet long and weighs 2,000 pounds. Other than its strange eyes and mannerisms, it physically resembles a massive saltwater crocodile, though it flourishes as well in the brackish waters of the district and the Lyme. Though it carries the Between-touched template from the time it spent in that realm, it long ago lost its temporary hit points associated with that template and has never been able to return to Between to replenish them.

Copyright Notice

Hooded Raven

This ash-gray raven is as large as an eagle, and has glossy black plumage over its head as well on the backs of its wings and tail, which give it an appearance of wearing an executioner's hood and robes. Its eyes are unusually large for a raven, and seem to be almost mesmerizing in their depths.

The sight of the hooded raven flying overhead is seen as an ill omen and that someone soon will perish. These creatures, like all carrion birds, have clawed talons and sharp beaks perfect for tearing flesh. Their enhanced eyesight allows them to spot a meal from great distances, and they typically swoop down the wide lanes of city streets high above the ground in search of a ripening carcass or a live mouse.

The hooded raven is omnivorous, with a diet similar to that of the carrion crow, and is a constant scavenger. It drops mollusks and crabs to break them after the manner of the crow, and the common name for empty sea urchin shells is "crow's cups." It also feeds on small mammals, scraps, smaller birds, and carrion. The raven has the habit of hiding food, especially meat or nuts, in places such as rain gutters, flowerpots, or in the earth under bushes to feed on later, and sometimes on the insects that have meanwhile been attracted to it.

These large cousins of normal ravens generally weigh between 6 and 8 pounds, with a wingspan of up to 4 feet.

A hooded raven uses the standard raven stat block but with the added trait **Prognostication (1/day):** Hooded ravens have a natural ability to predict the immediate future. Once per day, it gets a +10 bonus on any die roll (including a damage roll) or to its AC. The bonus can be applied after dice are rolled but before the final result is determined.

Copyright Notice
Author Jeffrey Swank, based on material by Richard Pett.

Horde, Larva

This hideous mass is composed of bloated, human-size maggots that curl and twist in a tangle of disgusting bodies. Worse is the fact that each of these worm-things has a human face — that of a man or a woman, mouth agape, and distorted into an expression of utmost horror and suffering.

Larva Horde

Large monstrosity, chaotic evil

Armor Class 10
Hit Points 88 (16d10)
Speed 30 ft.

STR	DEX	CON	INT	WIS	CHA
16 (+3)	10 (+0)	11 (+0)	4 (-3)	8 (-2)	4 (-3)

Saving Throws Con +3, Wis +1, Cha +0
Damage Resistances acid, cold, lightning
Damage Immunities charmed, grappled, paralyzed, petrified, prone, restrained
Senses darkvision 60 ft., passive Perception 8
Languages understands Abyssal but can't speak
Challenge 8 (3,900 XP)

Ferocity. When the larva horde drops to 0 hit points, it immediately makes one bite attack against every creature within 5 feet as a reaction before dying.
Horde. The horde can occupy the same space as other creatures. *Up to four Medium or smaller creatures can share the same space as the larva horde, or one Large creature.* All creatures that are in the larva horde's space at the start of the horde's turn take 6d6 slashing damage and, if they aren't grappled already, must make a successful DC 14 Strength saving throw or be grappled (escape DC 13).

ACTIONS
Multiattack. The horde bites four times, regardless of how many creatures it has grappled.
Bite. *Melee Weapon Attack:* +6 to hit (reach 5 ft.; one creature). *Hit:* 2d6 + 3 piercing damage, and the creature must make a successful DC 14 Strength saving throw or be grappled (escape DC 13) and pulled into the horde's space.
Burst of Bile. All creatures in the larva horde's space or within 10 feet of it take 3d6 acid damage, or half damage with a successful DC 14 Dexterity saving throw.

ECOLOGY
Environment any (Abyss)
Organization solitary, ball (2–5), or judgment (6–15)

The souls of chaotic evil peoples find their way to the Abyss where they become a type of petitioner called a larva. Though sentient, these worm-like proto-demons find themselves subjected to every form of degradation imaginable, until their minds break and they become little more than animalistic embodiments of torment and rage. Those that survive being devoured by demons, stolen by night hags, sacrificed by liches, or struck down by the myriad unnatural hazards of that realm are forced to sup upon the foul effluvia that drains to its lowest gutters, unfit even for the demons' guard beasts. Those larvae that are able to endure these torments and that consume enough of this Abyssal filth eventually find themselves transformed into the lowest of demons from where they can begin their improbable opportunity to rise to power within the Abyss. Most never last that long, and on many occasions when large numbers of larvae are present, they gather together into a massive tangled horde both for mutual **DEFENSE** and to feed upon each other as a pleasant change from their normal diet. On some occasions, a larva that is able to fend off and consume an entire horde of its brethren may find itself elevated to the ranks of demons much sooner than would otherwise be possible, so larvae attempt to form a horde whenever possible in order to increase that possibility.

Hydra-Hag

She could be one of the many destitute poor found in the many alleys and doorways of the city except for the five snakelike necks protruding from her shoulders, each of which ends in the head of a ghastly crone.

Hydra-Hag

Medium monstrosity (aquatic), chaotic evil

Armor Class 14 (natural armor)
Hit Points 110 (13d8 + 52)
Speed 20 ft., swim 30 ft.

STR	DEX	CON	INT	WIS	CHA
19 (+4)	14 (+2)	18 (+4)	14 (+2)	12 (+1)	18 (+4)

Skills Perception +5
Damage Resistances bludgeoning, piercing, and slashing from nonmagical weapons
Senses darkvision 90 ft., passive Perception 15
Languages Common, Deep Speech, Giant
Challenge 8 (3,900 XP)

Hag Heads. Each surviving head can always bite, but only one can use its special ability on the hydra-hag's turn. Roll 1d5 at the start of the hydra-hag's turn to determine which head is dominant (uses its special ability) that turn. If that head is gone, roll again until a surviving head is chosen. Hags are immune to all these effects.

Flue Hag—Soot Breath. The flue hag head belches out a 20-foot-cloud of blinding, choking soot. All creatures in the cloud must make a successful DC 15 Constitution saving throw or be blinded for 1 minute. The creature can repeat the saving throw at the end of each of its turns, ending the effect on itself on a success.

Green Hag—Mimicry. The green hag head imitates a sound it has heard. This is largely a "gift" for the characters, who get a 1-round break from the more dangerous attacks of the other heads. If, however, the hydra-hag has heard a sound that has the potential to frighten or confuse characters—a friend screaming in pain, a trusted ally yelling for help—it uses that against the PCs, who must make successful DC 15 Wisdom saving throws to not be fooled by the sound.

Mute Hag—Shaping Touch. If mute hag's bite attack hits and the creature fails its saving throw, in addition to the usual effect, the creature also suffers a debilitating change in its physical form. Roll 1d4: 1 = speed halved (legs twisted or shortened), 2 = -2 on attacks (arms twisted or shortened), 3 = -2 on Perception checks (face altered so vision is obscured or distorted), 4 = -2 on Constitution saving throws (midsection com-

pressed or distorted). These penalties are permanent until removed by *greater restoration* or comparable magic.

Sea Hag—Evil Eye. Every humanoid within 30 feet of the hydra-hag must make a successful DC 15 Wisdom saving throw or be frightened of the hydra-hag for 1 minute. A frightened creature repeats the saving throw at the end of its turn, ending the effect on itself with a success. Subsequent saves are made with disadvantage while the sea hag head is alive and within sight.

Winter Hag—Frost Breath. The winter hag head exhales a 30-foot cone of frost. Every creature in the cone takes 4d6 cold

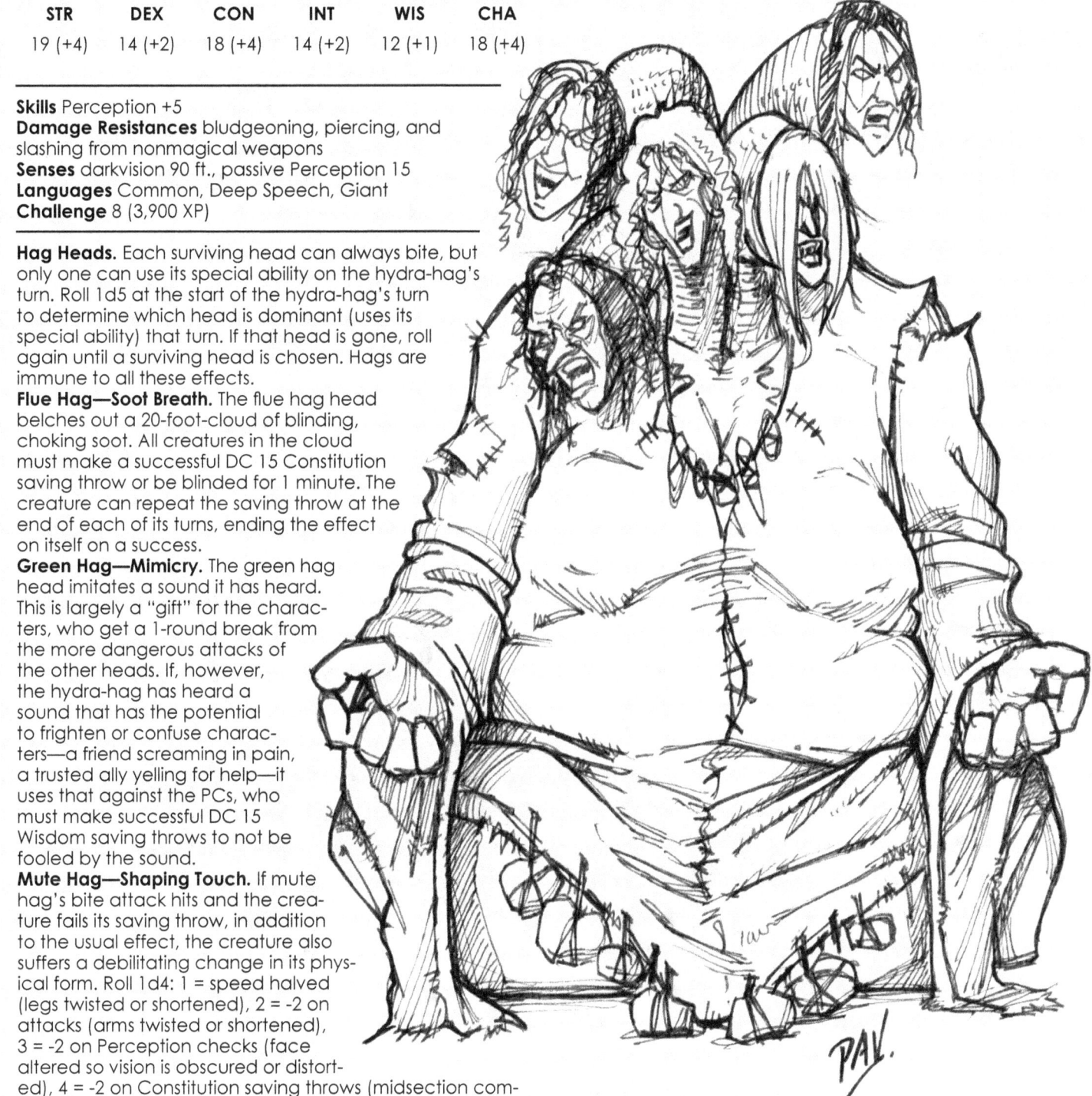

damage and is blinded for 1 minute. The creature can repeat the saving throw at the end of each of its turns, ending the effect on itself on a success.

Multiple Heads. An attack against the hydra-hag that does 20 or more damage destroys one of the hydra-hag's heads, selected at random. For each head that's missing at the start of the hydra-hag's turn, roll 1d6; on a roll of 5 or 6, that head grows back immediately. If all five heads are gone at the same time, the hydra-hag dies. While the hydra-hag has more than one head, it has advantage on saving throws against blindness, charm, deafness, fright, stunning, and unconsciousness.

ACTIONS

Multiattack. They hydra-hag uses the special ability of one randomly-chosen head, then each of its surviving heads bites once.

Flue Hag Bite. *Melee Weapon Attack:* +7 to hit (reach 5 ft.; one creature). *Hit:* 1d8 + 4 piercing damage plus 1d6 fire damage.

Green Hag Bite. *Melee Weapon Attack:* +7 to hit (reach 5 ft.; one creature). *Hit:* 1d8 + 4 piercing damage.

Mute Hag Bite. *Melee Weapon Attack:* +7 to hit (reach 5 ft.; one creature). *Hit:* 1d8 + 4 piercing damage, and a creature must make a successful DC 18 Wisdom saving throw or have disadvantage on attacks against the hydra-hag until the end of the creature's next turn.

Sea Hag Bite. *Melee Weapon Attack:* +7 to hit (reach 5 ft.; one creature). *Hit:* 1d8 + 4 piercing damage, and a creature must make a successful DC 15 Wisdom saving throw or be frightened of the hydra-hag until the end of the creature's next turn.

Winter Hag Bite. *Melee Weapon Attack:* +7 to hit (reach 5 ft.; one creature). *Hit:* 1d8 + 4 piercing damage plus 1d10 cold damage.

ECOLOGY

Environment urban (the Blight)
Organization solitary

Considered a "successful" experiment in the unnatural manipulation of living flesh, the hydra-hag is a truly horrifying creature. The fact that it has managed to breed true is additionally disturbing, especially when one stops to consider what serves as its breeding stock. Not many such creatures are known to prowl the byways of the city, but those who do know are well advised to stay clear. The personalities of the different heads of a hydra-hag vie for control, and while one day a hydra-hag may feel content to root through the garbage of a landfill or simply enjoy the eddies and currents of Sister Lyme, it is just as likely to unleash its powers at any moment upon those who had previously allied with it. The fact that the hydra-hag's diet other than rats and stray cats is humanoids — especially street urchins — is not lost on most who encounter them and live to tell of it. However, despite their abominable appearance, hydra-hags are adept at staying out of sight during the day, so the half-hearted efforts made in the past to find them and round them up have met with limited success.

The five differing heads of the hydra-hag make its daily life a constant battle for control and does a lot to ensure that the creatures not truly rise to power in the city's underworld. They are too fractured within their own minds to manage much in the way of an organized plan. The heads of a hydra-hag cannot constitute a coven on their own, and multiple hydra-hags together have proven unable to do so either because of the chaos inherent to that many disparate personalities.

Hydra-hags are universally corpulently obese, which has much to do with having five different mouths that all crave to be fed but only one body between them to process what is eaten. And without the massive body or metabolism of a true hydra, they are simply not able to handle their intake. It is not at all uncommon to find a hydra-hag vomiting its last meal from multiple heads as its gastric system rebels at the abuse. Whether this contributes to their overall surliness is suspect, but they clearly lead a very uncomfortable existence in the unnatural form they were given. Despite their notoriously voracious appetites, hydra-hags actually have bite attacks only with two of their heads — the mute hag head and the flue hag head. Only the flue hag head has the searing bite.

Hydra-hags stand about 6 feet high at the shoulder with another 3 feet of neck and head. They typically weigh close to 350 pounds.

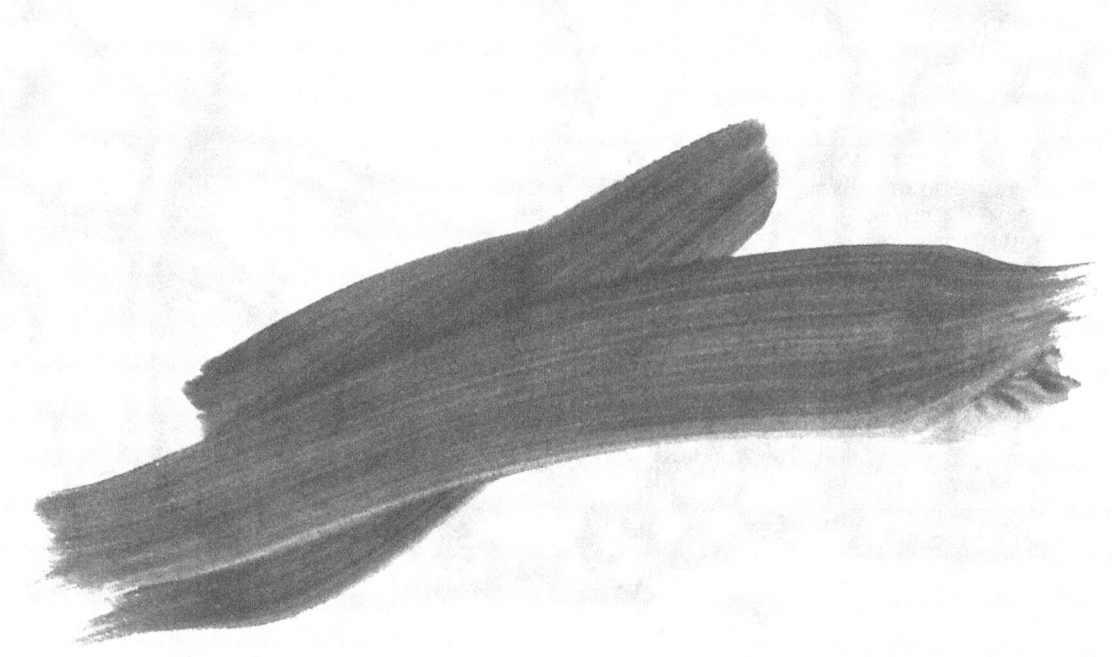

Living Disease, Bloody Flux

A dark mist roils and retracts, probing its environment with ephemeral tendrils.

Bloody Flux

Medium swarm of Tiny monstrosities, unaligned

Armor Class 12
Hit Points 22 (5d8)
Speed fly 10 ft., swim 10 ft.

STR	DEX	CON	INT	WIS	CHA
1 (-5)	14 (+2)	10 (+0)	1 (-5)	6 (-2)	1 (-5)

Skills Stealth +6
Damage Resistances bludgeoning, piercing, slashing
Damage Immunities force
Condition Immunities blinded, charmed, deafened, exhaustion, frightened, grappled, incapacitated, paralyzed, petrified, prone, stunned, unconscious
Senses blindsight 60 ft., passive Perception 8
Languages none
Challenge 1 (200 XP)

Amorphous. The swarm can move through gaps as small as 1 square inch without penalty. It can move through and remain in spaces occupied by other creatures without hindrance.

Blend Into Darkness. A swarm of bloody flux is invisible in dim light.

Bloody Flux. A creature that starts its turn in the same space as a swarm of bloody flux must make a successful DC 10 Constitution saving throw or contract the disease bloody flux. A creature that contracts bloody flux gains 1 level of exhaustion immediately and must make a DC 10 Constitution saving throw after every long rest. If the saving throw fails, the creature gains another level of exhaustion; if it succeeds, the creature recovers from 1 level of exhaustion. The disease ends when the creature has no levels of exhaustion or when it receives a *lesser restoration* spell or comparable magic.

Regeneration. The swarm heals 5 hit points at the start of its turn. This ability doesn't function if it took cold or poison damage since its previous turn.

Vulnerability to Healing. A *lesser restoration* spell cast on a living disease kills the swarm instantly.

ACTIONS

Swarm. *Melee Weapon Attack:* +7 to hit (reach 5 ft.; one creature). *Hit:* 1d8 + 2 piercing damage.

ECOLOGY

Environment urban (the Blight)
Organization solitary or plague (2-7)

Living diseases are swarms of harmful bacteria or viruses that have supernaturally gained limited sentience under exceedingly foul or magical conditions. They seek out hosts to propagate their contagion. Their individual components are microscopic; the only reason they can be seen is because they form swarms containing billions of individual organisms.

A living disease has the appearance of a floating shadow or dimness with indistinct edges. It offers no resistance to solid objects that enter its space; it can't be felt even as a subtle dampness (like a mist) or coolness (like a shadow). They make no sound whatsoever. They're most dangerous at twilight and nighttime, when their presence in a dimly-lit campsite or hovel is almost impossible to detect.

Living diseases are extremely rare, but they are also highly varied. There are potentially as many different kinds of living diseases as there are diseases. Only bloody flux is described here, but it can be used as a model for others. A living disease instinctively avoids undead, oozes, plants, constructs, and other creatures that aren't suitable hosts.

This disease is endemic to the Sinks district of Castorhage, with a major outbreak occurring every few years though largely remaining contained to that portion of the city. On occasion, it spreads to other poor, overcrowded areas of the city where clean water is in short supply. Bloody flux is generally contracted through exposure to water that's been contaminated with fecal matter from someone already suffering from the disease or, as is the case in the Sinks, the presence of one or more bloody flux living diseases that travel through sewers and along filthy gutters lining the streets. The disease enters the intestinal tract of the victim and causes inflammation resulting in fever, painful cramping, and frequent bloody diarrhea that leads to severe dehydration and eventually death.

Lyme Angler (Slop-Shark)

This ugly, bloated fish has a glowing, fleshy protrusion that extends from the top of its skull and dangles in front of its wide-mouth, which is filled with needle-like fangs.

Lyme Angler

Large beast (aquatic), unaligned

Armor Class 12 (natural armor)
Hit Points 51 (6d10 + 18)
Speed 0 ft., swim 30 ft.

STR	DEX	CON	INT	WIS	CHA
18 (+4)	13 (+1)	16 (+3)	1 (-5)	10 (+0)	2 (-5)

Condition Immunities prone
Senses darkvision 30 ft., passive Perception 10
Languages none
Challenge 3 (700 XP)

Brine Misery. This infection is an extremely sore, itchy, red inflammation around the site of the lyme angler bite. An infected creature gains 1 level of exhaustion immediately. There is no other effect, but the disease can be cured only with a *lesser restoration* spell or comparable magic.

Lantern Lure. A bioluminescent lure dangles from the lyme angler's forehead, giving off dim light within 15 feet. Creatures within that distance and able to see the light must make a successful DC 13 Wisdom saving throw or be charmed by the lyme angler. While charmed this way, an air-breathing creature won't surface to take a fresh breath of air. A charmed creature repeats the saving throw at the end of its turn, ending the effect on itself with a success. A creature that makes a successful save is immune to all lyme angler lantern lures for 24 hours.

ACTIONS

Bite. *Melee Weapon Attack:* +6 to hit (reach 5 ft.; one creature). *Hit:* 2d4 + 4 piercing damage and the creature must make a successful DC 13 Constitution saving throw or contract brine misery (see above).

ECOLOGY

Environment sea
Organization school (1-100)

Also known as a slop-shark to those along the River Lyme, the Lyme angler is among the most ferocious of predatory fish in and around that waterway. Lyme anglers have a luminescent organ called a lantern lure at the tip of a modified dorsal ray (or fishing rod). The organ serves not only the purpose of luring prey in the warm, shallow, polluted water of the Lyme, but also serves to call males' attention to the females to facilitate mating. The source of luminescence in this organ is a symbiotic species of brine shrimp that lives in and along the Lyme and has an affinity for the lantern lure organ of the Lyme angler. Through a complex chemical reaction, the Lyme angler is able to agitate these brine shrimp and cause them to illuminate its lure at will.

These diseased things of corruption and toxin are common in the Lyme. They have fanged-filled mouths, and their bodies are riddled with sores, infestations, and chemical burns — proof that there are places even they cannot swim safely. One of the most notorious man-eaters of the river, the biggest Lyme anglers can reach lengths of more than 20 feet and weigh up to 5,000 pounds.

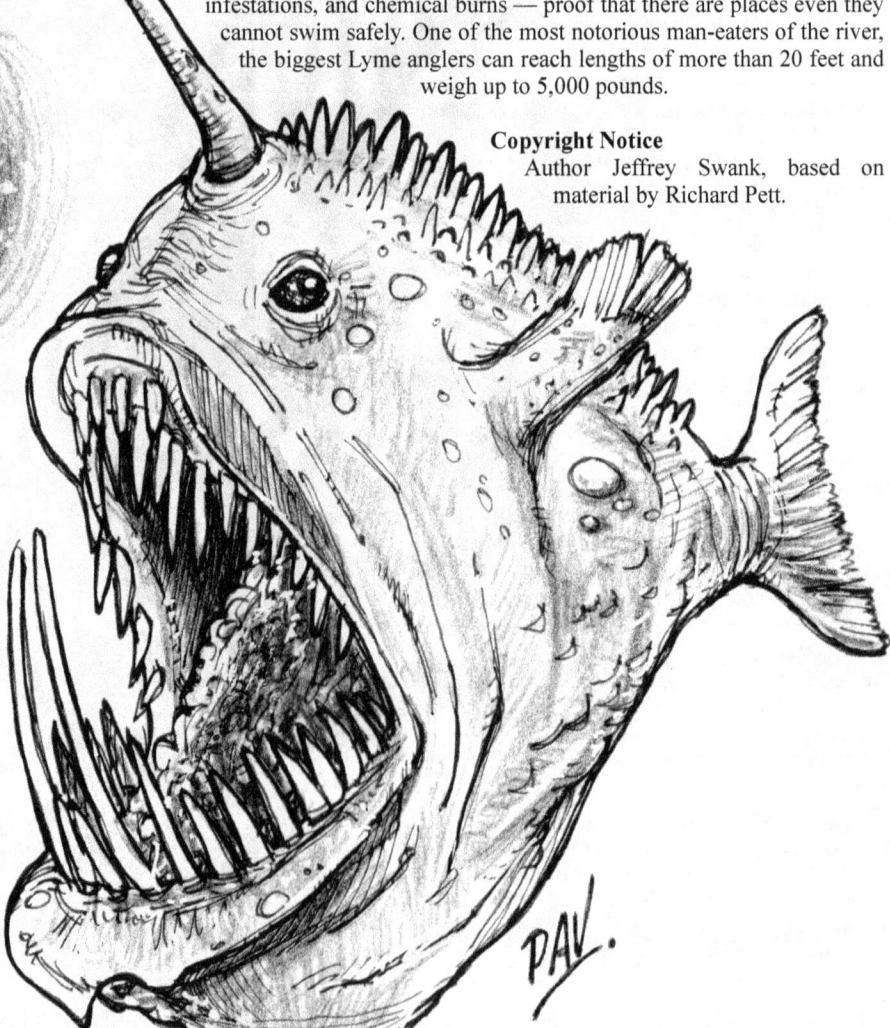

Lyme Walrus

Thick folds of fleshy blubber encase this massive sea creature. Yet despite its bestial appearance, its eyes reveal calculating intelligence, and it holds itself upright with unusual dignity. The illusion of a man would almost be convincing were it not for the long tusks that protrude from its whiskered mouth.

Lyme Walrus

Large humanoid, chaotic neutral

Armor Class 12 (natural armor)
Hit Points 93 (11d10 + 33)
Speed 20 ft., swim 40ft.

STR	DEX	CON	INT	WIS	CHA
19 (+4)	11 (+0)	17 (+3)	10 (+0)	12 (+1)	16 (+3)

Skills Perception +3, Performance +7, Persuasion +5
Damage Resistances cold; bludgeoning, piercing, and slashing from nonmagical weapons
Senses darkvision 60 ft., passive Perception 13
Languages Common
Challenge 4 (1,100 XP)

Fascinating Story. A Lyme walrus can manipulate its guttural voice while weaving a fascinating story. Creatures within 60 feet that can see and hear the Lyme walrus for 1 minute or longer must make successful DC 13 Charisma saving throws or be charmed and stunned for as long as the Lyme walrus continues speaking. Combat and other severe distractions prevent the ability from working. A creature that saves successfully is immune to Fascinating Story for 24 hours. Any potential threat allows a charmed creature to repeat the saving throw, ending the effect on itself with a success. Taking damage breaks the effect automatically on the injured creature. A creature need not understand Common for this ability to work; the power is in how the Lyme walrus modulates the sound of its voice, not in the words it speaks.

Innate Spellcasting. The Lyme walrus can use the following spell-like abilities, using Charisma as its casting ability (DC 13). The Lyme walrus needs only vocal components to use these abilities.

At will: *minor illusion*
3/day each: *disguise self, major image*

ACTIONS
Multiattack. The lyme walrus bites twice.
Bite. *Melee Weapon Attack:* +6 to hit (reach 5 ft.; one creature). *Hit:* †

ECOLOGY
Environment coast
Organization solitary or team (1 Lyme walrus with 1–6 scouts, spies, or master thieves)

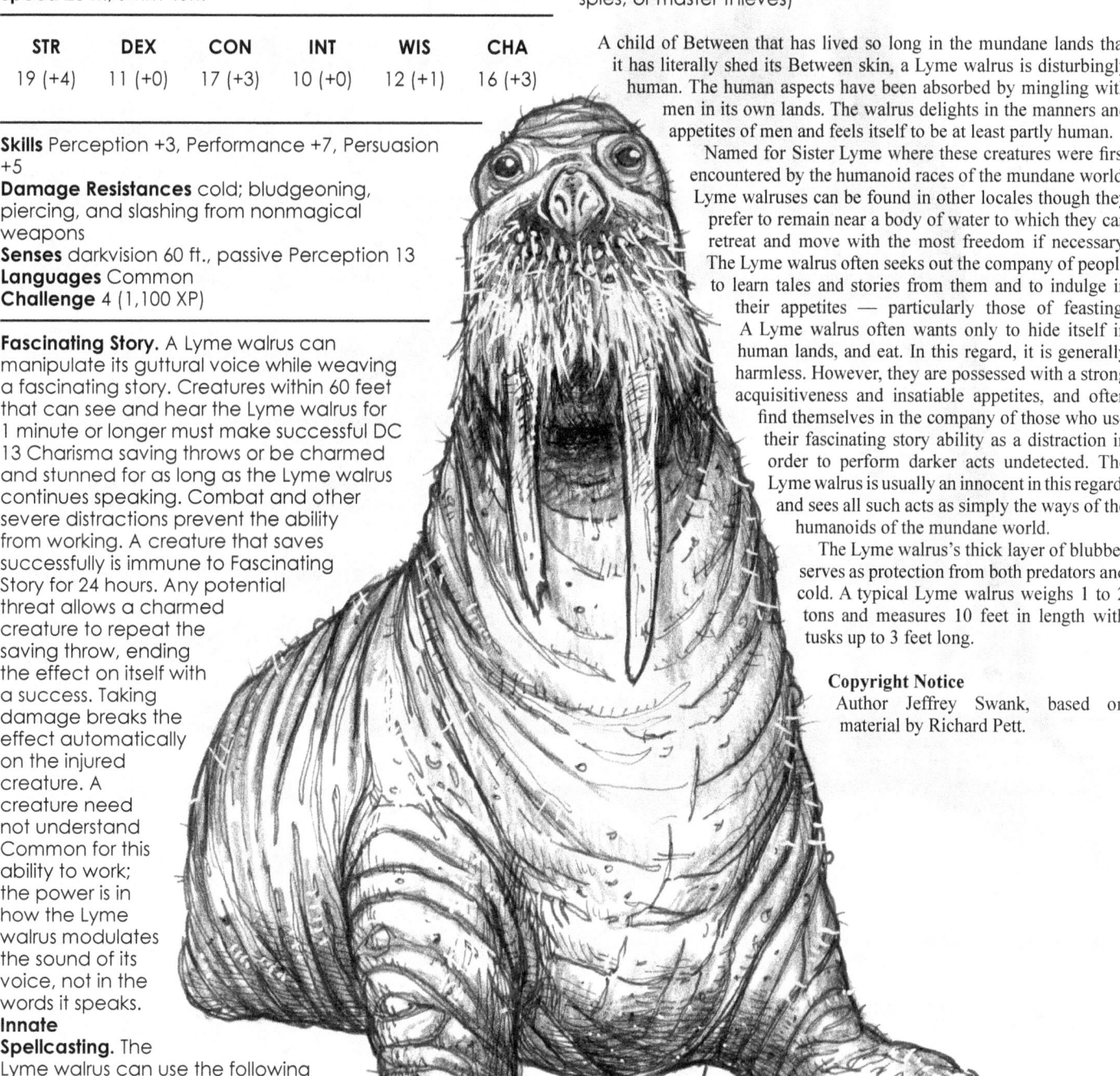

A child of Between that has lived so long in the mundane lands that it has literally shed its Between skin, a Lyme walrus is disturbingly human. The human aspects have been absorbed by mingling with men in its own lands. The walrus delights in the manners and appetites of men and feels itself to be at least partly human.

Named for Sister Lyme where these creatures were first encountered by the humanoid races of the mundane world, Lyme walruses can be found in other locales though they prefer to remain near a body of water to which they can retreat and move with the most freedom if necessary. The Lyme walrus often seeks out the company of people to learn tales and stories from them and to indulge in their appetites — particularly those of feasting. A Lyme walrus often wants only to hide itself in human lands, and eat. In this regard, it is generally harmless. However, they are possessed with a strong acquisitiveness and insatiable appetites, and often find themselves in the company of those who use their fascinating story ability as a distraction in order to perform darker acts undetected. The Lyme walrus is usually an innocent in this regard, and sees all such acts as simply the ways of the humanoids of the mundane world.

The Lyme walrus's thick layer of blubber serves as protection from both predators and cold. A typical Lyme walrus weighs 1 to 2 tons and measures 10 feet in length with tusks up to 3 feet long.

Moon Angel

This thin, stretched creature has gangly, long limbs that bend in unusual ways. Its skin is pale and sickly with its face shrunken in its drooping, hairless head. Pointed ears rise high above the crown of its head, and its eyes are sunk deep beneath its brow like two bottomless pits. Its toothless mouth hangs open, jaw slack, as it incessantly licks its withered lips.

Moon Angel

Large fey, neutral evil

Armor Class 14
Hit Points 97 (13d10 + 26)
Speed 30 ft., swim 30 ft.

STR	DEX	CON	INT	WIS	CHA
13 (+1)	18 (+4)	15 (+2)	8 (-1)	10 (+0)	16 (+3)

Saving Throws Wis +3
Skills Stealth +7
Damage Resistances bludgeoning, piercing, and slashing from nonmagical weapons
Damage Immunities cold, poison
Condition Immunities disease; poisoned
Senses blindsight 30 ft., darkvision 60 ft., passive Perception 10
Languages Aquan, Common, Deep Speech
Challenge 5 (1,800 XP)

Hypnotic Song. A moon angel's song has the power to entrance those that hear it. All creatures aside from other moon angels within 300 feet of a singing moon angle must make a successful DC 14 Wisdom saving throw or be charmed by all moon angels. While charmed this way, a creature's speed is 0. A creature that successfully saves is immune to the hypnotic singing of all moon angels until the following sunrise. This effect lasts for as long as the moon angel continues singing and for 1 full round after it stops. A charmed creature is willing to accept a moon angel's Drowning Kiss.

ACTIONS

Multiattack. The moon angel attacks twice with its claws.
Claw. *Melee Weapon Attack:* +7 to hit (reach 5 ft.; one creature). *Hit:* 2d6 + 4 slashing damage plus 1d8 cold damage, and the creature must make a successful DC 13 Constitution saving throw or be paralyzed for 1 minute. A paralyzed creature repeats the saving throw at the end of its turn, ending the effect with a success.
Drowning Kiss. A moon angel can flood the lungs of a willing, sleeping, helpless, or hypnotized creature by touching it (traditionally by kissing the creature on the lips). If the target cannot breathe water, it immediately begins suffocating from drowning. A drowning creature makes a DC 13 Constitution saving throw at the end of its turn, coughing up the water and ending the effect with a success.

ECOLOGY

Environment sea
Organization solitary or school (2-5)

Oftentimes folk who fall into the river, even in the relative shallows, are never seen again even if help was close at hand. At such times, folk who dwell near the riverside make the sign against the evil eye and blame the disappearance on hidden currents carrying the victim into the depths or the normal fauna that makes the Great Lyme a graveyard for hundreds of citizens of Castorhage every year. However, sometimes the cause of the disappearance is more sinister than either of those. Sometimes it is the work of a moon angel.

The moon angel is a rare creature that lurks in the deepest, coldest waters of the Lyme, fond of rising to the surface and quietly watching the goings-on ashore, waiting for the unfortunate soul who loses his footing or is more drunk than careful and falls into the dark waters of the river. When it locates such a victim, it quickly moves to hypnotize him and draw him deeper into the waters where it can feed at its leisure.

A creature of the coldest fathoms of the river where depth and pollution block the sun, a moon angel cannot stay long near the warm surface while it waits for prey. It becomes uncomfortable from the heat and light, and can even develop severe sunburns on its pale skin when remaining too close to the surface for long. For this reason, the depredations of the moon angels remain relatively rare. The occurrences do increase in the winter months when a thin sheet of ice often covers the river's edges, though they still love the daylight no better then than they do in summer.

Occasionally on moonless nights, a moon angel may leave the river under the cover of darkness to hunt additional victims on land. At these times, such a creature tends to clamber along the rooftops to find open windows to take meat from within, with any household survivors the next morning describing only dreams of a strange crooning song echoing through their sleep. As with those who disappear into the river when a moon angel pays a visit, the unfortunate soul that has garnered its attention is never seen again. It for these incidences that the twisted fey known as moon angels gain their name, though few if any folk have made a connection between these nighttime disappearances and those that occur more frequently in the river.

Extremely tall and awkwardly gangly, the moon angel stands eight feet in height but weighs barely 250 lbs.

Naga, Blight

An exotically featured woman's head tops this snakelike creature. Its scales range in color from deep purple to black, with the creature's underside colored a lighter shade of violet. Ten arms protrude from the snake body's flanks, though they are spindly and frail in their musculature.

Blight Naga

Large aberration, chaotic neutral

Armor Class 14 (natural armor)
Hit Points 65 (10d10 + 10)
Speed 30 ft.

STR	DEX	CON	INT	WIS	CHA
8 (-1)	12 (+1)	12 (+1)	16 (+3)	7 (-2)	19 (+4)

Saving Throws Dex +3, Con +3, Wis +0
Skills Deception +6, Insight +2, Perception +0, Persuasion +6
Damage Immunities poison
Condition Immunities charmed, poisoned
Senses darkvision 60 ft., passive Perception 10
Languages Common, Deep Speech, Meeruwahn
Challenge 2 (450 XP)

Change Shape (3/day). A Blight naga can take the form of a human as an action. Each transformation lasts 10 minutes. If the naga impersonates a specific person, it must make a Deception check when it meets people who know the person being simulated.

Innate Spellcasting. The Blight naga can use the following spell-like abilities, using Charisma as its casting ability (DC 14). The Blight naga doesn't need material components to use these abilities.

At will: *comprehend languages, detect magic*
3/day each: *dispel magic, identify, magic aura, suggestion*
1/day: *dominate person*

ACTIONS
Bite. Melee Weapon Attack: +3 to hit (reach 5 ft.; one creature). *Hit:* 1d6 + 1 piercing damage plus 5d6 poison damage, or half poison damage with a successful DC 11 Constitution saving throw.

ECOLOGY
Environment urban (the Blight)
Organization solitary, pair, or family (2–4 adults and 1–3 young)

Blight nagas are aesthetes and artists that as a race have existed in the city for as long as anyone remembers. Whether they were indigenous inhabitants, early visitors from Between, or immigrants from a distant land is argued, but they have seemingly always been there. Most Blight nagas claim ancestry from the exotic lands of Far Jaati and

go so far as to learn that land's language, though this has yet to be proven and is refuted by some members of the Blight naga community who, in fact, steadfastly deny this origin. The fact that members of the race can move among the humanoid populace indistinguishably in humanoid form further lends to this confusion.

Art Collectors. Blight nagas relish the arts, including the arcane arts. They have a propensity for identifying magical items, as well as the skill and capriciousness to fabricate such items (or fake versions of them to foist upon the unwary). Likewise, many a Blight naga has coaxed or cajoled a fine piece of artwork or rare magical item out of the hands of its owner, augmenting their skills in such tasks with magic as necessary. When rolled together, this means Blight nagas are sought out for the keen ability to identify and appraise artwork and magical trinkets, yet held at arm's length once the object is identified.

Nagas with Arms. Blight nagas are frailer than their more common cousins. However, they make up for this frailty, at least in part, with an odd evolutionary feature other types of nagas lack—arms. While the arms of a Blight naga don't have much in the way of musculature, they are well suited to fine craftwork and the ability to wield magical items such as wands and staves.

In Plain Sight. Blight nagas delight in hiding in plain sight among the humanoids of the city, usually using their change shape ability to take the form of a humanoid female so as to mingle freely. Still, while using this ability they must be wary of the passage of time lest they find themselves transforming back to their natural state at an awkward moment. A typical Blight naga is 12 feet long, resting on a coil of two-thirds of its body so that it stands only around 6 feet in height, and weighs 275 pounds on average.

Night-Slug

The creature is roughly the size of a halfling. Its skin is a blotchy gray color with a few sporadic tufts of muddy-brown hair. The scraps of ragged clothes it wears are covered in filth, clearly not having been washed in weeks — if ever. Its arms are thin and elongated, hanging almost limp.

None are as naturally capable of the fine art of breaking and entering as the night-slug. Fortunately for society, few are also as cowardly. Night-slugs maintain their existence simply by avoiding notice. They often reside in small crawlspaces or even the hollows between the outer masonry and inner plaster and lathe of a house. Those who are not lucky enough to acquire such grand accommodations typically live in places that allow them to avoid notice — the city dump, a gable hanging over a small alleyway, and so forth.

Night-slugs are capable of maneuvering their bodies through seemingly impossible spaces. Their ligaments and tendons are exceptionally elastic, allowing a night-slug to elongate its arms and legs, and in the process pulling what muscle it has closer to its frame. In addition, night-slugs have a "collapsible" skeleton; its bones are composed primarily of cartilage, allowing the creature to squeeze into incredibly small areas.

A typical night-slug stands around 3-1/2 feet tall and weighs 40 pounds.

Night-Slug Society

Night-slugs are scavengers living on the fringes of other societies. They prefer densely populated urban areas for the increased number of hiding places and resources from which to scrounge their needs. Most night-slugs are loners because of the limited resources available to them; mated couples rarely stay together beyond the birth of a brood of whimps (as their young are called), and mothers generally abandon their young as soon as they reach maturity after 3 years.

While most humanoids despise night-slugs and find their presence loathsome, few actually fear the creatures. More than one urban goodwife has walked into a room of her house at night to find a night-slug crouched in the corner chewing on a lace table runner and staining the rug with its noxious skin secretions. While the typical reaction certainly includes a scream, rather than flight it just as often concludes with her grabbing a broom and chasing the creature until it manages to squeeze back through a crack in the baseboards to the safety of the inner walls. In some cities plagued by these creatures, there is an entire industry for exterminators hired to enter homes and buildings to clear out night-slug infestations.

Unlike their skulk cousins, who possess a more violent bent, night-slugs are inherently cowardly and rarely a threat

to even those who would otherwise find themselves at their mercy. There are examples, however, of individuals who have overcome this innate fearfulness and gone on to become highly proficient thieves and even assassins, in some cases.

Night-Slug Characters

Night-slug player characters have the following racial **traits**.

Ability Score Increase. Your Dexterity score increases by 4, but your Intelligence is reduced by 2 and your Charisma is reduced by 4. No score can be raised above 20 or reduced below 3.

Age. Night-slugs are able to survive on their own by age 3. By age 5, they're considered adults, and they seldom live more than 30 years.

Alignment. Most night-slugs have no strong ethical convictions of any kind. They survive by stealing, so they tend toward Chaos and Neutrality.

Size: Night-slugs are Small creatures. Because they're so flexible and able to squeeze themselves into their surroundings, they make Stealth checks with =advantage.

Darkision: Night-slugs have darkvision (60 feet).

Sly Crawler: While prone, a night-slug has a Crawl speed of 20 feet, and crawling doesn't slow it down even in difficult terrain. A crawling night-slug doesn't trigger opportunity attacks for movement.

Slime Coat: The skin of a night-slug secretes a thin fluid resembling slimy perspiration that has a musty odor and leaves a stain on most fabrics. This coating protects the night-slug against grappling; other creatures have disadvantage when trying to grapple a night-slug, and a night-slug has advantage on its attempts to escape from grappling. It also makes night-slugs easy to track; Survival checks to follow a night-slug's trail across any type of terrain are made with advantage.

Compression: Night-slugs can move through spaces one size category smaller than themselves without squeezing, and they can squeeze through openings two size categories smaller.

Languages: Night-slugs begin play speaking Common.

Night-Slug Burglar

Small humanoid, neutral

Armor Class 14
Hit Points 11 (2d6 + 4)
Speed 25 ft., crawl 20 ft.

Str	Dex	Con	Int	Wis	Cha
10 (+0)	19 (+4)	14 (+2)	8 (-1)	13 (+1)	6 (-2)

Skills Sleight-of-hand +6, Stealth +6
Senses darkvision 60 ft., passive Perception 11
Languages Common
Challenge 1/2 (100 XP)

Compression. The night-slug can move through spaces one size category smaller than itself without squeezing, and it can squeeze through openings two size categories smaller.

Slime Coat. Other creatures have disadvantage when trying to grapple a night-slug, and the night-slug has advantage on attempts to escape from grapples. Survival checks to follow a night-slug's trail across any type of terrain are made with advantage.

Sly Crawler. Crawling doesn't slow down a night-slug, even in difficult terrain. A crawling night-slug doesn't trigger opportunity attacks for movement.

Sneak Atttack. A night-slug burglar's dagger attack does an extra 1d6 piercing damage if the night-slug has advantage on the attack or if another night-slug is within 5 feet of the target and able to attack.

Thief. The night-slug burglar has proficiency with thief's tools and is never without them.

ACTIONS

Dagger. *Melee Weapon Attack:* +6 to hit (reach 5 ft.; one creature). *Hit:* 1d4 + 4 piercing damage.
Dagger. *Ranged Weapon Attack:* +6 to hit (range 20 ft./60 ft.; one creature). *Hit:* 1d4 + 4 piercing damage.

ECOLOGY

Environment urban
Organization solitary, pair, or gang (3–6)

Primate, Blight

Two different species of primate call the streets and rooftops of the city of Castrohage home. Whether they were once truly wild animals or not is unknown, but what is known is that, whether through the corruption or the sophistication of the city, each has developed very differently into something else.

Blight Ape

This creature looks like a strange caricature of a gorilla. Standing barely 4 feet tall, it superficially resembles a tawny-colored version of that animal save for its height. However, the resemblances end there. Rather than the look and posture of an animal, the creature carries itself with a sense of dignity. It stands straight (or as straight as possible for a creature whose knuckles drag the ground), and it wears a formal black vest. Its simian face is carefully composed, with its eyes bearing the look of long-suffering patience of a professional manservant.

Blight Ape
Small monstrosity, lawful neutral

Armor Class 13
Hit Points 26 (4d6 + 12)
Speed 20 ft., climb 20 ft.

STR	DEX	CON	INT	WIS	CHA
13 (+1)	17 (+3)	12 (+1)	6 (-2)	14 (+2)	10 (+0)

Saving Throws Int +0, Wis +4, Cha +4
Skills Insight +4, Perception +4
Condition Immunities charmed, frightened
Senses darkvision 60 ft., passive Perception 14
Languages understands Common but can't speak
Challenge 1/8 (25 XP)

Blight Monkey Mange Vulnerability. Blight apes are especially susceptible to the mange carried by Blight monkeys. A Blight ape makes saving throws against the disease with disadvantage. If a Blight ape contracts Blight monkey mange, it loses great patches of its fur as the disease's characteristic rash spreads across its body, eventually infiltrating the ape's respiratory system. If a Blight ape's Dexterity or Constitution score is driven down to 0 as a result of the disease, it dies from suffocation.

ACTIONS
Slam. *Melee Weapon Attack:* +5 to hit (reach 5 ft.; one creature). *Hit:* 1d4 + 3 bludgeoning damage.

ECOLOGY
Environment urban (the Blight)
Organization solitary

It is speculated that Blight apes probably originated as some species of Libynosi ape transported en masse over the years to Castorhage to serve in assorted menageries of the well-to-do, circuses for the common folk, and as game animals in the hunting preserves of the truly decadent. Whatever type of ape they are descended from is unknown because no further specimens have been found in recent centuries, and they are presumed to be extinct in their natural habitat due to hunting as well as the wholesale capture and exportation of them. Over the years, their numbers proliferated in the city of Castorhage, and they took readily to the ways of their captors, literally aping their mannerisms and habits. At some point in

the last century, bored nobles who had long ago taken to dressing them in finery in mockery of their near-human appearance realized that the Blight apes were no longer simply mimicking their human masters, they were in fact carrying out their own activities in the same manner as the humans around them. They had evolved into an entirely new species, no longer truly animals.

Loyal and Smart. With the realization of the evolution of the Blight ape came the discovery that they were both intelligent (if not truly smart) but also of an extremely lawful and peaceful nature. Likewise, though they can understand the Common tongue well enough, they never developed the ability to use language of their own beyond a few simple grunts and hand motions. It soon became in vogue to keep the creatures as scullions and servants, which developed over time into actually hiring them into trusted positions as butlers and governesses with a known penchant for keeping their mouths shut about any internal secrets they might learn. By whim of Castorhage law, Blight apes receive the same wage as any other hireling in their position and are now often seen as actual family members by some of the more benevolent folk of the city. However, there are far more Blight apes than there are staff positions in well-to-do households, so most Blight apes find themselves relegated to menial jobs and poor treatment. Most are actually employed by the city, since few businesses choose to hire a Blight ape over a human or other humanoid race if they're going to have to pay the same rate anyway, but there are some exceptions — particularly for jobs where a combination of extreme loyalty and extreme discretion are desirable.

Despised Cousins. Blight apes despise Blight monkeys with a passion, and the little cretins are one of the few things that can truly rouse a Blight ape to anger. Some of the Blight apes hired by the city are actually armed for the purpose of hunting down and exterminating nests of Blight monkeys among the city rooftops, an occupation which they pursue with relish. For their part, Blight monkeys enjoy humiliating and even killing a Blight ape whenever possible.

Blight Monkey

This dark-furred monkey has slightly lighter fur around its face and chest, but all of it is matted with reeking filth. It hangs by its prehensile tail as it prepares to throw a handful of the filth that it wears so copiously.

Blight Monkey
Tiny monstrosity, chaotic neutral

Armor Class 14
Hit Points 5 (2d4)
Speed 20 ft., climb 30 ft.

STR	DEX	CON	INT	WIS	CHA
6 (-2)	18 (+4)	10 (+0)	3 (-4)	10 (+0)	6 (-2)

Skills Perception +2, Stealth +6
Condition Immunities frightened
Senses darkvision 60 ft., passive Perception 12
Languages none
Challenge 1/8 (25 XP)

Blight Monkey Mange. A creature infected with this disease must make a successful DC 10 Constitution saving throw every time it completes a long rest. On a failure, the creature's Dexterity score is reduced by 1d2 and its Constitution score is reduced by 1. The disease ends when the creature's Constitution saving throw succeeds two days in a row or when it receives a *lesser restoration or comparable magic. Once the disease ends, the creature's ability scores recover at a similar rate.*

ACTIONS

Bite. *Melee Weapon Attack:* +6 to hit (reach 5 ft.; one creature). *Hit:* 1d3 + 4 piercing damage, and the creature must make a successful DC 10 Constitution saving throw or contract Blight monkey mange (see above).

Excrement. *Ranged Weapon Attack:* +6 to hit (range 10 ft./30 ft.; one creature). *Hit:* the creature must make a successful DC 10 Constitution saving throw or contract Blight monkey mange (see above).

Enraged Screech. The Blight monkey emits a harsh screech. Creatures within 30 feet that hear the screech must make a successful DC 10 Wisdom saving throw or be frightened until the end of its next turn. Once a creature makes a successful saving throw, it's immune to the screeching of Blight monkeys for 24 hours.

ECOLOGY

Environment urban (the Blight)
Organization solitary, pair, band (3–9), or troop (10–40)

Like Blight apes, these little beasts are believed to have originated in distant Libynos and were originally brought to Casterhage as part of menageries, but unlike the apes no one wanted to continue importing the creatures after their nasty disposition was discovered. Somehow, it seems, they just kept creeping unseen onto ships in Libynosi ports and disembarking upon reaching the city. There was a time when seeing dozens of the things scampering across yardarms and hawser lines to reach the docks from ships newly arrived from the East was a common sight. When the true extent of their colonization of Castorhage was realized and their disease-ridden nature fully grasped, the city took steps to curtail this mass immigration. However, despite its best efforts the city's efforts were far too late, and now thousands, if not tens of thousands, of the creatures clamber unseen — though certainly not unheard — across the city's maze of rooftops.

Twisted by Blight. Something about the city's influence appears to have corrupted the creatures and changed them from previously mischievous and unruly animals to actual beasts with just enough intelligence to have a taste for cruelty and a strong penchant for chaos. Despite their nimbleness and glimmerings of intelligence, all attempts by folk to domesticate them and spellcasters to take them as familiars have failed as they invariably turn against their would-be masters at the first chance. They routinely destroy books and valuables, and attack family pets. Their habit of biting off the fingers and toes of humanoid infants sleeping in their cribs has earned them the eternal ire of Blight apes everywhere who always attack them on sight. Blight monkeys share this animosity, going out of their way to ambush or abuse Blight apes at every opportunity even flinging themselves into suicidal attacks in their attempts to bring harm to the apes. They are truly fearless in their stupefying anarchy and attack a creature much larger than themselves, using their grating screech to summon more of their kind to join in the attack. It is fortunate for the city that Blight monkeys appear to be a favored prey of gable spiders and festering Lyme rats, because otherwise the fecund beasts would likely plague the city to an even greater degree.

Blight Monkey Mange. All Blight monkeys are a carrier of a disease that is transmitted through their bite and through contact with their excrement. This disease causes the disgusting monkeys to lose patches of fur in clumps, but otherwise appears to cause them no harm. To others infected with Blight monkey mange, it causes a red, scaly rash in the crooks of elbows and knees and in the armpits. The rash is itchy and raw, causing pain and limiting movement until it clears up. Blight apes are known to be particularly susceptible to the ravages of this disease (see Blight ape).

Protyugh

The creature is a horrible mix of otyugh and ... something. It has the basic tripod shape of an otyugh with its fanged maw on the side of its central body, but instead of a tentacle and an eyestalk, it has an arcing tail with thick spikes down its entire length. In addition, two arms ending in wicked claws emerge from the mouth of the beast to grope at whatever it can make its next meal.

Protyugh

Large aberration, chaotic neutral

Armor Class 15 (natural armor)
Hit Points 140 (14d10 + 70)
Speed 30 ft.

STR	DEX	CON	INT	WIS	CHA
17 (+3)	12 (+1)	20 (+5)	6 (-2)	13 (+1)	6 (-2)

Skills Perception +4
Saving Throws Con +8, Cha +1
Damage Resistances lightning
Damage Immunities acid
Condition Immunities disease
Senses blindsight 30 ft., darkvision 60 ft., passive Perception 14
Languages Otyugh; understands Common but can't speak it
Challenge 7 (2,900 XP)

Magical Attacks. A protyugh's attacks count as magical.
Protean Form. The protyugh is immune to effects that would alter its form.
Regeneration. If the protyugh has at least 1 hit point at the start of its turn, it heals 5 hit points.
Swallow. If a protyugh starts its turn with a creature grappled in its claws, it immediately makes a claws attack as a bonus action. If the attack hits, the creature takes 3d6 slashing damage and is swallowed. A swallowed creature is blinded and restrained. It takes 1d6 bludgeoning damage plus 1d8 acid damage automatically at the start of each of the protyugh's turns. One Large, two Medium, or four Small creatures can be inside the protyugh at one time, thanks to its unstable form. A swallowed creature is unaffected by anything happening outside the protyugh or by attacks from outside it. A swallowed creature can get out of the protyugh by using 5 feet of movement, but only after the protyugh is dead.

ACTIONS

Multiattack. The protyugh attacks once with its tail and once with its claws.
Tail. *Melee Weapon Attack:* +6 to hit (reach 10 ft.; one creature). *Hit:* 2d8 + 3 bludgeoning damage, and the creature must make a successful DC 16 Wisdom saving throw or be confused (per the confusion spell) until the end of its next turn. Chaotically-aligned creatures have advantage on this saving throw.
Claws. *Melee Weapon Attack:* +6 to hit (reach 5 ft.; one creature). *Hit:* 2d10 + 3 slashing damage, and the creature must make a successful DC 14 Strength saving throw or be grappled (escape DC 13).

ECOLOGY

Environment underground (the Blight)
Organization solitary

Aberrations are notoriously difficult for physicians to use in experiments, but their discovery of the unique chaos properties of proteans and the ever-endurable pliability for which otyughs are known within their ranks proved to be the key to finally crafting a mortal-aberration cross. The resulting protyugh, an otyugh with an infusion of naunet protean, has bred true and become an extremely interesting experiment, even if its utility is limited by the randomness that is inherent to its very nature. Even the feasibility of using otyugh as guard beasts in sewers and abattoirs is somewhat lost since the protyugh gained none of the naunet's intellect but also lost the otyugh's territorial instincts. A protyugh is just as likely to wander away as to establish a lair in any given location. Despite these setbacks, the physicians still consider its existence to be one of their greatest successes and continually seek ways to further enhance the species.

Beyond Disgusting. Like otyughs, protyughs are primarily offal eaters. However, unlike otyughs, their palate is even less refined, causing them to try to ingest anything from garbage and corpses to former allies and even furniture and large pieces of masonry. The result is that protyughs manage to keep few allies (most either flee or are eventually eaten), and they are continually regurgitating previous meals because of the inedible nature of so much that is placed in their maws. Certain scavengers have learned that if one is cautious enough, it is often beneficial to follow behind a protyugh and search through its regurgitated past meals because there are often items of value that it has ingested and then left carelessly behind after they proved to be indigestible.

Rat, Festering Lyme

This revolting, diseased-looking rat is the size of a small dog. It is covered in lice that visibly swarm in its filthy, matted fur.

Festering Lyme Rat

Small monstrosity, unaligned

Armor Class 12
Hit Points 9 (2d6 + 2)
Speed 30 ft.

STR	DEX	CON	INT	WIS	CHA
8 (-1)	14 (+2)	12 (+1)	2 (-4)	10 (+1)	4 (-3)

Damage Resistances acid
Condition Immunities disease
Senses darkvision 60 ft., passive Perception 11
Languages none
Challenge 1/4 (50 XP)

Delusional Infestation. A creature that starts its turn within 5 feet of a festering Lyme rat and can see it must make a successful DC 11 Wisdom saving throw or have disadvantage on attack rolls and ability checks until the end of its turn, as it imagines thousands of bugs crawling over it. A successful save leaves a creature immune to Delusional Infestation for 24 hours.
Filth Fever. A creature with filth fever becomes sick 1d4 days after being infected. At that time, the creature gains 1 level of exhaustion. It also regains only half the usual number of hit points from spending Hit Dice and no hit points from resting. Once symptoms appear, the infected creature must make a DC 11 Constitution saving throw after every long rest. If it fails, the creature gains 1 level of exhaustion; if it succeeds, the creature loses 1 level of exhaustion. The disease is cured when the creature has no exhaustion.
Pack Attack. The festering Lyme rat has advantage on its attack roll if the target is within 5 feet of another Lyme rat or giant rat that's able to attack.

ACTIONS

Bite. *Melee Weapon Attack:* +4 to hit (reach 5 ft.; one creature). *Hit:* 1d4 + 2 piercing damage, and the creature must make a successful DC 11 Constitution saving throw or be infected with filth fever (see above).

ECOLOGY

Environment urban (the Blight)
Organization solitary or pack (2–20)

Festering Lyme rats inhabit the sewers, canals, and subterranean waterways of the blighted city of Castorhage. Similar in appearance to giant rats, the Lyme rat, possibly through the Blight's proximity to Between, can affect those who see it with a momentary delusion of parasitic infestation.

Copyright Notice
Author Alistair Rigg, based on material by Richard Pett.

Rat, Giant Rat of Shabbis

This black-furred rat is the size of a bear. It has a long, hairless tail, and its oversized jaws are crammed with yellow fangs pitted with decay and tangled with strands of hair and filth caught between them.

Giant Rat of Shabbis
Large monstrosity, unaligned

Armor Class 14 (natural armor)
Hit Points 102 (12d10 + 36)
Speed 40 ft., climb 30 ft., swim 30 ft.

STR	DEX	CON	INT	WIS	CHA
19 (+4)	11 (+0)	17 (+3)	3 (-4)	13 (+1)	6 (-2)

Skills Perception +3
Damage Vulnerabilities cold
Damage Immunities acid
Condition Immunities disease
Senses darkvision 60 ft., passive Perception 13
Languages none
Challenge 4 (1,100 XP)

Wererage. When a giant rat of Shabbis is reduced to half or fewer of its starting hit points, it immediately enters wererage (no action required) lasting 1 minute. The giant rat gains a +2 bonus on attack rolls and damage rolls, it gains resistance to damage from nonmagical weapons, and its Armor Class drops by 2. In addition, creatures damaged by the giant rat's claw attacks must make a successful DC 13 Constitution saving throw or be infected by wererat lycanthropy.

ACTIONS
Multiattack. The giant rat of Shabbis bites once and makes one claws attack.
Bite. *Melee Weapon Attack:* +6 to hit (reach 5 ft.; one creature). *Hit:* 1d8 + 4 piercing damage, and a creature must make a successful DC 13 Constitution saving throw or be infected with Shabbisian plague (see sidebox).
Claws. *Melee Weapon Attack:* +6 to hit (reach 5 ft.; one creature). *Hit:* 3d6 + 4 slashing damage. If the giant rat is in wererage, the target creature must also make a successful DC 13 Constitution saving throw or be infected by wererat lycanthropy.

ECOLOGY
Environment urban (the Blight)
Organization solitary

Fabled Shabbis-Beyond-The-Sea, the Green City of Jasper, is said to be the home of a thousand wonders and feared as the source of a thousand plagues. Shabbis, recognized by many yet known to few, is a port of distant Libynos, whose wharves lie among malarial swamps and whose ships ply the tepid coastal waters of the Boiling Sea. Shabbis provides a direct, unrestricted route to access the riches of the central lands of Libynos without interference by a major local power such as Khemit or Alcaldar, and has long proved a tempting destination for traders seeking to make a quick fortune on a risky venture. The fact that it is also known as a haven of unimaginable disease only adds to the allure of those adventure-seekers who would risk all at one roll of the dice. Because of its extremely remote location, few states of Akados have managed to successfully establish trade with this distant cornucopia, which is all well and good, because those few who do inevitably receive an unwanted visit by the hideous Shabbisian Plague.

One or Many. The equally fabled Giant Rat of Shabbis is, mercifully, a rare visitor to the city of Castorhage. Many argue whether there is a single Giant Rat that populates all of their tales or whether it is an entire species of gargantuan rats from that distant land. Though the latter is likely the truth, thankfully their appearance is rare to the point that there has never been more than one seen at a time. It is thought that if a true species, the giant rat must not be so large in its distant homeland or it would have long ago either decimated the human population or been hunted to extinction. Most proponents of the "rat species" theory assume that some quality of either a shipborne voyage to or taking up residence in western lands that somehow agrees with their foreign physiology causes them to thrive to the point that they grow to such prodigious size. Those more in the know whisper one word to account for their theory of unnatural growth: "Between ..."

Plague and Lycanthropy. Despite its size, a Giant Rat of Shabbis is able to squeeze into tiny spaces and is therefore found in the same sorts of places as other rats: sewers, disused subterranean structures and caverns, and in the holds and bilges of ships from where it swims to enter new ports. They are greatly feared as they are known to spread plague and the curse of lycanthropy, even though they are not lycanthropes themselves. This strange fact has led some scholars to speculate that the Giant Rat of Shabbis may be the original source of wererat lycanthropy. Whatever the case, those who succumb seem to become only hybrids of dire rats or festering Lyme rats, and not of a Giant Rat of Shabbis itself.

Blockade and Quarantine. Shabbisian Plague has long been a scourge of the city-states of the Boiling Sea so that most have enforced a trade embargo of the Libynosi nations against the Green City of Jasper. This is primarily enforced by the Kingdom of Khemit by land and the Empire of Alcaldar by sea. This has, in turn, resulted in even greater access to ships of Akados for the trade-hungry merchant lords of Shabbis who, as said traders, likewise risk the life and limb of all to enrich themselves and their houses.

Tenacious Plague. The teeming swarms of rats and foul insects that infest the tidal swamps and dismal slums of Shabbis are known to be carriers of Shabbisian Plague, but prove incredibly difficult to root out or eradicate from ships that make port in the Green City. The priesthood of the deity Bast conducts an ongoing, almost crusadelike, campaign against the folk of that city who travel abroad, and their multitude of feline minions have done more to stem the tide of plague in locations as far away as Bard's Gate than any other measures ever taken. But even they at best can only keep the omnipresent threat of plague in Castorhage temporarily at bay, as it waits for just a moment of lassitude to unleash its foul effects upon the unsuspecting populace. For their part, the merchant lords of Shabbis see the waves of plague that sweep through the overflowing shanty towns within their city as a sort of urban renewal. What the royal family of Castorhage thinks of such events remains speculative at best, but it is unlikely to be far from a similar mindset.

Disease: Shabbisian Plague

Victims of Shabbisian Plague begin experiencing symptoms 3d4 hours after being bitten by the carrier, whether it be a rat or some tiny insect such as a flea or mosquito. Its victims experience high fever and suffer teeth-rattling chills while at the same time their muscles spasm painfully and tendons tighten, causing limbs to draw up into an almost fetal position. In addition, the victim develops a purplish rash on cheeks, forehead, neck, armpits, and groin that eventually blisters and breaks open, causing oozing wounds that leave scars and can lead to further serious infections. Those that recover from the plague usually bear discolored scars from this rash as a memento, and frequently move with an uneven gait or have a slightly twisted arm caused by permanent tendon damage.

The victim's Dexterity is reduced by 1d4 and Charisma is reduced by 1d2 when the symptoms kick in. The victim must make a successful DC 15 Constitution saving throw after completing each long rest or lose another 1d4 Dexterity and 1d2 Charisma. The disease ends if the character's Constitution saving throw succeeds two days in a row.

If the victim's Dexterity or Charisma reaches 0 from this, they die. Once they have made successful Constitution saving throws two days in a row, disease ends. The Dexterity and Charisma damage will be restored after a long rest following the disease ending.

After a victim recovers from Shabbisian plague, the disease comes back 2d4 days later unless a successful DC 10 Constitution saving throw is made at that time. Subsequent bouts are identical to the first bout, except the DC for daily Constitution saves is 10. The disease always recurs 2d4 days after recovery until the initial DC 10 Constitution saving throw succeeds and staves it off permanently, or it's cured with *lesser restoration or comparable magic.*

Satyrmouther

This hairless, gray-skinned man with goatlike legs and horns like a ram's is covered in a mass of staring eyes and countless, fanged maws that yammer ceaselessly.

Satyrmouther

Medium aberration, chaotic evil

Armor Class 12
Hit Points 71 (11d8 + 22)
Speed 40 ft.

STR	DEX	CON	INT	WIS	CHA
11 (+0)	14 (+2)	14 (+2)	10 (+0)	10 (+0)	16 (+3)

Saving Throws Dex +4, Con +5, Wis +3
Skills Deception +5, Perception +3, Performance +5, Persuasion +5
Damage Resistances bludgeoning, piercing, and slashing from nonmagical weapons
Senses darkvision 60 ft., passive Perception 13
Languages Common, Deep Speech, Sylvan
Challenge 3 (700 XP)

Magic Resistance. The satyrmouther has advantage on saves against magic.
Ravenous Embrace. At the start of the satyrmouther's turn, a creature that is grappling the satyrmouther or is grappled by it takes 2d4 piercing damage plus 2d6 necrotic damage.
Suasive Song. A satyrmouther can sing a cacophony of maddening sound (no action required). All creatures other than aberrations within 60 feet that hear the song must make a DC 13 Wisdom saving throw. For each creature that fails, roll 1d4 to determine the effect: 1 = confusion (per the spell), 2 = incapacitated (by despair), 3 = unconscious, 4 = frightened. An affected creature repeats the saving throw at the end of its turn, ending the effect on itself with a success. The effect ends automatically if the satyrmouther stops, or is prevented from, singing. A creature that saves successfully is immune to the Suasive Song of satyrmouthers for 24 hours.

ACTIONS

Multiattack. The satyrmouther makes two attacks, each of which must be different, all while singing its Suasive Song.
Shortsword. *Melee Weapon Attack:* +4 to hit (reach 5 ft.; one creature). *Hit:* 1d6 + 2 piercing damage.
Head-butt. *Melee Weapon Attack:* +4 to hit (reach 5 ft.; one creature). *Hit:* 2d4 + 2 bludgeoning damage.
Shortbow. *Ranged Weapon Attack:* +4 to hit (range 80 ft./320 ft.; one creature). *Hit:* 1d6 + 2 piercing damage.
Spittle (recharge 5-6). *Ranged Weapon Attack:* automatic hit (range 30 ft.; one creature). *Hit:* the creature must make a successful DC 13 Constitution saving throw or be blinded for 1 minute. The affected creature can attempt a saving throw at the end of each of its turns. A successful save ends the effect.

ECOLOGY
Environment underground (the Blight)
Organization solitary

The satyrmouther is a strange and rare mix of aberration and fey. It sings songs that madden, sadden, lull, and terrify. Unlike a satyr, the creature is interested only in fostering negative emotions, lying, and bullying; it disdains charm and diplomatic persuasion. And unlike a gibbering mouther, it's a being of insidious intellect whose mouths sing and manipulate rather than simply inducing temporary insanity.

Skulking Manticore (Mulk)

No larger than a mountain lion, this dusky gray, leonine creature slinks through the shadows, its humanlike head set in a scowl of concentration, its batlike wings folded neatly against its flanks. It holds its tail aloft, and the tip of it gleams with the dull glint of unpolished iron.

Skulking Manticore
Medium monstrosity, lawful evil

Armor Class 15 (natural armor)
Hit Points 102 (12d10 + 36)
Speed 30 ft., fly 50 ft.

STR	DEX	CON	INT	WIS	CHA
16 (+3)	19 (+4)	16 (+3)	7 (-2)	12 (+1)	6 (-2)

Saving Throws Wis +4, Cha +2
Skills Stealth +7
Senses darkvision 60 ft., passive Perception 11
Languages Common
Challenge 5 (1,800 XP)

Chameleon Blend. A skulking manticore can Hide as a bonus action at the end of its turn, if it's lightly obscured. It always has advantage on Stealth checks and initiative rolls.
Untrackable. Any creature trying to follow a skulking manticore through forest or underground territory has disadvantage on skill checks for trailing or tracking.

ACTIONS
Multiattack. The skulking manticore attacks three times, either biting once and clawing twice, or using its tail spikes three times.
Bite. *Melee Weapon Attack:* +6 to hit (reach 5 ft.; one creature). Hit: 1d10 + 3 piercing damage.
Claw. *Melee Weapon Attack:* +6 to hit (reach 5 ft.; one creature). Hit: 1d8 + 3 slashing damage.
Tail Spike. *Ranged Weapon Attack:* +7 to hit (range 100 ft./200 ft.; one creature). Hit: 1d10 + 4 piercing damage.

ECOLOGY
Environment non-arctic land, urban (the Blight)
Organization solitary

The successful infusion of the chameleonlike abilities of a skulk into a line of manticores has proven to be a useful and popular experiment in Castorhage. The resulting breed is smaller than a typical manticore and much more discreet in its presence. The inherent cowardliness of skulks seems to also have had an effect, removing much of the wildness found in manticores and making then much more biddable and useful as guardian beasts but without making them craven or too skittish to fight off intruders if needed. Oftentimes owners have them broken (see the Broken Creature template in Appendix B) to ensure their docility toward their masters.

Chameleonic. A skulking manticore has a featureless gray hide that is able to adopt the color of its surroundings like a chameleon. A typical skulking manticore is 4 feet long and weighs 120 pounds.

Slithering Bulette

The massive creature has four legs thick as a tree trunk and the vague suggestion of armored plates over its head and back. A great, toothless maw opens at the front of its head. Its back plate rises up between its shoulders into a finlike dorsal hump. Even stranger, however, the entire creature appears to be composed entirely of some transparent gelatinous substance that has difficulty holding its form.

Slithering Bulette

Huge monstrosity, unaligned

Armor Class 15 (natural armor)
Hit Points 103 (9d12 + 45)
Speed 30 ft.

STR	DEX	CON	INT	WIS	CHA
21 (+5)	10 (+0)	20 (+5)	5 (-3)	9 (-1)	2 (-4)

Skills Perception +5
Damage Immunities psychic
Condition Immunities blinded, exhaustion, frightened, paralyzed, poisoned, prone, stunned
Senses darkvision 60 ft., tremorsense 60 ft., passive Perception 15
Languages Undercommon
Challenge 6 (2,300 XP)

Amorphous. A slithering bulette can move through gaps as small as 4 square feet without penalty.
Sealed Mind. Even though a slithering bulette is intelligent, it's immune to mind-affecting effects such as charms, domination, illusions, and phantasms.
Transparent. Because of its lack of coloration, a motionless slithering bulette can be spotted only with a successful DC 15 Wisdom (Perception) check. The creature is spotted automatically if it moves, attacks, or contains an engulfed creature. Creatures that blunder into an unseen slithering bulette are surprised.

ACTIONS
Bite. *Melee Weapon Attack:* +8 to hit (reach 5 ft.; one creature). *Hit:* 5d12 + 5 piercing damage, and a creature must make a successful DC 16 Constitution saving throw or be paralyzed for 1 minute. A paralyzed creature repeats the saving throw at the end of its turn, ending the effect with a success.
Engulf. The slithering bulette moves up to its full speed. It can enter spaces occupied by Large or smaller creatures as it moves. If the creature whose space is being entered makes a successful DC 16 Dexterity saving throw, the creature moves safely out of the slithering bulette's path. If the saving throw fails, the creature is engulfed: it takes 2d6 acid damage immediately, is restrained, can't breathe, and takes 4d6 acid damage at the start of each of the slithering bulette's turns. An engulfed creature can use an action on its turn to try to escape from the slithering bulette; the creature escapes if it makes a successful DC 15 Strength check. A creature adjacent to the slithering bulette can use an action to try to pull one engulfed creature free. The rescue succeeds if the creature makes a successful DC 15 Strength check, and the creature making the check takes 2d6 acid damage whether it succeeds or fails. A slithering bulette can engulf two Large creatures, four Medium creatures, or 16 Small creatures in any combination.

ECOLOGY
Environment underground (the Blight)
Organization solitary

The slithering bulette is a great oddity among the work of the physicians in that while it appears to have the form of one creature — a bulette, to be precise — it is entirely composed of the oozelike proto-matter of the slithering tracker and the gelatinous cube. Somehow, the strange creature combines the most dangerous qualities of both creature types.

Engulf and Drain. The creature's preferred attack is to overrun and engulf opponents into its body to drain their plasma and dissolve their matter. It then continues fighting with its ferocious bite while any creature trapped within is carried along for the ride as it fights. The slithering bulette continues to favor this tactic as long as it is able and is generally too dumb to retreat from a battle. However, if it sustains more than 50 points of damage in a single attack, the dim intellect that drives it kicks in and it tries to retreat.

Genetic Memory. Though a slithering bulette retains the tremorsense of a bulette, it does not possess its burrowing ability. If it retreats, there is a 20% chance that a slithering bulette spends a full round unsuccessfully trying to burrow into whatever is under it. After a round of fruitless effort, the slithering bulette realizes its error and makes a run for it. If an opponent escapes from a battle, leaving a slithering bulette victorious, the creature's instinct to track takes over and for the next 1d4 days it attempts to follow the trail of the escaped opponent to finish the kill.

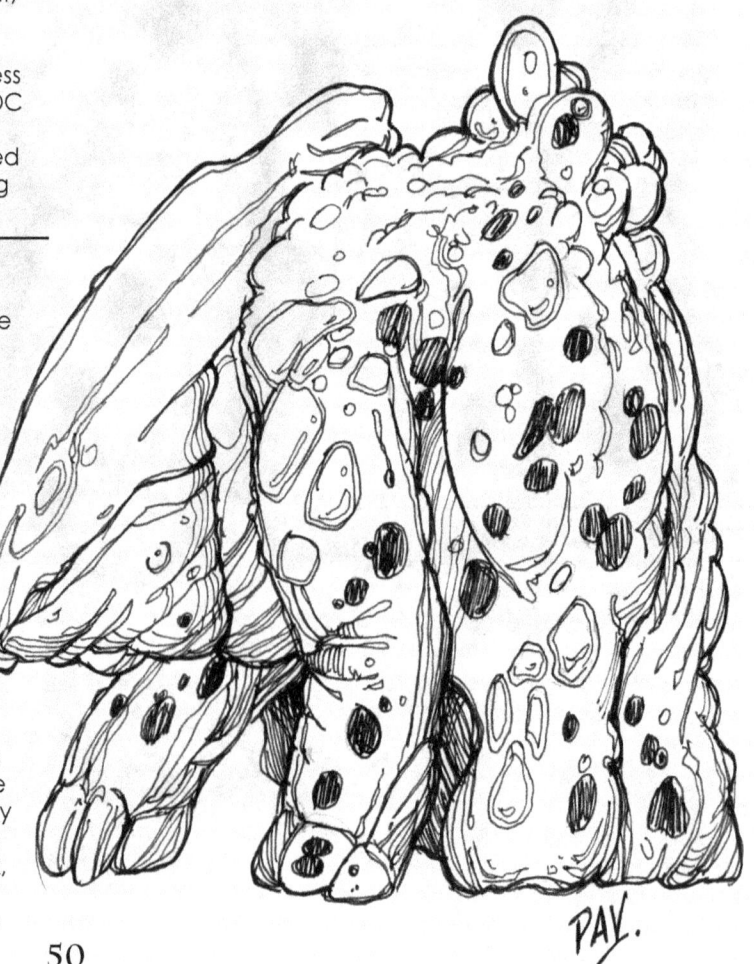

Slithering Tangle

A sinister serpentine tangle of rotting vines ends in an approximation of a humanoid head, its maw lined with slime-dripping thorns.

Slithering Tangle
Large plant, chaotic evil

Armor Class 16 (natural armor)
Hit Points 136 (14d10 + 56)
Speed 30 ft., swim 20 ft.

STR	DEX	CON	INT	WIS	CHA
19	11	18	11	13	18
(+4)	(+0)	(+4)	(+0)	(+1)	(+4)

Saving Throws Dex +3, Wis +4
Damage Resistances fire
Damage Immunities lightning, psychic
Condition Immunities charmed, frightened, prone, stunned, unconscious
Senses darkvision 60 ft., passive Perception 11
Languages Common
Challenge 8 (3,900 XP)

Constrict. A grappled creature takes 1d8 + 4 bludgeoning damage at the start of the slithering tangle's turn.
Electric Fortitude. When a slithering tangle is hit by an attack that causes lightning damage, it gains temporary hit points equal to half the lightning damage.
Spellcasting. The slithering tangle is an arcane spellcaster that uses Charisma as its spellcasting ability (DC 15, attack +7). It doesn't need material or vocal components to cast spells.

> Cantrips (at will): *dancing lights, light, mage hand, minor illusion, shocking grasp*
> 1st level (x4): *color spray, ray of sickness, shield, silent image, thunderwave*
> 2nd level (x4): *hold person, misty step, scorching ray, suggestion*
> 3rd level (x2): *lightning bolt, stinking cloud*

ACTIONS
Multiattack. Because the slithering tangle needs only somatic components to cast spells and it has hundreds of shoots, it can bite and cast a spell on the same turn.
Bite. *Melee Weapon Attack:* +7 to hit (reach 5 ft.; one creature). *Hit:* 2d6 + 4 piercing damage plus 2d8 poison damage, and the creature must make a successful DC 15 Strength saving throw or be grappled (escape DC 14). A slithering tangle can have up to two Medium or smaller creatures grappled at one time. Maintaining grapples doesn't interfere with the slithering tangle's ability to bite or cast spells.
Fascinating Cloud (1/day). The slithering tangle emits a transparent cloud of pollen as a bonus action. Breathing creatures within 20 feet of the slithering tangle must make a successful DC 15 Charisma saving throw or be charmed for as long as the creature remains in the cloud, which lasts 5 rounds unless dispersed sooner by wind. A charmed creature that's not in the cloud repeats the

saving throw at the end of its turn, ending the effect on itself with a success.

ECOLOGY
Environment swamp, underground (the Blight)
Organization solitary or nest (2–4)

Slithering tangles appear to be snakelike tangles of rotting vegetation, but like shambling mounds, they are actually intelligent, carnivorous plants akin to animate tangles of creeping parasitic vines. They are morbid, hateful creatures shunned for their loathsome sorcerous powers.

Foul Lairs. These repulsive creatures lair in despoiled forests and fetid swamps where they blend in with the surrounding terrain while they wait to ambush their prey. They also can be found underground living among damp fungal thickets. They are able to draw sustenance by parasitizing other plants and by sending rootlets into the soil to absorb raw nutrients, but they prefer to consume flesh and bone from animals crushed in their coils.

Sough-Eel

This massive eel, nearly 20 feet long, has pale hide almost translucent like a fish's belly that is marred by great areas of sloughing flesh that hang loose in rotten folds. It is eyeless, with a row of small black nodules extending back from its snout, and has several small vestigial fins growing sporadically along the length of its body. Its mouth however, is the most noticeable feature, occupying nearly a quarter of its length and splayed wide with a crowd of jagged fangs.

Sough-Eel

Huge beast (aquatic), unaligned

Armor Class 15 (natural armor)
Hit Points 126 (12d12 + 48)
Speed 10 ft., swim 30 ft.

STR	DEX	CON	INT	WIS	CHA
22 (+6)	10 (+0)	18 (+4)	1 (-5)	12 (+1)	8 (-1)

Skills Perception +3, Stealth +3
Damage Resistances piercing
Damage Immunities poison
Condition Immunities blinded, poisoned, prone
Senses blindsight 30 ft., passive Perception 13
Languages none
Challenge 5 (1,800 XP)

ACTIONS

Bite. *Melee Weapon Attack:* +9 to hit (reach 10 ft.; one creature). *Hit:* 2d10 + 6 piercing damage, and a creature must make a successful DC 15 Constitution saving throw or contract sight rot. A Medium or smaller target is also grappled (escape DC 16) and restrained. The sough-eel can't bite a different target while it has a creature grappled.

Gnaw. *Melee Weapon Attack:* +9 to hit (one creature already grappled at the start of the sough-eel's turn). Hit: 1d8 + 6 piercing damage. The sough-eel makes this attack as a bonus action at the start of its turn. A creature that's hit on 2 consecutive rounds by the sough-eel's gnaw attack may be swallowed (see below).

Swallow. The sough-eel makes its bite attack against a Medium or smaller creature it is grappling and that it's hit with 2 consecutive gnaw attacks. If the bite attack hits, the creature takes the bite damage and is swallowed. A swallowed creature is blinded and restrained, and it's unaffected by anything happening outside the sough-eel or by attacks from outside it. It takes 4d6 acid damage at the start of each of the sough-eel's turns. Up to two Medium or smaller creatures can be inside the sough-eel at one time. If the sough-eel takes 30 or more damage on a single turn from a creature inside it, the sough-eel must succeed on a DC 14 Constitution save at the end of that turn or regurgitate all swallowed creatures, which fall prone in a space within 10 feet of the slough-eel. A swallowed creature can get out of the sough-eel by using 15 feet of movement, but only after the sough-eel is dead.

ECOLOGY

Environment sea
Organization solitary or school (4-8)

These vile predators are found exclusively in the dark, filthy waters of the Great Lyme River and Fetid Sea in the vicinity of the City-State of Castorhage. Some have speculated that they were once a temperate water variety of moray eel that was indigenous to the area until the Lyme was tainted by the noxious effluvia from the metropolis known colloquially as the Blight. Unlike most aquatic species that were unable to survive the poisoning of the waters, the sough-eel population managed to endure the deadly influx but was changed in the process. Immune to most disease and poison, the sough-eels — carriers of their own endemic pathogen — are now affected by it chronically so that their hide is in a constant state of dying and sloughing off in large swaths and layers. This has not seemed to affect their ability to survive in their harsh environment, and every native of the Blight knows better to enter the water of the Lyme for fear of the voracious attacks of the ever-present sough-eels.

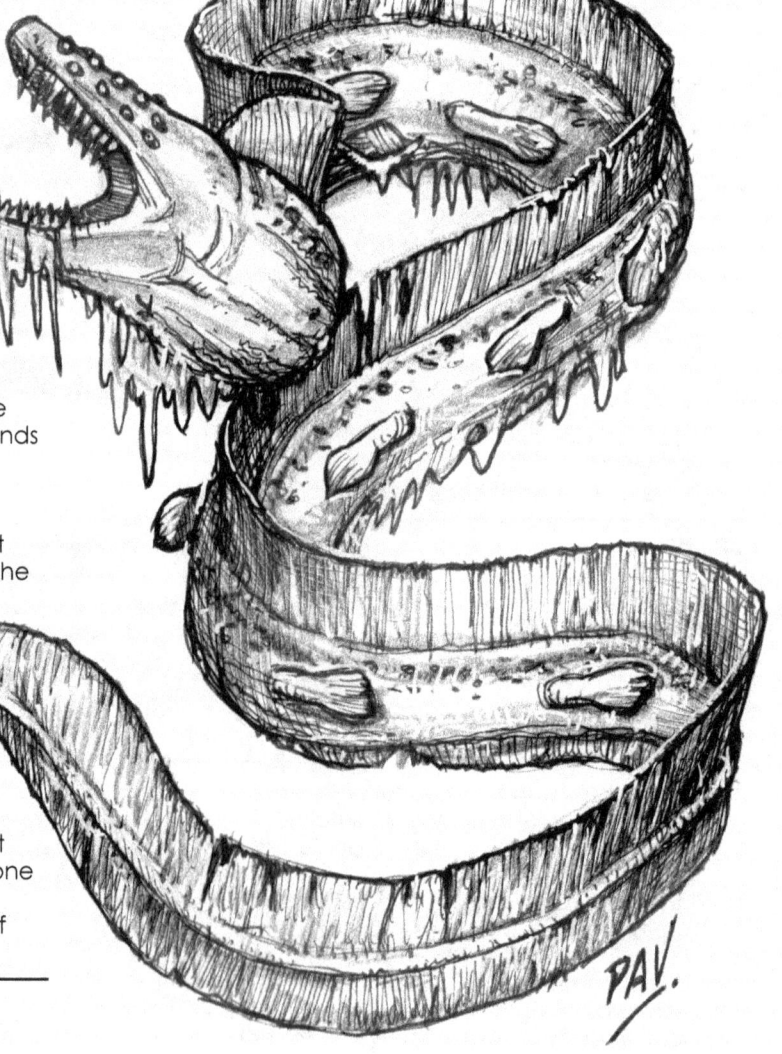

Spider, Chymic

The body of this spiderlike creature is a mass of humanoid faces caught in drawn-out, hideous screams. Ten spindly legs rise unevenly from the bulbous mass. Between tufts of bristly hair hang needle-sharp fangs that drip with a bitter-smelling, thick red liquid.

Chymic Spider

Small aberration, neutral evil

Armor Class 15 (natural armor)
Hit Points 52 (8d6 + 16)
Speed 30 ft., climb 30 ft.

STR	DEX	CON	INT	WIS	CHA
7 (-2)	15 (+2)	15 (+2)	9 (-1)	16 (+3)	10 (+0)

Saving Throws Dex +4, Con +4, Wis +5
Skills Perception +6, Stealth +5
Damage Immunities psychic
Condition Immunities charmed, frightened
Senses darkvision 60 ft., passive Perception 16
Languages understands Common but can't speak, telepathy 100 ft. (dreams only)
Challenge 3 (700 XP)

Arachnophobia Aura. A chymic spider exudes a fear of arachnids that seeps into the psyche of all creatures within 1 mile of the chymic spider's lair. Creatures with Intelligence 3 or higher have disadvantage on saving throws against fright in this area.

Dream Telepathy. The chymic spider's telepathy allows it to communicate only with creatures that are asleep and dreaming. Most creatures interpret these exchanges as normal dreams, but characters are free to reach their own conclusions. The chymic spider can also choose to create nightmares in the sleeper, who must make a successful DC 13 Wisdom saving throw or be paralyzed for as long as the chymic spider maintains telepathic contact (it can be lost as concentration).

Egg Implantation. A chymic spider can implant eggs in a helpless or paralyzed creature. The eggs hatch 24 hours later. Once the eggs hatch, at the start of each of the host's turns, it takes 1d6 necrotic damage and must make a successful DC 12 Constitution saving throw or be paralyzed by pain and spiderling poison until the start of its next turn. This continues until the spiderlings are destroyed or removed. Spiderlings can be removed by inflicting 4d6 slashing damage on the host (halved with a successful DC 13 Wisdom (Medicine) check by the creature doing the damage) or destroyed with a *greater restoration spell* or comparable magic. If the host dies, a swarm of spiders bursts from the body.

ACTIONS

Bite. *Melee Weapon Attack:* +5 to hit (reach 5 ft.; one creature). *Hit:* 1d4 + 2 piercing damage plus 2d8 poison damage, and a creature must make a successful DC 12 Constitution saving throw or be paralyzed for 1 minute. A paralyzed creature repeats the saving throw at the end of its turn, ending the effect with a success.

Chyme Spray (recharge 6). The chymic spider expels the chymic juices from its stomach in a 15-foot cone. Creatures in the cone take 6d6 acid damage, or half damage with a successful DC 11 Dexterity saving throw. The juice sticks to creatures that failed their saving throws, and they take 3d6 acid damage at the ends of their next 2 turns unless the acid is removed by using an action to make a successful DC 13 Wisdom (Medicine) check, or is neutralized with vinegar, alcohol, or a similar substance.

ECOLOGY
Environment urban (the Blight)
Organization solitary

Chymic spiders are not true spiders, but rather born from the fear that spiders instill within many intelligent humanoids and inherently linked to the fabric of fear. These cunning aberrations sneak through the city rooftops and await their prey for days on end. Anyone who wanders into the chymic spider's 1-mile radius that might be the least bit fearful of spiders is quickly identified, and the chymic spider begins methodically stalking the victim, waiting for its chance to make dream contact.

Urban Predators. These rare creatures lurk along the edges of Sister Lyme, hiding in gables, chimneys, and under eaves and seemingly found nowhere else in the world. Composed from the latent fears of arachnids somehow given life, the creature is able to project these primal fears into any living creature. It simply prefers to stalk and prey on those who fear it most. It is able to project these nightmares and can cause victims to be paralyzed while it enters their lairs, and lays its eggs within them. The baby spiders within whisper to their new host, wanting to be fed, obsessing about food, and within 24 hours they erupt to feed on their host before separating to make their own lairs. After a chymic spider successfully reproduces, it quickly withers and dies, leaving behind only a spiderlike husk that the crows and vermin of the city quickly consume. Newborn chymic spiders don't begin their own reproduction hunts for 1d3 years after birth.

Copyright Notice
Author Jeffrey Swank, based on material by Richard Pett.

Spider, Gable

A spider the size of an alley cat scampers up the side of a tenement building. In its mandibles, it drags what appears to be a clothesline, with many of the garments still dangling limply behind.

Tiny Gable Spider

Tiny beast, unaligned

Armor Class 13
Hit Points 2 (1d4)
Speed 15 ft., climb 15 ft.

STR	DEX	CON	INT	WIS	CHA
1 (-5)	16 (+3)	10 (+0)	1 (-5)	6 (-2)	2 (-4)

Skills Perception +0, Stealth +5
Damage Immunities psychic
Condition Immunities charmed
Senses darkvision 30 ft., tremorsense in web, passive Perception 10
Languages none
Challenge 1/4 (50 XP)

Web Construct. A creature that falls prone, is restrained, or is pushed into a gable spider web construct becomes restrained by the sticky material and can escape by using an action to make a successful DC 10 Strength saving throw. A web construct is no more flammable than the material it's made from, but each 5-foot-square section has AC 8 and 5 hit points. A gable spider can move across any web construct without hindrance.

ACTIONS
Bite. *Melee Weapon Attack:* +5 to hit (reach 0 ft.; one creature). *Hit:* 2d4 poison damage, or half damage with a successful DC 10 Constitution saving throw.
Sticky Globule (recharge 4-6). *Ranged Weapon Attack:* +5 to hit (range 10 ft.; one creature). *Hit:* the creature must make a successful DC 10 Strength saving throw or be restrained. A restrained creature repeats the saving throw at the end of its turn, ending the effect on itself with a success.

ECOLOGY
Environment urban (the Blight)
Organization solitary, pair, or colony (3-10)

Small Gable Spider

Small beast, unaligned

Armor Class 13
Hit Points 18 (4d6 + 4)
Speed 20 ft., climb 20 ft.

STR	DEX	CON	INT	WIS	CHA
4 (-3)	16 (+3)	12 (+1)	1 (-5)	6 (-2)	2 (-4)

Skills Perception +0, Stealth +5
Damage Immunities psychic

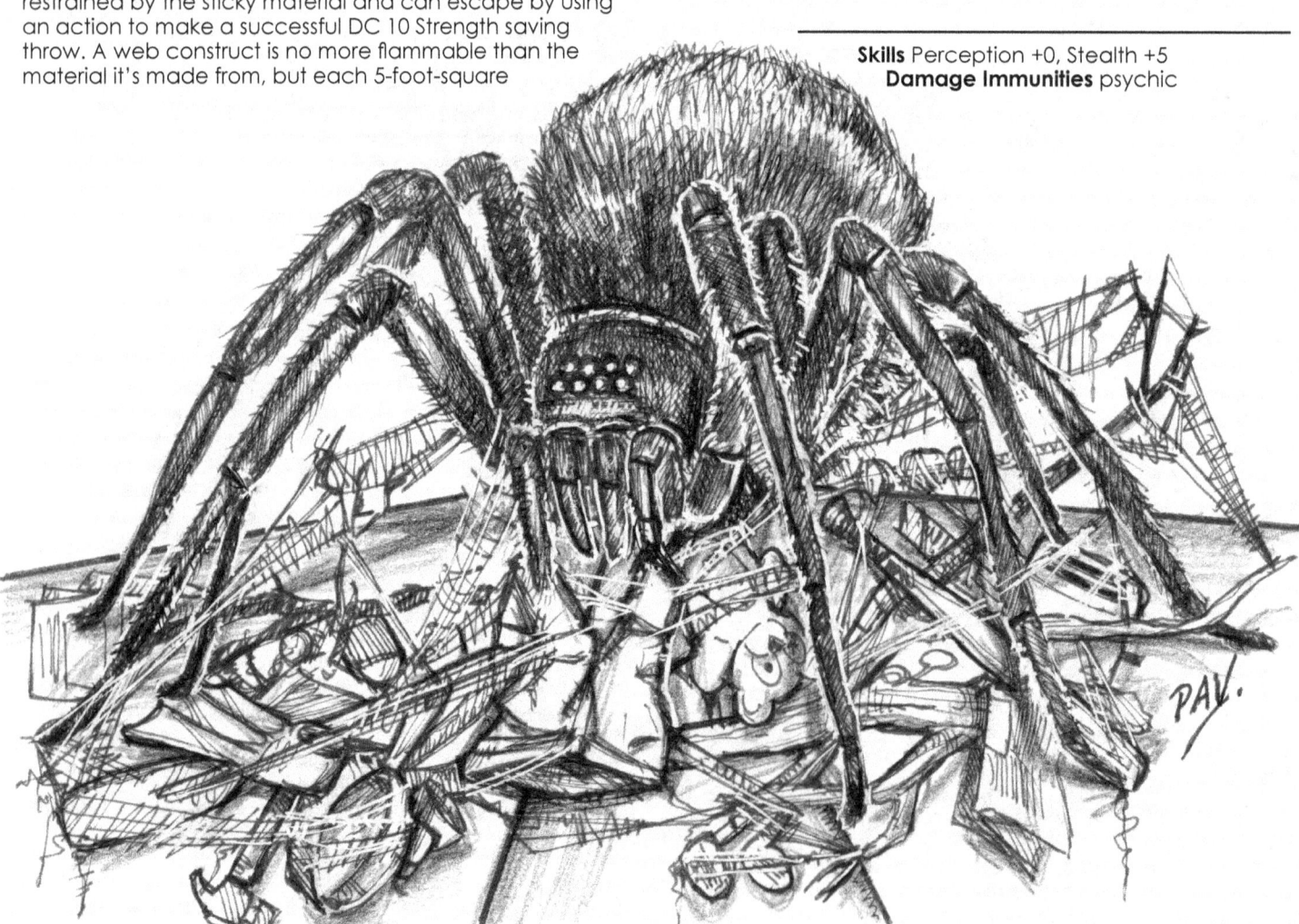

Condition Immunities charmed
Senses darkvision 30 ft., tremorsense in web, passive Perception 10
Languages none
Challenge 1/2 (100 XP)

Web Construct. A creature that falls prone, is restrained, or is pushed into a gable spider web construct becomes restrained by the sticky material and can escape by using an action to make a successful DC 10 Strength saving throw. A web construct is no more flammable than the material it's made from, but each 5-foot-square section has AC 8 and 5 hit points. A gable spider can move across any web construct without hindrance.

ACTIONS

Bite. *Melee Weapon Attack:* +5 to hit (reach 0 ft.; one creature). *Hit:* 1d8 + 3 piercing damage plus 2d6 poison damage, or half damage with a successful DC 11 Constitution saving throw.
Sticky Globule (recharge 4-6). *Ranged Weapon Attack:* +5 to hit (range 10 ft.; one creature). *Hit:* the creature must make a successful DC 11 Strength saving throw or be restrained. A restrained creature repeats the saving throw at the end of its turn, ending the effect on itself with a success.

ECOLOGY

Environment urban (the Blight)
Organization solitary, pair, or colony (3-10)

Medium Gable Spider

Medium beast, unaligned

Armor Class 13
Hit Points 52 (8d8 + 16)
Speed 30 ft., climb 30 ft.

STR	DEX	CON	INT	WIS	CHA
8 (-1)	16 (+3)	14 (+2)	2 (-4)	10 (+0)	2 (-4)

Skills Perception +2, Stealth +5
Damage Immunities psychic
Condition Immunities charmed
Senses darkvision 30 ft., tremorsense in web, passive Perception 12
Languages none
Challenge 2 (450 XP)

Web Construct. A creature that falls prone, is restrained, or is pushed into a gable spider web construct becomes restrained by the sticky material and can escape by using an action to make a successful DC 10 Strength saving throw. A web construct is no more flammable than the material it's made from, but each 5-foot-square section has AC 8 and 5 hit points. A gable spider can move across any web construct without hindrance.

ACTIONS

Bite. *Melee Weapon Attack:* +5 to hit (reach 0 ft.; one creature). *Hit:* 1d10 + 3 piercing damage plus 4d8 poison damage, or half damage with a successful DC 12 Constitution saving throw.
Sticky Globule (recharge 4-6). *Ranged Weapon Attack:* +5 to hit (range 10 ft.; one creature). *Hit:* the creature must make a successful DC 12 Strength saving throw or be restrained. A restrained creature repeats the saving throw at the end of its turn, ending the effect on itself with a success.

ECOLOGY

Environment urban (the Blight)
Organization solitary, pair, or colony (3-10)

Large Gable Spider

Large beast, unaligned

Armor Class 14
Hit Points 102 (12d10 + 36)
Speed 40 ft., climb 40 ft.

STR	DEX	CON	INT	WIS	CHA
14 (+2)	18 (+4)	16 (+3)	3 (-3)	10 (+0)	2 (-4)

Skills Perception +2, Stealth +6
Damage Immunities psychic
Condition Immunities charmed
Senses darkvision 30 ft., tremorsense in web, passive Perception 12
Languages none
Challenge 4 (1,100 XP)

Web Construct. A creature that falls prone, is restrained, or is pushed into a gable spider web construct becomes restrained by the sticky material and can escape by using an action to make a successful DC 10 Strength saving throw. A web construct is no more flammable than the material it's made from, but each 5-foot-square section has AC 8 and 5 hit points. A gable spider can move across any web construct without hindrance.

ACTIONS

Bite. *Melee Weapon Attack:* +6 to hit (reach 0 ft.; one creature). *Hit:* 1d10 + 4 piercing damage plus 4d12 poison damage, or half damage with a successful DC 13 Constitution saving throw.
Sticky Globule (recharge 4-6). *Ranged Weapon Attack:* +5 to hit (range 10 ft.; one creature). *Hit:* the creature must make a successful DC 13 Strength saving throw or be restrained. A restrained creature repeats the saving throw at the end of its turn, ending the effect on itself with a success.

ECOLOGY

Environment urban (the Blight)
Organization solitary, pair, or colony (3-10)

Gable spiders are different from other varieties of giant spiders, and it is for this reason that the whole of the city isn't shrouded in endless sheets of webbing. Gable spiders are not web spinners. Although they don't spin webs, gable spiders do have glands that produce a sticky fluid. This natural glue is used to string together the detritus they find in the city's dumps and alleys—frayed ropes, sail cordage, clothesline, twisted rags, curtains, discarded cloth, and more—into weblike structures. Even lengths of chain and broken lumber can be found in the weblike contrivances the gable spiders build. They combine this myriad material in twisting, knotted mazes of suspended lines that rival the largest spider webs for complexity. They knot and anchor these mismatched lines among the rooftops, between sagging buildings, and with each other to create swaying but stable webs of junk. Anything foolish enough to enter one of their gluey web constructions is unlikely ever to leave.

Salvaged Webs. The spiders also coat lengths of rope, cloth, sawdust, straw, or any other soft material with their fluid, wad it into a ball, and fling it at prey or at creaatures they're fighting. The sticky mass can glue a creature in place, making it easy prey for the gable spider's poison.

Squarpy (Sessile's Singing Terror)

At first glance, this creature looks like an "ordinary" giant squid of prodigious size. A closer look, however, shows a small, beaked mouth near the tip of each of its tentacles, and its two longer arms each end in great, birdlike talons.

Squarpy

Huge aberration (aquatic), chaotic evil

Armor Class 15 (natural armor)
Hit Points 172 (15d12 + 60)
Speed 20 ft., swim 60 ft.

STR	DEX	CON	INT	WIS	CHA
20 (+5)	14 (+2)	18 (+4)	7 (-2)	12 (+1)	17 (+3)

Saving Throws Dex +6, Con +8, Wis +5
Skills Perception +5
Condition Immunities blinded, prone
Senses darkvision 60 ft, tremorsense 30 ft. (underwater only), passive Perception 15
Languages Common
Challenge 10 (5,900 XP)

Captivating Song. The beaked tentacles of the squarpy all sing the song of kelpies as a bonus action. However, the combination of eight such voices and the strange way that the sound travels through the water causes the captivating harmony to become even more haunting and strange. All creatures within 300 feet of the squarpy (underwater or out of the water) must succeed on a DC 15 Wisdom saving throw or be charmed by the squarpy. While charmed this way, the creature is also incapacitated, and it moves toward the squarpy using the most direct means available. The charm lasts for as long as the squarpy maintains the song (it can be lost as concentration) or until it's broken with *dispel magic or comparable magic*. A charmed creature repeats the saving throw when it takes damage or when it begins suffocating, ending the effect on itself with a success.

Constrict. Grappled creatures take 2d8 bludgeoning damage plus 1d6 piercing damage at the start of the squarpy's turn.

Ink Cloud (recharge 6). As a reaction to being attacked, the squarpy emit a cloud of ink around itself while underwater. The ink extends 20 feet beyond the squarpy's space, and its area is heavily obscured. The ink persists for 1 minute and is stationary; it doesn't move with the squarpy.

Jet. When the squarpy dashes, it jets in a straight line up to 180 feet.

ACTIONS

Multiattack. The squarpy bites once and attacks twice with its tentacles.

Bite. *Melee Weapon Attack:* +9 to hit (reach 5 ft.; one creature). *Hit:* 3d6 + 5 piercing damage.

Tentacle. *Melee Weapon Attack:* +9 to hit (reach 15 ft.; one creature). Hit: 3d8 + 5 bludgeoning damage, and the target must make a successful DC 17 Dexterity saving throw or be grappled (escape DC 15). The squarpy can grapple up to eight creatures at one time. Maintaining grapples doesn't interfere with the squarpy's bite or tentacle attacks.

ECOLOGY

Environment sea (the Blight)
Organization solitary

It Hungers. Perhaps the most infamous creation of the physician Simon Sessile, this great beast is kept in the great aquarium at the Capitol, where its huge water tank enclosure is encased in thick, iron-reinforced, soundproof glass. The only access is through a second room on the floor above, which is simply a small metal cage with tightly spaced bars in which food-carcasses can be loaded and then dropped into the tank by pulling a lever to release the bottom of the cage. Nevertheless, despite all of these precautions, it seems that an aquarium keeper or night watchman disappears in the vicinity of the aquarium at least once a year. Sometimes some remnant of the missing person's clothing is spotted resting at the bottom of the great tank, but usually there is no evidence of their fate other than, perhaps, a faint red haziness in the water the next morning. How the squarpy is able to lure these individuals into its sealed tank is unknown, but few doubt that it is doing just that.

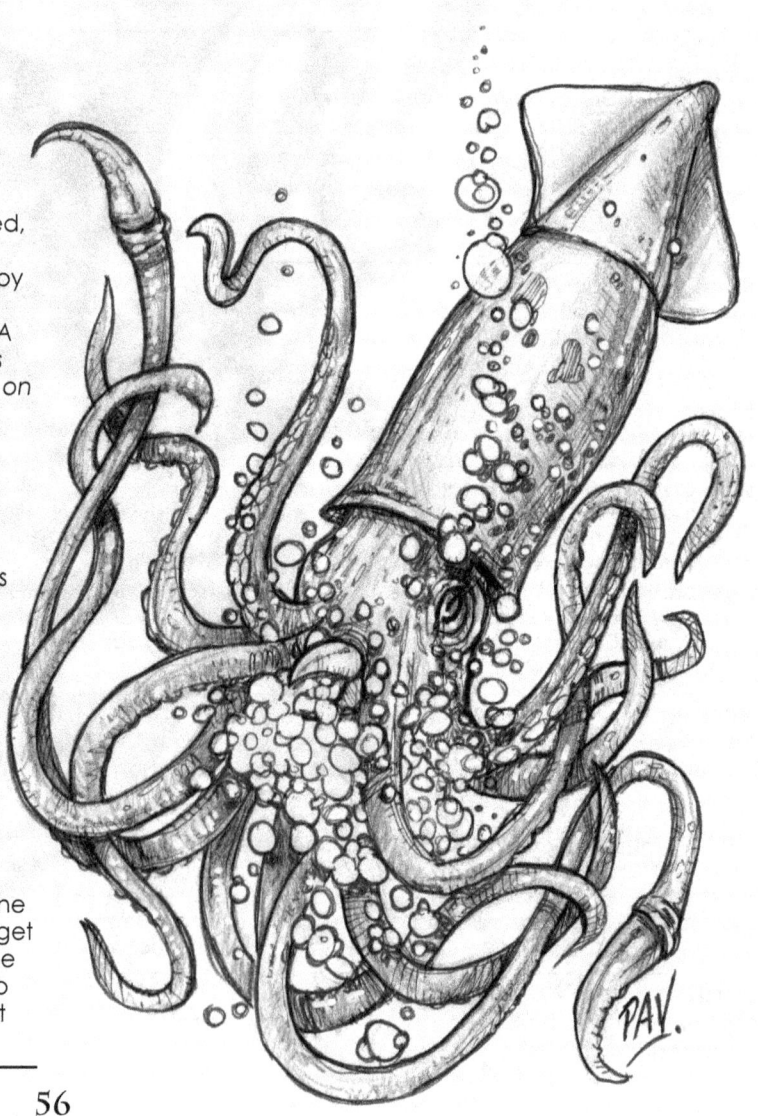

Stegocentroper

A massive, lumplike creature bursts from the cavern floor. It is has a huge, fanged maw flanked by mandibles, above which is a single, insectlike eye. Four chitinous tentacles emerge from its body behind its head, and the body itself is covered in bony plates with a double row of sharpened crests running down its back. Numerous centipede legs propel it forward as it continues pouring out of its burrow.

Stegocentroper

Huge monstrosity, unaligned

Armor Class 16 (natural armor)
Hit Points 104 (11d12 + 33)
Speed 30 ft., burrow 20 ft., climb 20 ft.

STR	DEX	CON	INT	WIS	CHA
19 (+4)	10 (+1)	17 (+3)	6 (-2)	14 (+2)	4 (-3)

Skills Perception +6
Damage Resistances cold
Damage Immunities lightning
Senses darkvision 60 ft., tremorsense 30 ft., passive Perception 16
Languages none
Challenge 9 (5,000 XP)

Spines. A stegocentroper raises its spine-plates during combat and moves rapidly back and forth while fighting. Creatures within 5 feet of the stegocentroper at the start of the monster's turn, and creatures that make melee attacks against the stegocentroper from 5 feet or less, must make successful DC 13 Dexterity saving throws or take 2d8 + 1 slashing damage.

Swallow. A swallowed creature is blinded and restrained. It takes 1d8 + 3 bludgeoning damage plus 1d8 acid damage automatically at the start of each of the stegocentroper's turns. Only one Medium creature or two Small creatures can be inside the stegocentroper at one time. A swallowed creature is unaffected by anything happening outside the stegocentroper or by attacks from outside it. A swallowed creature can get out of the stegocentroper by using 5 feet of movement, but only after the stegocentroper is dead.

ACTIONS

Multiattack. The stegocentroper bites once, stings once, and attacks twice with tentacles.

Bite. *Melee Weapon Attack:* +8 to hit (reach 5 ft.; one creature). *Hit:* 1d10 + 4 piercing damage. If the target is also grappled by the stegocentroper, it must make a successful DC 16 Dexterity saving throw or be swallowed (see "Swallow" above).

Sting. *Melee Weapon Attack:* +8 to hit (reach 10 ft.; one creature). *Hit:* 3d6 + 4 piercing damage plus 2d8 poison damage.

Tentacles. *Melee Weapon Attack:* +8 to hit (reach 30 ft.; one creature). *Hit:* 3d8 + 4 bludgeoning damage, and the target must make a successful DC 16 Strength saving throw or be grappled (escape DC 14). The stegocentroper can have up to two creatures grappled at one time, but the stegocentroper is prevented from making one tentacle attack for each creature it has grappled at the start of its turn.

ECOLOGY
Environment underground (the Blight)
Organization solitary

This abominable cross between a roper and a stegocentipede is a true nightmare of the deep places of the earth. It inherited the fierceness and strength of both species, magnified in its combination. Fortunately, it did not inherit the roper's intelligence, having only the dim awareness of the lower forms of life. It lives to eat and believes virtually anything it meets to be potentially edible. Its first instinct in combat is always to try to swallow opponents in its ceaseless hunger. Fortunately, the aggressiveness of these creatures prevents them from mating very frequently, so while they are naturally long-lived, they seldom reproduce.

Stircatrice

The creature flaps its batlike wings awkwardly through a series of bounding leaps, its red-rimmed eyes fixated in rage on its target. Beneath these eyes in its insectoid head, a long beaklike proboscis extends forward seemingly testing the air, with a pitch-black wattle dangling below. The body of the creature is lean like that of a cockerel with feathers as black as its wattle and six insectlike legs with jagged, grasping claws. A long, serpentine tail extends behind the creature, also feathered in the same inky plumes.

Stircatrice

Small aberration, unaligned

Armor Class 13 (natural armor)
Hit Points 33 (6d6 + 12)
Speed 20 ft., fly 40 ft.

STR	DEX	CON	INT	WIS	CHA
6	15	13	2	10	6
(-2)	(+2)	(+1)	(-4)	(+0)	(-2)

Skills Stealth +4
Condition Immunities petrified
Languages none
Senses darkvision 60 ft., passive Perception 10
Challenge 1 (200 XP)

Blood Drain and Calcification. A grappled creature takes 1d6 + 2 necrotic damage from blood loss at the start of the stircatrice's turn. It must also make a successful DC 11 Constitution saving throw or be restrained by rapid calcification of its tissue. A restrained creature repeats the saving throw at the end of its turn, ending the effect on itself with a success. If a restrained creature fails a second Constitution saving throw at the start of a grappling stircatrice's turn, the creature is petrified instead. A petrified creature makes another DC 11 Constitution saving throw every 24 hours, and returns to normal on a success.
Leaping Lunge. If a stircatrice moves at least 60 feet straight toward a target by dashing, it can make a tail attack against that target as a bonus action. It gets advantage on the tail attack and, if the tail hits, on the followup wing hook attack.

ACTIONS
Multiattack. A stircatrice stabs with its tail once. If the tail hits, the creature attacks the same target with its wing hooks as a bonus action.
Tail. *Melee Weapon Attack:* +4 to hit (reach 5 ft.; one creature). *Hit:* 1d4 + 2 piercing damage, and the stircatrice attacks the same creature with its wing hooks as a bonus action.
Wing Hooks. *Melee Weapon Attack:* +4 to hit (reach 5 ft.; one creature). *Hit:* the target is grappled (escape DC 8).

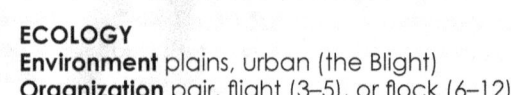

ECOLOGY
Environment plains, urban (the Blight)
Organization pair, flight (3–5), or flock (6–12)

Bloodless Entertainment. These aberrant creatures are prone to sudden rages and are nearly mindless in their aggression. They routinely attack creatures larger than themselves to feed on their blood. They are clumsy flyers at best, preferring to move in great leaping hops that appear gangly and uncoordinated but actually cover distance very quickly. Kept in menageries throughout the city, stircatrices are usually kept in double-walled cages since even a peck of their long, slender beak can spread a fatal infection.

Some yogis and entertainers of a more dramatic nature enter a stircatrice's cage to meditate or prove their mastery over the fearsome creature. An equal number of these have ended up as bloodless corpses as have emerged alive — to the raucous approval of their audience.

Swarm, Blindingcrow

This screeching whirlwind is a tumultuous mass of black feathers, talons, and pecking beaks.

Blindingcrow Swarm

Medium swarm of Tiny monstrosities, unaligned

Armor Class 12
Hit Points 22 (5d8)
Speed 10 ft., fly 40 ft.

STR	DEX	CON	INT	WIS	CHA
5 (-3)	14 (+2)	10 (+0)	3 (-4)	12 (+1)	6 (-2)

Skills Perception +3
Damage Resistances bludgeoning, piercing, and slashing
Condition Immunities blinded, charmed, frightened, grappled, paralyzed, petrified, prone, restrained, stunned
Languages none
Senses darkvision 30 ft., passive Perception 13
Challenge 1 (200 XP)

Blinding Sickness. A creature infected with blinding sickness must make a DC 9 Constitution saving throw after completing each long rest. On a failure, the infected creature gains 1 level of exhaustion; on a success, it loses 1 level of exhaustion. The disease is cured when the creature has 0 levels of exhaustion, or through *lesser restoration* or comparable magic. The real danger from the disease, however, is blindness. When a creature reaches 3 levels of exhaustion caused by blinding sickness, or when it has taken 3 or more necrotic damage in less than 10 minutes from blindingcrows, the creature is permanently blinded. Greater restoration or comparable magic is needed to cure this blindness.

Swarm. The blindingcrow swarm can occupy another creature's space and vice versa. The swarm can move through an opening large enough for an individual blindingcrow. The swarm never regains hit points or gains temporary hit points.

ACTIONS

Beaks. *Melee Weapon Attack:* +4 to hit (reach 0 ft.; one creature). *Hit:* 2d6 piercing damage, and the creature must make a successful DC 9 Constitution saving throw or take 1 necrotic damage and contract blinding sickness (see above). Piercing damage is 1d6 if

the swarm has half or fewer of its starting hit points.

ECOLOGY
Environment non-arctic land
Organization solitary or cluster (2-4)

A blindingcrow swarm is a mass of such birds mobbing together to defend against a predator or some other individual that has sufficiently antagonized them, usually through approaching too near a roosting murder of the birds or with loud noises. Only when blindingcrows mob something and form a swarm does the threat of blindness become really serious.

Blindingcrow swarms have the same general characteristics and habitat of normal blindingcrows.

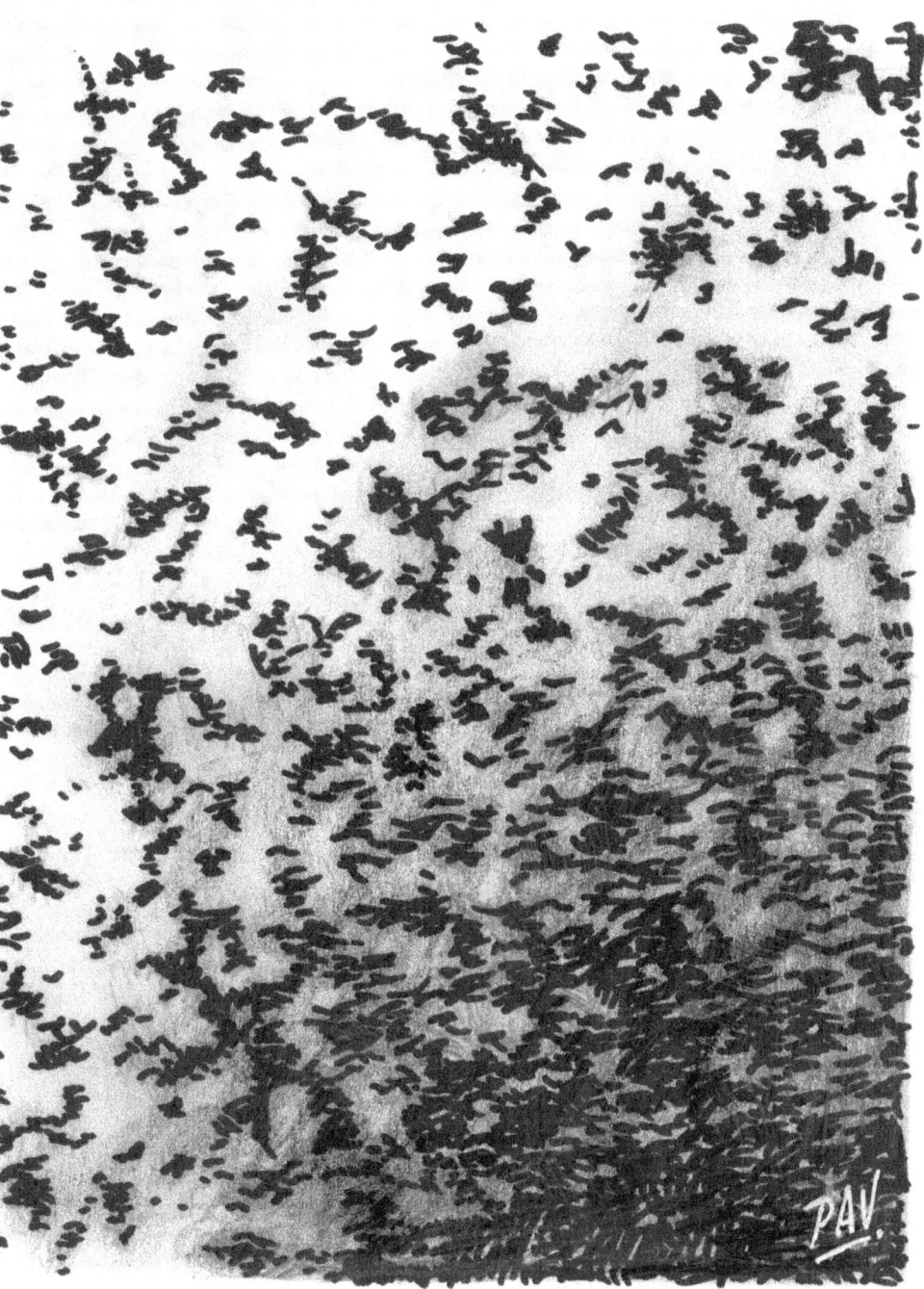

Woerm

This wormlike monster's eyeless head has a hooked jaw and large, pointed ears. Its scaly hide is dull gray with a crest on its head and along its back to its tail, along which its shrunken, vestigial legs hang limply. Its long, multi-jointed arms are like slimy spider legs tipped with elongated, clawed hands.

Woerm

Medium aberration, chaotic evil

Armor Class 11
Hit Points 38 (7d8 + 7)
Speed 40 ft., burrow 10 ft., climb 30 ft.

STR	DEX	CON	INT	WIS	CHA
16 (+3)	13 (+1)	13 (+1)	10 (+0)	12 (+1)	8 (-1)

Skills Acrobatics +3, Athletics +5, Stealth +3
Senses blindsense 30 ft. (blind beyond 30 ft.), passive Perception 11
Languages Undercommon
Challenge 1 (200 XP)

Blind. Woerms rely entirely on blindsight. They are immune to gaze attacks, visual effects, illusions, and other effects that interact with normal sight.
Filth Fever. A creature with filth fever becomes sick 1d4 days after being infected. At that time, the creature gains 1 level of exhaustion. It also regains only half the usual number of hit points from spending Hit Dice and no hit points from resting. Once symptoms appear, the infected creature must make a DC 11 Constitution saving throw after every long rest. If it fails, the creature gains 1 level of exhaustion; if it succeeds, the creature loses 1 level of exhaustion. The disease is cured when the creature has no exhaustion.
Pack Attack. A woerm has advantage on its attack roll if the target is within 5 feet of another woerm that's able to attack.
Regeneration. A woerm heals 5 hit points at the start of each of its turns. This ability doesn't function if it took acid or fire damage, or was exposed to sunlight, since its previous turn.
Stench. A creature (other than a woerm or troglodyte) that starts its turn within 5 feet of a woerm must make a successful DC 11 Constitution saving throw or be poisoned until the start of its next turn. A creature that saves successfully is immune to woem Stench for 24 hours.

ACTIONS

Multiattack. The woerm bites once and claws once.
Bite. *Melee Weapon Attack:* +5 to hit (reach 5 ft.; one creature). *Hit:* 1d4 + 3 piercing damage, and the creature must make a successful DC 11 Constitution saving throw or be infected with filth fever (see above).
Claws. *Melee Weapon Attack:* +5 to hit (reach 5 ft.; one creature). *Hit:* 2d6 + 3 slashing damage.
Disorientating Scream. Woerms communicate with their own kind via high-pitched screams. Creatures other than woerms within 15 feet of a screaming woerm must succeed at a DC 11 Wisdom saving throw or be incapacitated for 1 round. A character who makes this saving throw successfully is immune to woerms' Disorientating Screams for 24 hours.

ECOLOGY

Environment underground
Organization solitary, pair, gang (3–12), or cult (13+)

Woerms are an aggressive, insular race who constantly hunger for flesh and who have become adept at survival in the crippling and stifling confines of the Underneath. Originally spawned of cursed unions between morlocks and troglodytes, they are rarely encountered and never above ground, as sunlight repels them.

Careful Hunters. Woerms are cautious when hunting, striking prey as they rush forth from hidden holes and disappear into others. This tactic has led to an impression that they enjoy playing with their prey — earning them the name "Welcomers Below" — but woerms delight only in eating.

Social Horrors. Woerms are surprisingly sophisticated and intelligent — or at least, more sophisticated and intelligent than they look — and have complex and powerful clans and groups; two opposing groups of woerms never work together, but occasionally a great leader forges a larger kingdom of the creatures. These clans can last for decades or even centuries, and the feasting halls that rarely have been discovered have shown their appetites and successes. Occasionally, the insular woerms form an alliance with, or more often enslave, a race of subterranean dwellers, typically their morlock or troglodyte forebears.

Appendix A:

Between Creatures

Between Dream

This ghostlike figure is composed of nightmarish imagery and screaming faces.

Between Dream

Small aberration (larval Between), neutral evil

Armor Class 13
Hit Points 28 (8d6)
Speed 0 ft., fly 40 ft.

STR	DEX	CON	INT	WIS	CHA
1 (-5)	17 (+3)	10 (+0)	10 (+0)	15 (+2)	17 (+3)

Skills Stealth +7
Damage Resistances cold, force, thunder; bludgeoning, piercing, and slashing from nonmagical weapons
Damage Immunities poison
Condition Immunities disease; exhaustion, grappled, paralyzed, petrified, poisoned, prone, restrained, stunned, unconscious
Languages telepathy 100 ft.
Senses darkvision 60 ft., passive Perception 12
Challenge 1 (200 XP)

Incorporeal. A Between dream can move through gaps as small as 1 square inch without penalty. It can move through solid objects and other creatures as if they were difficult terrain. The Between dream takes 1d10 force damage if it is still inside something solid at the end of its turn.

Innate Spellcasting. The Between dream can use the following spell-like abilities, using Charisma as its casting ability (DC 13, attack +5). The Between dream needs no components to use these abilities.

> 3/day each: *fear, sleep, crown of madness, misty step*
> 1/day each: *confusion, dimension door, phantasmal force, sleep*

Vanish. The Between dream can Hide as a bonus action at the end of its turn, even when it's in plain sight.

ACTIONS

Nightmare Curse. *Melee Weapon Attack:* +5 to hit (reach 5 ft.; one creature). *Hit:* 2d6 + 3 psychic damage, and a creature must make a successful DC 13 Charisma saving throw or gain 1 level of exhaustion.

ECOLOGY

Environment any (Between)
Organization solitary

Between dreams are weak, semi-sentient dreams that form in Between rather than on the Ethereal Plane. Their true appearances are vague and nebulous, but they react to the fears and emotions of those around them, taking on increasingly nightmarish appearances that differ for each viewer. Between dreams sometimes cooperate with other Between creatures such as Between vampires and gloams that have associations with dreams and nightmares.

Between-Cat

Vaguely feline, this hairless, pale creature has wrinkled, flaccid skin, a pair of stunted vestigial limbs extending from its flanks, and a ring of small tentacles around its neck. Its clawed forepaws each bear one wickedly hooked claw much larger than the others. Its eyes are dark voids, and a long, prehensile tongue extends from its mouth.

Between-Cat

Tiny aberration (larval Between), neutral

Armor Class 15 (natural armor)
Hit Points 15 (6d4)
Speed 30 ft., climb 20 ft.

STR	DEX	CON	INT	WIS	CHA
3 (-4)	15 (+2)	10 (+0)	20 (+5)	14 (+2)	16 (+3)

Saving Throws Dex +5, Con +3, Int +7, Wis +4, Cha +5
Skills Arcana +7, History +7, Perception +4, Stealth +4
Damage Resistances cold, lightning, thunder; bludgeoning, piercing, and slashing from nonmagical weapons
Damage Immunities poison
Condition Immunities disease; charmed, poisoned
Senses darkvision 60 ft., passive Perception 14
Languages Abyssal, Celestial, Common, Deep Speech, Infernal; telepathy 60 ft.
Challenge 3 (700 XP)

Dislocated. The Between-cat's form is made up of memories, which shift and change. The creature is continually under the effect of a *blur* spell (attacks against it are made with disadvantage unless the attacker has blindsight, truesight, or an equivalent). The Between-cat can suppress or reactivate this ability at will as a bonus action.

Dual Existence (recharge 4-6). The Between-cat can pass easily back and forth between the Between and the mundane world at will (no action required). This allows it to teleport up to 60 feet to a space it can see, or to escape into the Between until it chooses to return to the mundane world.

Innate Spellcasting. The Between-cat can use the following spell-like abilities, using Intelligence as its casting ability (DC 15). The cadaver doesn't need material components to use these abilities.

At will: *comprehend languages, tongues*
1/day: *detect magic, glyph of warding*

Nulltropy. A creature slain by a nulltropic claws attack can return to life only through a *wish* or *true resurrection* spell.

Shapechanger. In the Between, the Between-cat always assumes its natural shape. In other worlds, it appears as a normal cat unless it uses an action to adopt its natural shape, which it must maintain through concentration, like a spell.

ACTIONS

Multiattack. The Between-cat claws once and strikes once with its tongue.

Nulltropic Claws. *Melee Weapon Attack:* +5 to hit (reach 5 ft.; one creature). Hit: 2d4 + 2 slashing damage plus 1 force damage for every additional Between-cat within 60 feet of the target. Force damage can't be reduced by resistance, immunity, magic, or any other means.

Tongue. *Melee Weapon Attack:* +5 to hit (reach 5 ft.; one creature). Hit: 1d6 + 2 piercing damage plus 2d8 poison damage.

ECOLOGY

Environment any land (Between)
Organization solitary, pair, pack (3–6), hunt (7–10), brood (11–15), coven (16–30), or council (31–56)

PAV.

Cats have often enjoyed a vaguely mysterious and sinister reputation throughout many cultures, and the Between-cat may be the most deserving of this reputation. Catlike in name only due to its vaguely feline appearance, some scholars question whether Between-cats began as normal cats and were changed through exposure to the Between. Others think they are actual creatures of the Between that managed to gain a catlike appearance through their intimate contact with the mundane world, while some believe they are some entirely unrelated species that simply evolved concurrently to resemble the more mundane varieties of cats. Whatever the case, it seems that Between-cats hold no special affinity for true felines, and yet are able to move among them completely unnoticed by other cats without raising any alarm when in their mundane cat forms. Whatever the reason for their existence and their relationship to mundane felines, Between-cats are one of the few creatures that enjoys seemingly complete freedom in moving between the natural world and Between.

Feline Scholars. While their full agenda is not known, two facts about Between-cats are recognized among the most learned of scholars. First, they ceaselessly search through venerable tomes, petroglyphs, and other ancient writings in search of some unknown secret or secrets that they have revealed to no one. Second — whether related to the first item or not — Between-cats seek to completely unmake reality for their own hidden reasons. Nulltropic damage from their claws, amplified by the presence of other Between-cats, induces a loss of order and energy in the target and produces an overall breakdown of substance toward nothingness. More than mere entropy, which simply describes the loss of order and cohesion, the nulltropy of the Between-cat brings about a complete loss of existence in any form, albeit on a tiny scale. Armed with their nulltropic attack, Between-cats can accomplish their goal of unmaking reality one tiny piece at a time.

Terrifying in Groups. Fortunately for the sake of reality and all who live in it, the nulltropic damage caused by a single Between-cat is minuscule, and they are loathe to use it indiscriminately. They instead save it for enemies in battle or for certain artifacts and writings they have found over the years, as well as for aboleths, whom they consider bitter enemies. However, when more Between-cats get together, their nulltropic attack becomes terrifying. Thankfully, no one has ever reported encountering more than 56 Between-cats in one place. There is speculation, however, that if more did gather, then the nulltropic damage they could cause would continue to scale to an ever-accelerating degree. Most sober-minded theoreticians refuse to think too long on the dreadful implications of this line of thought.

Caul-Cuckoo

This is no ordinary human child, but an infection, something that leeched upon a living babe whilst in the womb and smothered it, becoming something partly human and partly from Between. Its form is fluid, oily almost, and the disturbing mixture of human and slug is revolting to behold.

Caul Cuckoo

Small aberration (larval Between), neutral

Armor Class 13
Hit Points 63 (14d6 + 14)
Speed 10 ft., burrow 5 ft., climb 10 ft., swim 10 ft.

STR	DEX	CON	INT	WIS	CHA
8 (-1)	16 (+3)	12 (+1)	9 (-1)	12 (+1)	18 (+4)

Saving Throws Dex +6, Con +4, Wis +4
Skills Perception +4, Stealth +6
Damage Resistances bludgeoning, piercing, and slashing from nonmagical weapons
Damage Immunities acid
Condition Immunities prone
Senses darkvision 60 ft., passive Perception 14
Languages Common, Deep Speech, Sylvan, telepathy 30 ft.
Challenge 5 (1,800 XP)

Change Shape. A caul cuckoo has two forms. Its natural form is that of a sluglike thing with a distorted humanoid head, but it can also take a humanoid form based on its mother. A caul cuckoo can shift between its forms as a bonus action. Equipment worn or carried on its humanoid form melds into its natural form.

Distorted. The caul cuckoo's internal anatomy is radically different from a normal humanoid's. Critical hits against the creature do a flat +1 damage but don't roll damage dice twice.

Horrific Appearance. Creatures that start their turn within 30 feet of a caul cuckoo in its natural form and who can see it see must make a successful DC 15 Wisdom saving throw or be poisoned. This is a psychological effect, not actual poison, so immunity to poison offers no protection. A poisoned creature repeats the saving throw at the end of its turn to end the effect. A successful saving throw makes the creature immune to the horrific appearance of caul cuckoos for 24 hours.

Salt Vulnerability. A handful of salt burns a caul cuckoo as though it was alchemist's fire, doing 1d4 fire damage at the start of the caul cuckoo's turn until it's extinguished by spending an action to make a successful DC 10 Dexterity check.

ACTIONS

Multiattack. The caul cuckoo makes three tongue attacks or sings its lullaby.

Tongue. *Melee Weapon Attack:* +5 to hit (reach 5 ft.; one creature). *Hit:* 1d4 + 3 piercing damage plus 1d6 acid damage.

Lullaby. When a caul cuckoo wails its lullaby, it has the same effect as a *confusion* spell that affects all creatures within 300 feet of the caul cuckoo who can hear the song. All potential targets must make successful DC 15 Wisdom saving throws or become confused. The confusion lasts for 1 minute or until the caul cuckoo stops singing or loses concentration on its lullaby. The creature can repeat the saving throw at the end of its turn, with a success ending the effect.

ECOLOGY

Environment any land (Between)
Organization solitary, pair, gang (3–8), or cult (9–20)

Caul cuckoos are the tragic result of an unborn child corrupted by a caul cuckoo syre while still in its mother's womb. When birthed by its human parent, a caul cuckoo is Tiny, but otherwise has all of its normal abilities. A caul cuckoo has a 50% chance of being in either of its two forms at birth. If in its human form, it usually waits until after nightfall to either escape into the night or murder its sleeping parents and then escape. If born in its sluglike form, it immediately attacks its mother and any others present in an attempt to escape.

Though the birth of these creatures is a rare occurrence, there is a reason that many old midwives carry a bag of salt with them whenever they attend a new delivery.

Caul Cuckoo Syre

This creature is a pallid pupa, no larger than a finger, with a tiny, twisted humanoid face.

Caul Cuckoo Syre

Tiny aberration (larval Between), neutral

Armor Class 11
Hit Points 1 (1d4 - 1)
Speed 5 ft., burrow 5 ft., climb 5 ft., swim 5 ft.

STR	DEX	CON	INT	WIS	CHA
1 (-5)	12 (+1)	8 (-1)	6 (-2)	10 (+0)	16 (+3)

Skills Stealth +5
Damage Resistances bludgeoning, piercing, and slashing from nonmagical weapons

Damage Immunities acid
Condition Immunities prone
Senses darkvision 60 ft., passive Perception 10
Languages Deep Speech, telepathy 30 ft.
Challenge 1/8 (25 XP)

Salt Vulnerability. A handful of salt burns a caul cuckoo syre as though it was alchemist's fire, doing 1d4 fire damage at the start of the caul cuckoo's turn until it's extinguished by spending an action to make a successful DC 10 Dexterity check.

ACTIONS

Lullaby. When a caul cuckoo syre wails its lullaby, it targets one creature within 30 feet which must succeed on a DC 13 Wisdom saving throw or fall unconscious. Creatures with 5 or more HD are immune. A creature that saves successfully is immune to all caul cuckoo syre lullabies for 24 hours. An unconscious creature wakes up after 1 minute, when it takes damage, or when another creature uses an action to awaken it.

ECOLOGY

Environment any land (Between)
Organization solitary

Caul cuckoo syres are the progenitors of caul cuckoos. They spend the majority of their lives stealthily searching out pregnant humanoid females to infest, so they can corrupt their unborn children into caul cuckoos.

Drawn to Mothers. A caul cuckoo syre can detect pregnant humanoids within 60 feet by smell. Strangely, caul cuckoo syres are also attracted by the odor of some ghouls, which consider caul cuckoo syres to be quite the delicacy. When a caul cuckoo syre locates a pregnant potential host, it crawls into the woman's womb while she's asleep. Over the course of the next five days, it slowly dissolves into the developing embryo, bathing it in unnatural hormones. The woman experiences severe morning sickness during those five days; a successful DC 13 Wisdom (Medicine) check made by a character with proficiency in Medicine spots the difference between this sickness and typical morning sickness. By the end of the five days, the syre is completely gone and the fetus is transformed into a caul cuckoo.

Dangerous Surgery. If the syre's presence is detected or even suspected, it can be removed with a successful DC 15 Wisdom (Medicine) check. The check can be repeated as many times as necessary, but if it fails by 5 or more, the host takes 1d6 slashing damage (which can easily kill a commoner with 4 or fewer hit points). Lesser restoration or comparable magic destroys a caul cuckoo syre automatically and restores the fetus to normal health.

Gloam

This black humanoid doesn't appear to have eyes, a nose, or ears, but its mouth, set in a permanently too-wide rictus smile, is filled with awful, jagged teeth which, just like its claws, appear to be composed of fragments of mirror.

Gloam

Medium aberration (adult Between), neutral evil

Armor Class 15
Hit Points 91 (14d8 +28)
Speed 60 ft., climb 40 ft.

STR	DEX	CON	INT	WIS	CHA
16 (+3)	20 (+5)	14 (+2)	15 (+2)	10 (+0)	20 (+5)

Saving Throws Dex +9, Con +6, Wis +4, Cha +9
Skills Medicine +4, Perception +4, Stealth +9
Damage Resistances cold, force, lightning; bludgeoning, piercing, and slashing from all weapons
Damage Immunities poison
Condition Immunities charmed, frightened, poisoned, stunned, unconscious
Senses blindsight 60 ft., darkvision 90 ft., passive Perception 14
Languages Common, Deep Speech, Undercommon
Challenge 11 (7,200 XP)

Bleeding Wound. A creature takes 1d4 necrotic damage at the start of its turn from each bleeding wound it has. A creature with one or more bleeding wounds makes a DC 15 Constitution saving throw at the end of its turn; all wounds stop bleeding on a success. All bleeding is also stopped if the wounded creature or an ally within 5 feet uses an action to make a successful DC 15 Wisdom (Medicine) check.

Dislocated. The gloam's form is made up of its memories, which shift and change. The creature is continually under the effect of a *blur* spell (attacks against it are made with disadvantage unless the attacker has blindsight, truesight, or an equivalent). The gloam can suppress or reactivate this ability at will as a bonus action.

Distorted. The gloam's internal anatomy varies from individual to individual and seldom makes any biological sense. Critical hits against a gloam do a flat +1 damage but don't roll damage dice twice.

Fear Gaze. A creature that sees the gloam's face within 30 feet must make a successful DC 17 Wisdom saving throw or be frightened of the gloam for 1 minute. While frightened, the creature is also stunned; it can only cower in fear. A frightened creature repeats the saving throw at the end of its turn, ending the effect on itself

with a success.

Innate Spellcasting. The gloam can use the following spell-like abilities, using Charisma as its casting ability (DC 13, attack +5). The gloam doesn't need material components to use these abilities.

At will: *misty step (can't teleport to or from bright light)*
1/day each: *dimension door, invisibility (self only, duration 1 minute)*

Magic Resistance (1/day). When the gloam fails a saving throw, it can choose to succeed instead.

Regeneration. A gloam heals 10 hit points at the start of each of its turns. This ability doesn't function if it took radiant damage since its previous turn.

Sneak Attack. A gloam's attack does an extra 3d6 damage if the gloam has advantage on the attack.

ACTIONS

Multiattack. The gloam bites once and claws twice, or attacks three times with mirror shards.

Bite. *Melee Weapon Attack:* +9 to hit (reach 5 ft.; one creature). Hit: 1d6 + 5 piercing damage, and the creature suffers a bleeding wound (see above).

Claws. *Melee Weapon Attack:* +9 to hit (reach 5 ft.; one creature). Hit: 2d8 + 5 slashing damage, and the creature suffers a bleeding wound (see above).

Mirror Shards. *Ranged Weapon Attack:* +9 to hit (range 60 ft.; one creature). Hit: 2d6 + 5 slashing damage, and the creature suffers a bleeding wound (see above).

ECOLOGY

Environment urban (Between)
Organization solitary

A gloam embodies the paralyzing terror of the unknown "thing in the darkness" combined with a stalking murderer. It is an emotionless entity composed of alien flesh and shadow that steps from Between to terrorize communities with serial killings. Its imaginative dismemberment and placing of it victims' bodies conveys the horror they experienced when they encountered it and the fear that ripples outward from a gloam's presence in the mundane world.

Unlike many Between creatures that are born elsewhere and transported to Between, indications are that the gloam is a native of that realm. Its teeth and claws are razor-sharp shards of mirrors, and it can conjure additional mirror shards at will to throw or spit like darts or shuriken.

Herald at the Threshold

A thing of sublime chaos, this creature seems to have no set form yet is composed of flaccid skin and a trio of grasping, tentacle-like limbs. Its form is partially made of boiling emotions that clothe the thing in waxy flesh. Its great limbs grip at its surroundings, lacerating stone in its grasp, while some sort of fetid opening surrounded by moist bones rises to a set of horns like demented curved instruments through which an agonizing, grating scream tears.

Herald at the Threshold

Large aberration (adult Between), neutral

Armor Class 17 (natural armor)
Hit Points 102 (12d10 + 36)
Speed 30 ft., climb 30 ft.

STR	DEX	CON	INT	WIS	CHA
20 (+5)	18 (+4)	16 (+3)	8 (-1)	13 (+1)	18 (+4)

Saving Throws Dex +9, Con +8, Wis +6
Skills Perception +4
Damage Resistances cold, fire, force, lightning, poison; bludgeoning, piercing, and slashing from nonmagical weapons
Condition Immunities charmed, frightened
Senses blindsight 90 ft., passive Perception 14
Languages understands Deep Speech but can't speak
Challenge 15 (13,000 XP)

Absorb. If a creature with 0 hit points fails a death saving throw while a herald at the threshold is in the same space with it, that creature dies and its body is entirely absorbed into the herald's. The herald gains temporary hit points equal to the creature's Constitution score. If the herald is subsequently killed, enough of an absorbed creature's corpse can be recovered for a spell such as *resurrection* to work, but not *revivify* or *raise dead*.

Dimensional Mastery. A herald at the threshold can cast *dimension door* as a bonus action.

Dislocated. The herald at the threshold's form is made up of its memories, which shift and change. The creature is continually under the effect of a *blur* spell (attacks against it are made with disadvantage unless the attacker has blindsight, truesight, or an equivalent). The herald can suppress or reactivate this ability at will as a bonus action.

Immune to Transformation. A herald at the threshold is immune to any effect that would alter its form..

Magic Resistance (1/day). When the herald fails a saving throw, it can choose to succeed instead.

Innate Spellcasting. The herald at the threshold can use the following spell-like abilities, using Charisma as its casting ability (DC 16). The herald doesn't need material components to use these abilities.
At will: *dimension door, freedom of movement*
3/day each: *blink, counterspell*
1/day each: *invisibility* (self only, duration 1 minute), *resilient sphere*

ACTIONS

Multiattack. The herald attacks three times with its claws.

Claw. *Melee Weapon Attack:* +10 to hit (reach 5 ft.; one creature). *Hit:* 2d6 + 5 slashing damage. If two claw attacks hit the same target on the herald's turn, that target takes an additional 3d6 slashing damage and gains 1 level of exhaustion.

Overwhelming Mind (recharge 5-6). The herald projects a telepathic assault in a 30-foot cone. Creatures in the cone must make a successful DC 17 Wisdom saving throw or be paralyzed for 1 minute. A paralyzed creature repeats the saving throw at the end of its turn, ending the effect on itself with a success. In addition, creatures that attempt to make mental contact with a herald, whether telepathically or through spells such as *detect thoughts* or *dominate monster*, are immediately subject to this attack.

Preternatural Horror (1/day). The herald reveals the full horror of itself to the minds of nearby creatures. All creatures within 60 feet of the herald must make a successful DC 17 Wisdom saving throw or be afflicted with madness. If the result of the saving throw is 12-16, the creature suffers a short-term madness; 7-11 results in long-term madness; 6 or less results in indefinite madness. No line of sight or visual contact is needed for this attack to work.

Screaming Pipes (1/day). The herald emits a psyche-blasting shriek through its hornlike appendages. All creatures within 30 feet of the herald and capable of hearing it must make a DC 16 Wisdom saving throw. If the saving throw fails, the creature is stunned for 1d4 rounds and permanently deafened; if it succeeds, the creature is deafened for 1d4 rounds and incapacitated until the end of its next turn.

LEGENDARY ACTIONS

The herald at the threshold can take up to three legendary actions per round. Legendary actions are taken at the end of another creature's turn, and only one can be taken after each turn.

Cast Spell. The herald casts an at-will spell.

Claw. The herald makes a claw attack.

Multiattack (costs 2 actions). The herald makes three claw attacks.

ECOLOGY

Environment any (Between)
Organization solitary

Born by the Beautiful to serve her needs as keepers of her thresholds from Between, the heralds are creatures that defy mortal and mundane reference.

Hyme

Superficially it could be a horse — certainly there is some horse in it — but the resemblance is unnatural. It's a dark thing, a thing the eye finds difficult to rest upon, with the anger and musk of a horse, but the shape is wrong. Its head is dark and long, and slaver drools from it onto the ground. And though it tosses its head like a horse, it has barbed teeth in its jaw.

Hyme
Large aberration (larval Between), unaligned

Armor Class 13 (natural armor)
Hit Points 30 (4d10 + 8)
Speed 60 ft.

STR	DEX	CON	INT	WIS	CHA
18 (+4)	13 (+1)	14 (+2)	2 (-4)	11 (+0)	7 (-2)

Senses darkvision 30 ft., passive Perception 10
Languages none
Challenge 2 (450 XP)

Dislocated. The hyme's form is made up of memories, which shift and change. The creature is continually under the effect of a *blur spell (attacks against it are made with disadvantage unless the attacker has blindsight, truesight, or an equivalent).* The hyme can suppress or reactivate this ability at will as a bonus action.
Distorted. A hyme's internal anatomy varies from individual to individual and seldom makes any biological sense. Critical hits against a hyme do a flat +1 damage but don't roll damage dice twice.<RULE>
Musk of Fear (1/day). As a bonus action, a hyme emits an unpleasant musk. All breathing creatures within 30 feet must succeed on a DC 12 Constitution saving throw or be poisoned while within 30 feet of the hyme. The effect lasts 1 minute. A creature that spends its entire turn more than 30 feet from the hyme repeats the saving throw, ending the effect on itself with a success. Other hymes and their masters are immune. Beasts have a -2 modifier on the saving throw; horses save with disadvantage.

ACTIONS
Multiattack. The hyme bites once and attacks once with its hooves.
Bite. *Melee Weapon Attack:* +6 to hit (reach 5 ft.; one creature). *Hit:* 1d4 + 4 piercing damage.
Hooves. *Melee Weapon Attack:* +6 to hit (reach 5 ft.; one creature). *Hit:* 2d6 + 4 bludgeoning damage.
Bray of Terror (recharge 5-6). All creatures within 60 of the hyme and that can hear it must make a successful DC 12 Wisdom saving throw or be frightened of the hyme for 1d4 rounds. Other hymes and their masters are immune. Beasts have a -2 modifier on the saving throw; horses save with disadvantage. A creature that saves successfully is immune to Bray of Terror for 24 hours.

ECOLOGY
Environment plains, swamp (Between)
Organization solitary, pair, or herd (3–12)

The first hyme came about one terrible night when a creature from Between was captured and held in a stable. Whilst the greedy captors sought to sell their prize to those who collect such creatures in peculiar menageries, something terrible happened, and when the hunters returned they simply found the creature gone and the horses within mad with terror. Cursing their bad luck, the hunters looked for new prey. A few months later, each mare in the stable birthed a horrible dark thing that resembled a foal but was certainly not of this world. The hunters went back to their original purchaser with their new creatures and sold them. These were the first hymes.

Between-Horses. A bastard union of the Between and the horse, the hyme combines the qualities of a horse with the aggression of a Between creature. They are hard to tame, but not impossible, and broken ones now regularly pull coarse cabs around the city. Initially, such terrible dray were the exclusive property of those aristocrats who could afford them, but their prodigious appetites created more hymes from unions with mares (hymes are born to both hyme-hyme and hyme-horse parents). They are now seen regularly, but most often on dark nights.

Rare Commodities. Hymes command very high prices, and are extremely rare to find for sale. Occasionally, one becomes available, but generally only particular dealers — such as Groppit, Swift & Humb: Hyme Dealers by Royal Appointment — sell them. A hyme sells for 6,500 gp.

Mantis-Thing from Between

It is fleshy, but in a revoltingly waxy, insectoid way. It staggers on several insect legs and drags itself along on two long limbs, making the thing look like it is obsequiously praying to some demented god as it moves. It has a vast, bloated head riddled with teeth, but moves with appalling speed despite its large size. As it moves, sinews, faces, and limbs of people bloat its flesh, and horribly distorted hands grope outward from this vile host. Wreathed about its sickening flesh are palpable manifestations of misery, regret, and bitter, dashed hope.

Mantis-Thing from Between
Large aberration (naiadic Between), chaotic neutral

Armor Class 16 (natural armor)
Hit Points 110 (13d10 + 39)
Speed 40 ft., climb 40 ft.

STR	DEX	CON	INT	WIS	CHA
20 (+5)	15 (+2)	16 (+3)	5 (-3)	14 (+2)	11 (+0)

Saving Throws Dex +5, Wis +5
Skills Perception +5

Damage Resistances bludgeoning, piercing, and slashing from nonmagical weapons
Senses darkvision 60 ft., passive Perception 15
Languages Between Mantis
Challenge 6 (2,300 XP)

Cocoon (1/day). The mantis-thing can encase a grappled, incapacitated creature of up to Medium size in a dense cocoon (AC 10, 30 hp, immune to all but slashing damage) composed of fibrous material spun out of its mouth. The process takes 1 minute for creatures smaller than Small, 2 minutes for Small creatures, and 3 minutes for Medium creatures.

Immune to Transformation. A mantis-thing is immune to effects that would alter its form.

Incubation. Once an egg is implanted, it releases enzymes that paralyze the victim for as long as the egg remains in the body. The egg hatches 1d4 days later. When it does, the young mantis-thing consumes the host's internal organs, killing the creature. Removing an egg takes 10 minutes and a successful DC 15 Wisdom (Medicine) check; a creature without proficiency in Medicine has disadvantage on the check. Each attempt also does 2d6 slashing damage to the host, whether the check succeeds or fails. Magic that cures disease, such as *lesser restoration* or a *potion of vitality*, also destroys the egg without harming the host, but immunity to paralysis or disease offers no protection.

Pack Attack. The mantis-thing has advantage on its attack roll if the target is within 5 feet of one or more allies of the mantis-thing that are able to attack.

ACTIONS
Multiattack. The mantis-thing makes two claw attacks.
Lunge (recharge 5-6). *Melee Weapon Attack:* +8 to hit (reach 20 ft.; one creature). Hit: 4d8 + 5 slashing damage, and the target must make a successful DC 16 Constitution saving throw or be stunned until the end of its next turn.
Claw. *Melee Weapon Attack:* +8 to hit (reach 5 ft.; one creature). Hit: 2d8 + 5 slashing damage. If both claw attacks hit the same target on the mantis-thing's turn, the target is grappled (escape DC 15) and the mantis-thing can make a proboscis attack against it as a bonus action.
Implant Egg. *Melee Weapon Attack:* +8 to hit (reach 5 ft.; one grappled creature). Hit: a mantis-thing egg is implanted in the creature, which is paralyzed and becomes subject to Incubation (see above).
Proboscis. *Melee Weapon Attack:* +5 to hit (one grappled creature). Hit: 1d4 + 2 piercing damage, and the creature must make a successful DC 14 Constitution saving throw or be paralyzed until the end of its next turn.

ECOLOGY
Environment any land (Between)
Organization solitary, pair, or nest (3–8)

Mantis-things are exaggerated versions of insects, distorted by the horror of parasitic infestation and the misery of hopelessness. They are semi-intelligent, and communicate via a language composed of clicks from their mouthparts, and the position and trembling of their patterned forelimbs.

Copyright Notice
Author Alistair Rigg, based on material by Richard Pett.

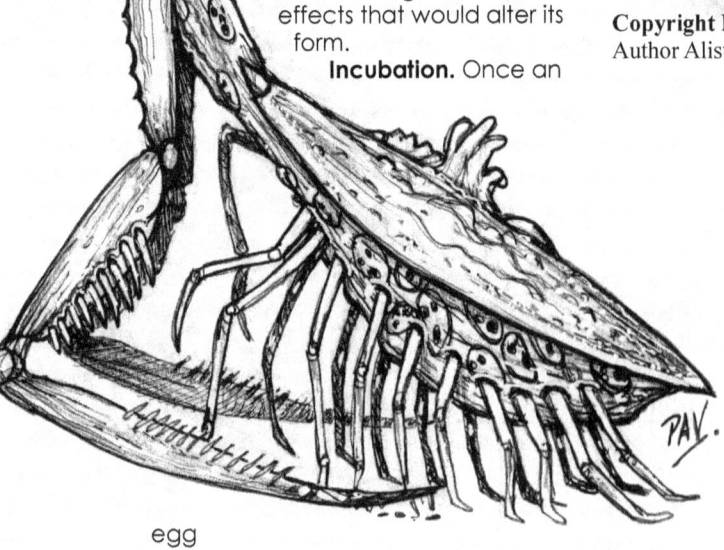

egg

Mockingbeast

This creature's former body is now a collapsed tangle of rubbery limbs and gnashing teeth that thrashes and gurgles as it drags itself about with claws and tentacles that have sprouted from random locations.

Mockingbeast
Large aberration (larval Between), chaotic neutral

Armor Class 13
Hit Points 133 (14d10 + 56)
Speed 20 ft., climb 10 ft.

STR	DEX	CON	INT	WIS	CHA
19 (+4)	16 (+3)	18 (+4)	8 (-1)	5 (-3)	16 (+3)

Saving Throws Dex +6, Con +7, Int +2, Cha +6
Damage Resistances bludgeoning, piercing, and slashing from nonmagical weapons
Senses darkvision 30 ft., passive Perception 7
Languages Common
Challenge 8 (3,900 XP)

Between Flux. A mockingbeast's body constantly shifts and changes in response to the Between plague that infuses it, reshaping and rebuilding it in hideous ways. At the start of each of the mockingbeast's turns, roll 1d10 and check the following table to see what effect the between flux has. All of the listed mutations last 1 minute except for results 9 and 10, which are instantaneous.

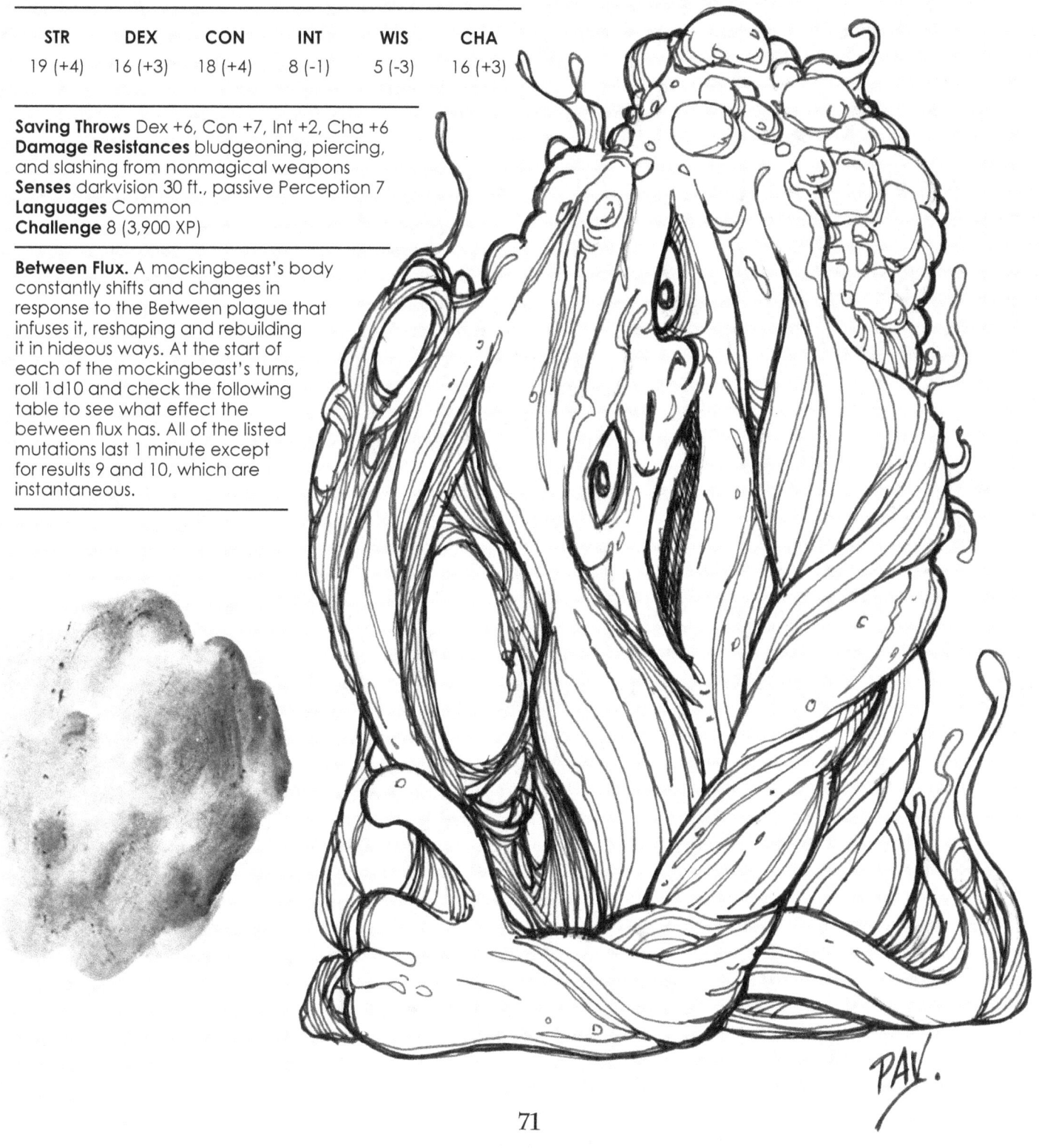

1d10	Result
1	The mockingbeast gains a +2 bonus on attack rolls and damage rolls (max +6).
2	The mockingbeast gains resistance to each damage type that strikes it, after taking the initial damage.
3	Creatures that do slashing or piercing damage to the mockingbeast from a distance of 5 feet or less take 1d6 acid damage (max 3d6) from digestive fluid spraying out of the wound.
4	The mockingbeast's AC increases by 2 (max 19).
5	The mockingbeast's Multiattack ability allows it to make one additional grab attack (max 6/turn).
6	The mockingbeast grows appendages that increase its standard and climb speeds by 10 feet each (max 50 ft., climb 40 ft.).
7	The mockingbeast gains 25 temporary hit points.
8	The mockingbeast gains blindsight 30 feet or the range of its blindsight increases by 30 feet (max 90 feet).
9	The mockingbeast emits a cloud of poisonous vapor. Creatures within 5 feet of the mockingbeast must make a successful DC 14 Constitution saving throw or be poisoned until the end of their next turn.
10	The mockingbeast unleashes a burst of psychic energy. Creatures within 30 feet of the mockingbeast must make a successful DC 14 Wisdom saving throw or be frightened of the mockingbeast until the end of their next turn.

Insanity. A mockingbeast's mind is a raw chaos of madness. It uses its Charisma modifier for Wisdom saving throws. Any attempt to contact a mockingbeast telepathically (including spells such as *detect thoughts* and *dominate monster*) produces a backlash that does 2d8 Psychic damage to the creature attempting the contact, or half damage with a successful DC 14 Wisdom saving throw.

Mocking Plague. Symptoms appear 1d6 hours after a creature is infected. At that time, the creature gains 1 level of exhaustion and its Charisma score is reduced by 2. The infected creature must make a DC 15 Constitution saving throw after every long rest. If the saving throw fails, the creature gains another level of exhaustion and its Charisma is reduced by 2. The disease can be cured by magic or when the infected creature succeeds on two consecutive Constitution saving throws. A victim that gains a 6th level of exhaustion or has its Charisma reduced to 0 by mocking plague must make a DC 10 Constitution saving throw. If it succeeds, the creature dies normally; if it fails, the creature instead transforms into a mockingbeast. Reduction in Charisma is not permanent and will be healed by completing a long rest

Resistant to Transformation. Effects that alter the mockingbeast's form end at the start of the mockingbeast's next turn, when it automatically returns to its normal form (no action required).

ACTIONS

Multiattack. The mockingbeast makes three grab attacks with its tentacles.

Grab. *Melee Weapon Attack:* +7 to hit (reach 15 ft.; one creature). Hit: 2d8 + 4 bludgeoning damage, and a Medium or smaller creature must make a successful DC 14 Dexterity saving throw or be grappled (escape DC 14) and pulled to within 5 feet of the mockingbeast. The mockingbeast makes an immediate Bite attack against a creature that was just grappled as part of the same action.

Bite. *Melee Weapon Attack:* +7 to hit (reach 5 ft.; one grappled creature). Hit: 2d4 + 4 piercing damage, and a creature must make a successful DC 15 Constitution saving throw or be infected with Mocking Plague (see above).

LEGENDARY ACTIONS

The mockingbeast can take up to three legendary actions per round. Legendary actions are taken at the end of another creature's turn, and only one can be taken after each turn.

Bite. The mockingbeast bites a grappled target.

Grab. The mockingbeast makes one grab attack.

Flux (uses 2 actions). The mockingbeast forces a mutation to occur. Roll on the Between Flux table.

ECOLOGY

Environment any (Between)
Organization solitary or pair

The mocking plague is a supernatural Between disease spread by Between vampires and some other Between creatures. Most creatures that contract this horrific infection die from the mutations it causes, but some are instead transformed into aberrations known as mockingbeasts. These monsters embody the biological chaos that the mocking plague causes, changing their forms to survive attacks they are subject to or to better spread the disease that created them.

Nightmare Choir (Between Peacock)

A fleshy sack, discolored with veins, sits amid and beneath a trio of gangling legs that bend in all the wrong places. A head is thrust back that looks part bird, part cockroach; its beak more akin to a stinger. Its peacocklike plume is littered with wretched-looking scraps of flesh topped by a grisly collection of severed harpy heads, the eyes of which watch you with tortured expressions.

Nightmare Choir
Large aberration (adult Between), unaligned

Armor Class 15
Hit Points 152 (16d10 + 64)
Speed 15 ft., fly 30 ft.

STR	DEX	CON	INT	WIS	CHA
15 (+2)	21 (+5)	18 (+4)	2 (-4)	12 (+1)	19 (+4)

Saving Throws Con +9, Int +1, Wis +6
Skills Perception +6
Damage Resistances cold, force, poison damage; bludgeoning, piercing, and slashing from nonmagical weapons
Condition Immunities disease; charmed, frightened
Senses darkvision 120 ft., passive Perception 16
Languages Deep Speech
Challenge 13 (10,000 XP)

Death Throes. When it drops to 0 hit points, a nightmare choir explodes in a mass of thorny, fleshy limbs riddled with teeth and hundreds of tiny filaments that hook into clothing, skin, and flesh. Creatures within 20 feet of the nightmare choir take 6d6 piercing damage and are restrained; a successful DC 15 Dexterity saving throw halves the damage and prevents being restrained. A restrained creature frees itself by using an action to make a successful DC 16 Strength (Athletics) check. The area becomes difficult terrain for 10 minutes, and a creature that ends its turn in the difficult terrain takes 1d6 slashing damage.

Magic Resistance (1/day). When it fails a saving throw, the nightmare choir can choose to succeed instead.

Swallow. A creature that ends its turn grappled by the nightmare choir is swallowed whole. A swallowed creature is blinded and restrained. It takes 3d8 necrotic damage automatically at the start of each of the nightmare choir's turns. Only one Medium creature or two Small creatures can be inside the nightmare choir at one time. A swallowed creature is unaffected by anything happening outside the nightmare choir or by attacks from outside it. A swallowed creature can get out of the choir by using 5 feet of movement, but only after the monster is dead. When the nightmare choir inverts or reverts to normal, swallowed creatures are ejected prone into adjacent, empty spaces.

ACTIONS
Multiattack. The nightmare choir makes one tongue attack and three claw attacks.
Claw. *Melee Weapon Attack:* +10 to hit (reach 10 ft.; one creature). *Hit:* 2d8 + 5 slashing damage.
Tongue. *Melee Weapon Attack:* +10 to hit (reach 15 ft.; one creature). *Hit:* the target is grappled (escape DC 15) and

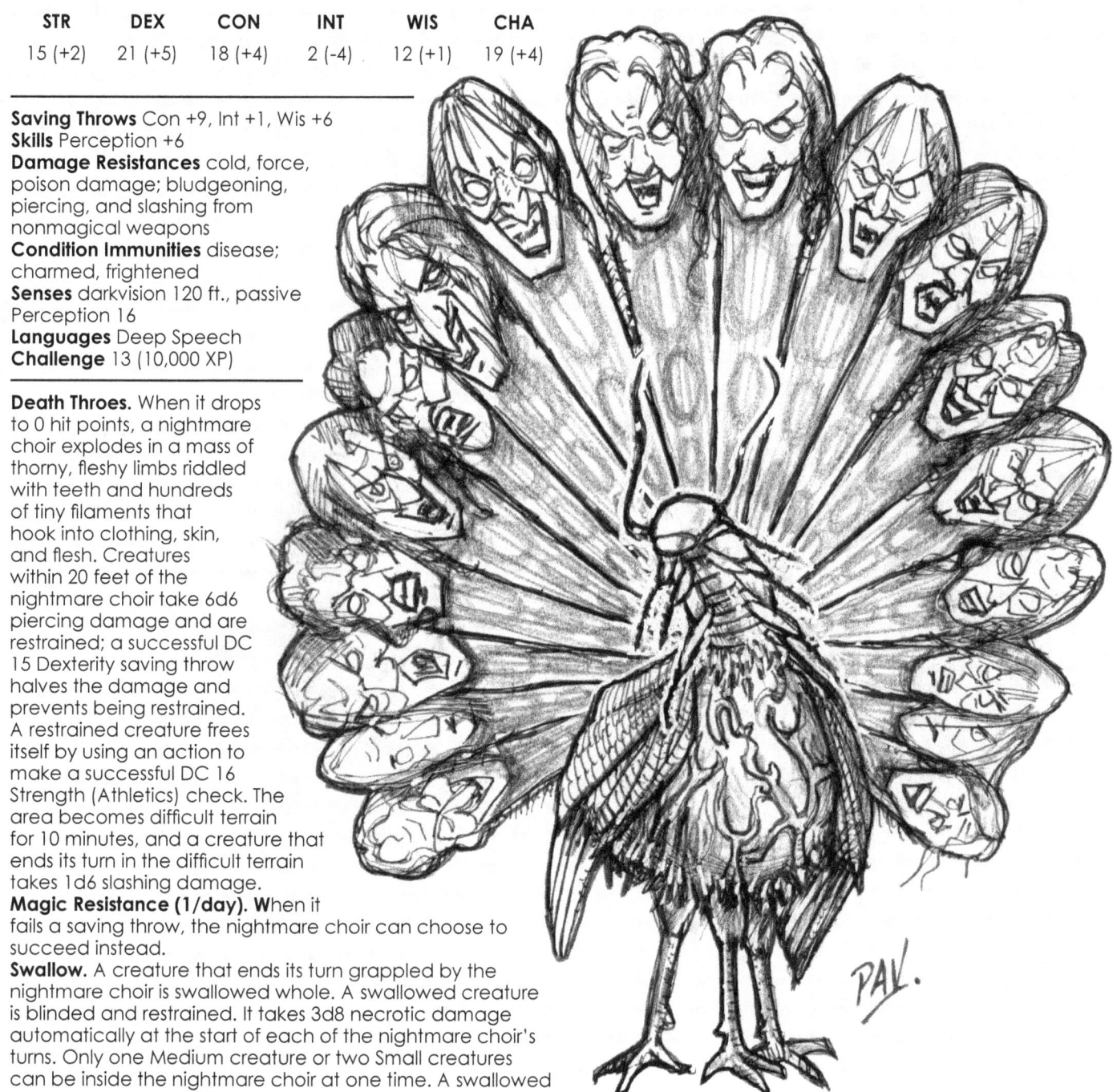

PAV.

pulled to within 5 feet of the nightmare choir, which then makes a bite attack against it as part of the same action.

Bite. *Melee Weapon Attack:* +10 to hit (reach 5 ft.; one grappled creature). *Hit:* 4d6 + 5 piercing damage plus 2d10 necrotic damage.

Captivating Hymn (1/day). The nightmare choir raises its harpy plumes, which begin singing. They continue singing as a bonus action for 1 minute. Creatures within 100 feet of the nightmare choir and able to hear it must make a successful DC 17 Wisdom saving throw or be charmed by the nightmare choir for as long as the singing continues. A charmed creature must move toward the nightmare choir along the most direct path, even if that takes them through dangerous terrain. A charmed creature that's within 5 feet of the nightmare choir is stunned. A charmed creature repeats the saving throw when it takes damage, ending the effect on itself with a success. Success on the saving throw leaves a creature immune to Captivating Hymn for 24 hours.

Horrific Inversion (recharge 6). The nightmare choir inverts itself, becoming a huge maw filled with hundreds of quivering, needlelike teeth. The choir makes a bite attack against every creature within 5 feet of it, regardless of grappling. Creatures within 30 feet that witness this transformation must make a successful DC 17 Wisdom saving throw or be afflicted with madness. If the result of the saving throw is 12-16, the creature suffers a short-term madness; 7-11 results in long-term madness; 6 or less results in indefinite madness. An inverted nightmare choir cannot fly or use Captivating Hymn. It can revert to its normal form as a bonus action. When it inverts or reverts to normal, swallowed creatures are ejected prone into adjacent, empty spaces.

ECOLOGY

Environment any land (Between)
Organization solitary

A nightmare choir is an animalistic predator that uses the mesmerizing songs of harpies to lure prey to its side. When prey is near — and prey is anything that the nightmare choir can drain blood from — the monster suddenly inverts its body to make a surprising attack. In its usual form, it appears as a veiny sack of rubbery, feather-flecked skin, with bony, feathered wings, a swan's neck tipped with a beaklike stinger, three skinny, multi-jointed legs tipped with talons, and long, peacocklike plumes tipped with the severed heads of harpies. When the monster inverts, it suddenly bloats into a balloon of flesh that rips apart to allow a great maw of hooked teeth to burst forward, and a long, sticky tongue to shoot out to draw its prey in. The collapsed flesh sack envelops its stinger, wings, and plume, which become unusable in this alternate form.

Arcane Feathers. The thirteen eye-feathers of the nightmare choir's plume are worth 100 gp each. If an eye-feather is used as an additional material component for a divination spell, the spell either takes effect as if cast with a spell slot 2 levels higher, or the saving throw against it is made with disadvantage (caster's choice).

Copyright Notice
Author Alistair Rigg, based on material by Richard Pett.

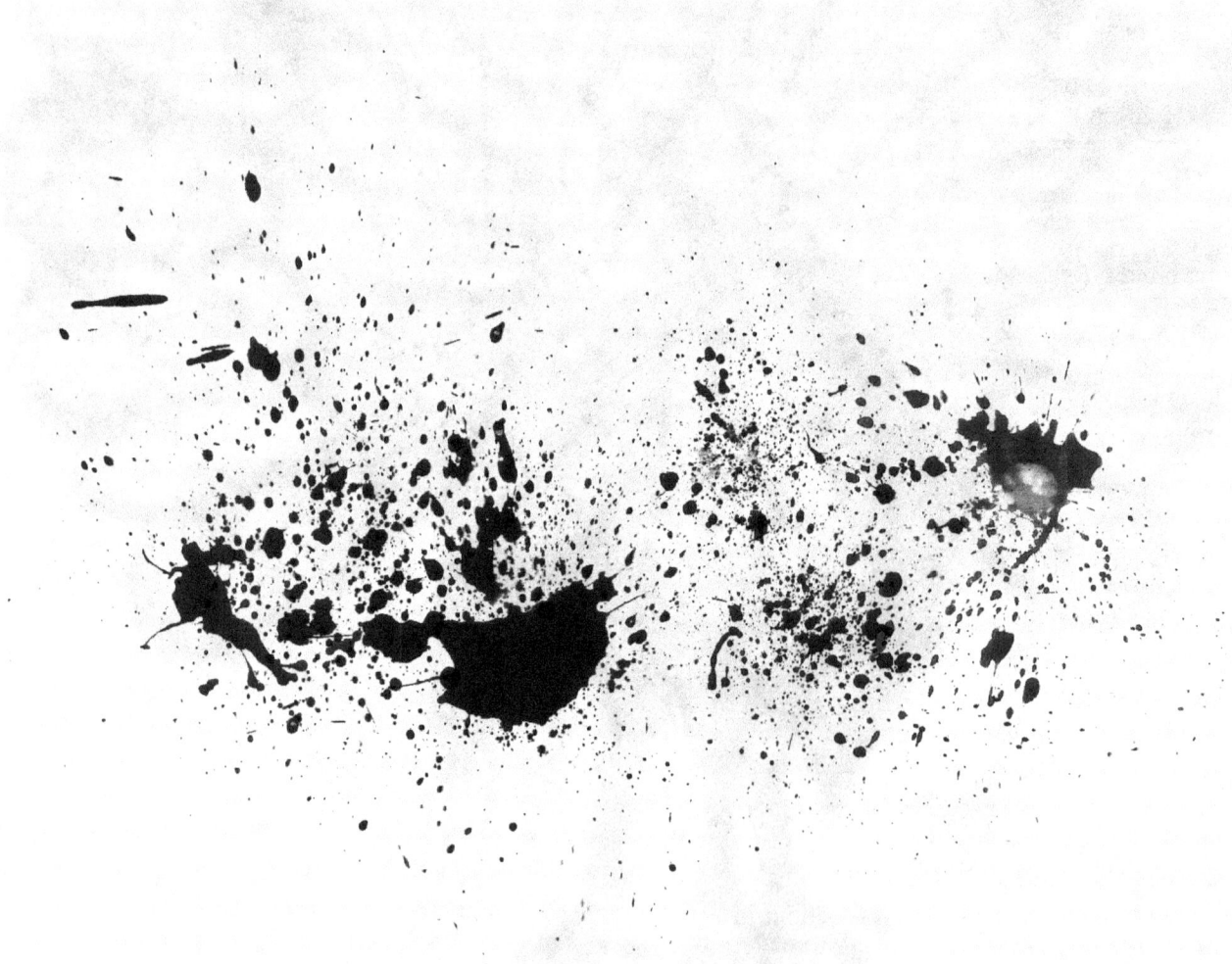

Nimb

A shimmering in the air, like a heat haze, describes the silhouette of a humanoid form.

Nimb

Medium aberration (larval Between), neutral

Armor Class 14
Hit Points 55 (10d8 + 10)
Speed 0 ft., fly 30 ft.

STR	DEX	CON	INT	WIS	CHA
5 (-3)	15 (+2)	12 (+1)	13 (+1)	12 (+1)	16 (+3)

Damage Resistances bludgeoning, piercing, and slashing from nonmagical weapons
Damage Immunities poison
Condition Immunities disease; paralyzed, poisoned, prone, stunned, unconscious
Senses darkvision 30 ft., passive Perception 11
Languages understands Common and Deep Speech but can't speak; telepathy 100 ft.
Challenge 2 (450 XP)

Distorted. A nimb's internal anatomy varies from individual to individual and seldom makes any biological sense. Critical hits against the creature do a flat +1 damage but don't roll damage dice twice.

Incorporeal. A nimb can move through gaps as small as 1 square inch without penalty. It can also move through solid objects and other creatures as if they were difficult terrain. The nimb takes 1d10 force damage if it is still inside something solid at the end of its turn.

ACTIONS

Multiattack.
Ectoplasmic Touch.
Melee Weapon Attack: +5 to hit (reach 5 ft.; one creature). *Hit:* 1d6 + 2 necrotic damage, and the target's hit point total is reduced by 5. In addition, the nimb gains temporary hit points equal to the necrotic damage.
Bond. The nimb bonds itself with a willing or incapacitated humanoid whose square it co-occupies. The nimb

takes control of the body if it wins a Charisma contest against the host. The host's consciousness remains and can communicate telepathically with the nimb, but the nimb controls the body, which gains the nimbated template (see Appendix B). The nimb can sever the bond on its turn (no action required), whereupon it appears in the closest empty square. If a nimb bonds with a host that has reduced hit points, the nimb can immediately restore the host's normal hit points. If the host dies, the bonded nimb is ejected into any empty space within 5 feet. If the nimb has temporary hit points when this happens, it loses those temporary hit points and generates a second nimb in an adjacent space with hit points equal to the temporary hit points.

ECOLOGY
Environment any (Between)
Organization solitary

The nimbi are incorporeal creatures from Between that appear as shimmering silhouettes of humanoid forms. They are strongly drawn to other intelligent beings, and step through mirrors and other reflective portals between the dimensions to follow those they feel connected to. Sometimes, a nimb telepathically communicates with its target, attempting to negotiate a bonding. Often, however, their alien mindsets and troubling requirements prove an insurmountable barrier to such discussions, and they resort to force, hoping that an agreement can be made after the bond has formed.

Spiboleth

A hideous, three-eyed fish creature with a lobsterlike tail, eight long spider legs extending from its flanks ending in sharp claws, and a strange globular gland just beneath its head drips a thick slime.

Spiboleth

Large aberration (larval Between, aquatic), lawful evil

Armor Class 15 (natural armor)
Hit Points 127 (15d10 + 45)
Speed 40 ft., climb 40 ft., swim 60 ft.

STR	DEX	CON	INT	WIS	CHA
19 (+4)	11 (+0)	17 (+3)	17 (+3)	14 (+2)	8 (-1)

Saving Throws Con +6, Int +6, Wis +5
Skills Perception +5
Senses tremorsense 60 ft., passive Perception 15
Languages Common, Deep Speech
Challenge 6 (2,300 XP)

All-Around Vision. A spiboleth's multiple eyes allow it to scan quickly in all directions. Attackers never gain advantage or bonus damage against it from the presence of nearby allies.
Innate Spellcasting. The spiboleth can use the following spell-like abilities, using Intelligence as its casting ability (DC 14, attack +6). The spiboleth doesn't need material components to use these abilities.

At will: *color spray, dancing lights, minor illusion, silent image*
  3/day: *charm person, hypnotic pattern, phantasmal force*
  1/day: *dominate monster*

Paralytic Poison. The spiboleth's mucus contains a paralytic poison. A creature that comes into contact with the mucus must make a DC 14 Constitution saving throw. If the save succeeds, the creature is poisoned until the end of its next turn; if it fails, the creature is paralyzed for as long as it remains in contact with spiboleth webbing, or for 1 minute. A paralyzed creature that's not in contact with webbing repeats the saving throw at the end of its turn, ending the effect on a success.

ACTIONS

Multiattack. The spiboleth attacks twice with its claws and once with its tail.
Claw. *Melee Weapon Attack:* +7 to hit (reach 5 ft.; one creature). *Hit:* 1d10 + 4 piercing damage, and the creature is exposed to the spiboleth's paralytic poison (see above).
Tail Slap. *Melee Weapon Attack:* +7 to hit (reach 5 ft.; one creature). *Hit:* 4d8 + 4 bludgeoning damage, and the target is knocked prone.
Mucus Web (recharge 4-6). The spiboleth launches globs of mucus at a target within 50 feet. The target must make a successful DC 14 Dexterity saving throw or be restrained and be exposed to the spiboleth's paralytic poison (see above). A restrained creature can break free by using an action to make a successful DC 13 Strength or Dexterity check. This attack is equally effective above

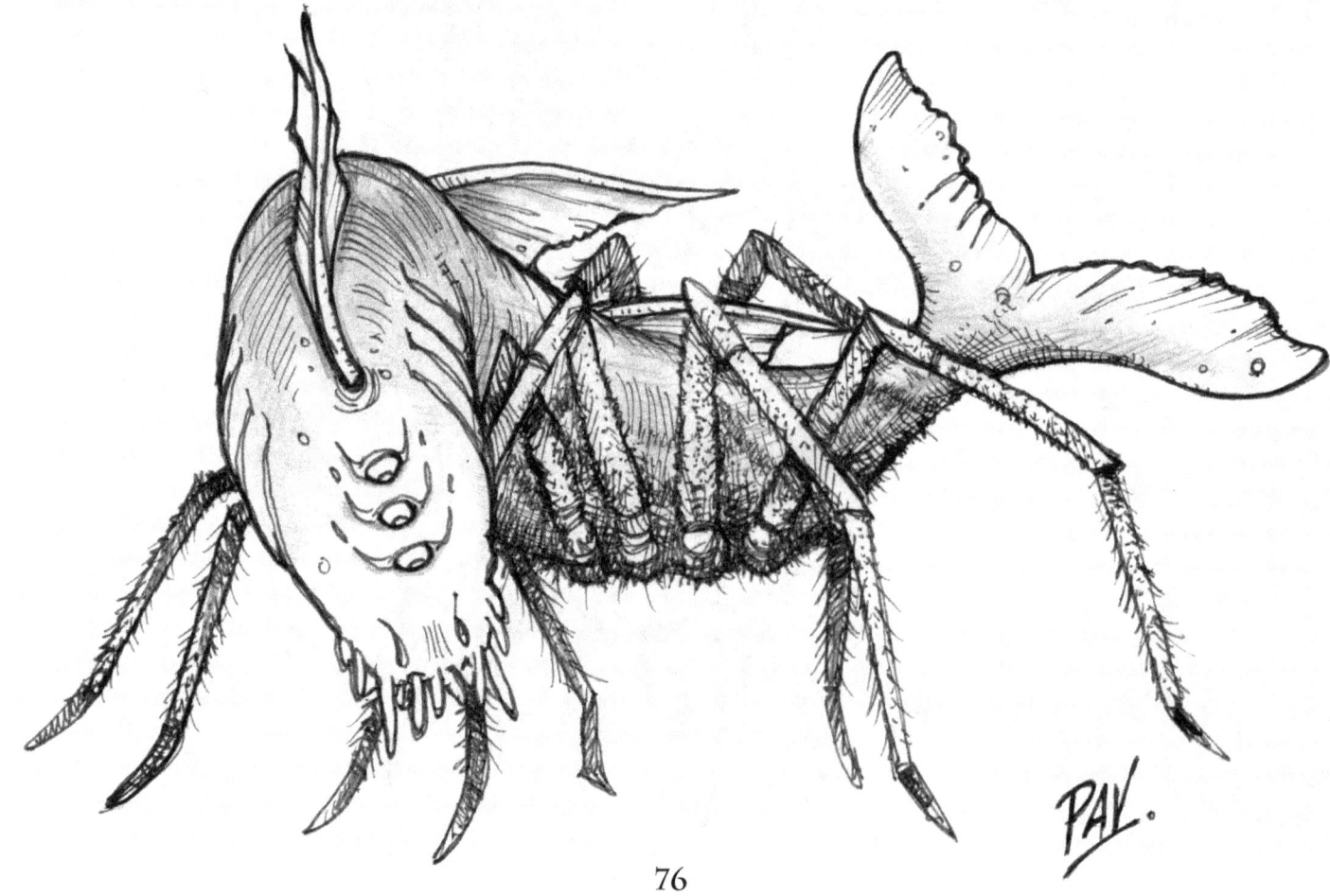

or under water.

ECOLOGY
Environment *coast, sea (Between)*
Organization *solitary, pair, or colony (3–8)*

It's unknown whether the physicians stole their ideas from the aboleths of the Unsea or the aboleths of the Unsea stole their concept from the physicians of Castorhage. What is known is that the spiboleths are essentially a golem-stitched mixture of aboleth and giant spider and that the physicians didn't create them. The spiboleths dwell primarily in the shallows of the Unsea where they work with the vile aboleths of that realm as almost-equal partners. They possess the same intellect and massive egos as the aboleths, but are slightly inferior in magical aptitude and physical prowess, a fact not lost on the aboleths who claim to be their original creators. The aboleths do not outright enslave the spiboleths, however, because the spiboleths are still relatively powerful and far too egotistical to accept such an arrangement without an outright rebellion. The spiboleths are much too useful to the aboleths as spies and agents to be sent to the mundane world. In the eyes of the aboleths, the spiboleths have value and they, therefore, bite back their prejudice and paternalism toward them, limiting it to occasional small hints of superiority and a secret knowledge among their own as to the truth of the matter. The spiboleths are well aware of the aboleths' thoughts on the matter, but they have not yet bred in numbers sufficient to overthrow the more-powerful aboleths. For now, it behooves both sides to cooperate and at least appear gracious toward one another even if always looking for some sign of weakness to exploit. This constant tension between aboleth and spiboleth is perhaps the greatest asset that the peoples of the mundane world have against their machinations.

Arachnoleths. Spiboleths superficially resemble a smaller version of the aboleths, but with chitin-covered, spiderlike legs instead of tentacles. In addition, though they have the same vertical arrangement of eyes, those of the spiboleth are actually multifaceted and provide the spiboleth with a greater field of vision. Though powerful in their own right, the spiboleths are still less powerful than their aboleth cousins, and they do not possess the same form-altering slime and mucus cloud as the aboleths. Instead, the spiboleths have the ability to live indefinitely out of the water, though they are more comfortable in damp places where they can keep their bodies moist, and they possess the ability to secrete a thick mucus from which they can construct great webs made from thick strands of the nearly translucent substance. The webs are somewhat sticky, but the mucus also has a paralytic poison that makes them much more dangerous.

Lurkers in Water. Though spiboleths hail from Between, many of them find their way into the mundane world and set up hidden lairs in the waters and along the coasts. There is no telling how many of the great docks or blind riverside alleys that seem empty at a glance actually hold the web-strung lairs of these spiderlike aberrations hidden behind the camouflage of mirage arcana or illusory walls as they watch their oblivious prey wandering by mere yards away and contemplate their murky thoughts of conquest.

Mucus Weavers. As befits their arachnid heredity, spiboleths have glands beneath their heads that secrete a thick mucus. The spiboleth forms this mucus into tough but flexible strands that it weaves into a web. This web can extend both above and below water, and with multiple spiboleths contributing to the construction, these webs can be made immense. Large air bubbles can be attached to the web below water, allowing air-breathing creatures to survive for up to 2 hours while caught in the web. Spiboleths can also create sheets of mucus webbing up to three times their own size. They usually position these to snare unwary creatures. Normally, approaching creatures could see one of these webs easily, but spiboleths usually camouflage them with illusions, hoping victims stumble into them and are quickly paralyzed. Each 5-foot section of mucus web has AC 8, 15 hit points, immunity to necrotic, poison, psychic, and radiant damage, and resistance to all other damage types except slashing. A spiboleth moves across mucus webbing without hindrance, and its tremorsense allows it to pinpoint the location of any creature touching the web.

Spite-Waif

The figure is childlike, but any sense of innocence is immediately overshadowed by the aura of malevolence that exudes almost palpably from it. Its flesh is gray and pasty, seemingly too loose for its body. Its head is hairless with a wide mouth and distended jaw full of needle-sharp teeth, and, though humanoid in shape, when it moves it scuttles about on all fours like some kind of insect with too many joints.

Spite-Waif

Small aberration (larval Between), neutral evil

Armor Class 13
Hit Points 36 (8d6 + 8)
Speed 20 ft.

STR	DEX	CON	INT	WIS	CHA
9 (-1)	16 (+3)	12 (+1)	10 (+0)	11 (+0)	13 (+1)

Skills Deception +5, Insight +2
Condition Immunities charmed
Senses darkvision 60 ft., passive Perception 10
Languages Common
Challenge 1 (200 XP)

Mirror Portal (1/day). A spite-waif can turn a normal mirror into a portal between the Material Plane and Between. The spite-waif must touch the mirror to be transformed. The portal forms behind the mirror, which must be pushed aside to get at the portal. The portal can be used by any creature that fits through it; the portal is the same size as the mirror. It remains open indefinitely or until the spite-waif creates a different mirror portal or the mirror is broken.

Create Mirror-Portal (1/day). A spite-waif can turn a normal mirror into a portal between the Material Plane and Between. To use this ability a mirror must be obtained from the Material Plane and taken to Between where the spite-waif must conduct a 1-hour ritual to attune the mirror and turn it into a device for scrying. It is then able to scry through any Material Plane mirror for a suitable location to use as a portal. Once a location has been determined, the *mirror-portal* is created and fixed between the two mirrors, and the spite-waif's mirror cannot be attuned to any other mirror. Once the mirrors have been attuned, the portal can be opened from either end by simply sliding the mirror aside as a part of movement and revealing the extradimensional portal behind it. Anyone can pass through the *mirror-portal* as long as they can fit through the dimensions of the mirror's pane. Once created, a *mirror-portal* remains open indefinitely until closed. If closed, it can no longer be opened except by the spite-waif that created it. If either mirror is destroyed, the *mirror-portal* is closed permanently.

Innate Spellcasting. The spite-waif can use the following spell-like abilities, using Charisma as its casting ability (DC 11). The spite-waif doesn't need material components to use these abilities.

At will: *alter self*
1/day: *sleep*

Perfect Copy. When a spite-waif uses *alter self*, it can assume the appearance of a specific individual. Unlike a doppelganger, when a spite-waif is killed it remains in its assumed form unless a *dispel magic* is cast on the corpse.

ACTIONS

Multiattack. The spite-waif bites once and claws once.
Bite. *Melee Weapon Attack:* +5 to hit (reach 5 ft.; one creature). *Hit:* 1d6 + 3 piercing damage.
Claw. *Melee Weapon Attack:* +5 to hit (reach 5 ft.; one creature). *Hit:* 2d4 + 3 slashing damage.

ECOLOGY

Environment any land (Between)
Organization solitary or gang (3–6)

These creatures are insidious changelings and infiltrators from Between. Spite-waifs are an immature stage in the development of a doppelganger that are native to that bizarre realm. While they have the doppelganger's ability to change shape, they lack its physical power and ability to read minds. As a result, they are used primarily as changelings to replace children of the Material Plane, and then grow up within that child's household and live its life. The reasons for these switches are manifold, but they are universally of malign intent. This is especially evident in the fact that unlike hags, who swap changelings out for real children and then raise the true child as its own, the spite-waif usually devours the child at the time of the switch.

Formless Children. Superficially, spite-waifs physically resemble a small humanoid child but with a doppelganger's characteristic gray and formless skin and features. Its jaw is able to distend to allow it to swallow creatures up to Medium size, and a mouthful of needle-sharp teeth help it grip its prey. Internally, the spite-waif's abdomen is an extra-dimensional space that can hold any amount of prey. Horrifically, the parents of switched children are frequently concerned about a possible stomach ailment afflicting their "child" when they change its bedclothes, not aware of the true source of its exceptionally soiled and sometimes bloody diapers.

Stolen Lives. A spite-waif can maintain its charade for years, altering its regularly as it "grows," and usually does so for the entire childhood and adolescence of the replaced child. In many ways, they become that child, assuming all of its roles and eventual responsibilities, though it always maintains some form of contact with its own kind — even if only a quick meeting once every few years — to stay current on the planned reasons for the switch. The reasons and plans for a changeling switch are always extremely far-reaching, taking decades to develop, and frequently involve replacing a child from a prominent family in order to attain a powerful position in government later in adulthood. While a spite-waif remains in Between, it doesn't mature physically or in Between Age. A spite-waif that dwells on the Material Plane grows at a rate comparable to the species it mimics. When a Material Plane-dwelling spite-waif reaches physical maturity (usually within 10–12 years), it attains Medium size and completes its transformation into a full non-Between doppelganger, becoming in all ways at this point a normal doppelganger, though likely maintaining any prior contacts with its Between compatriots.

Wallow-Whale

Something stirs in the sludge beneath, swimming through the arsenic poison that passes for water. It is vast, a seething globe of flesh, a mountain of rotting skin that hangs like a bridal train behind its back. It has at least a dozen eyes oddly spaced on its foul body, and a vast maw capable of swallowing a ship.

Wallow-Whale

Gargantuan aberration, neutral

Armor Class 17 (natural armor)
Hit Points 201 (13d20 + 65)
Speed swim 40 ft.

STR	DEX	CON	INT	WIS	CHA
22 (+6)	4 (−3)	21 (+5)	4 (−3)	10 (+0)	5 (−3)

Skills Perception +4
Damage Resistances bludgeoning, piercing, and slashing from nonmagical weapons
Damage Immunities thunder
Condition Immunities prone
Senses darkvision 60 ft., passive Perception 14
Languages none
Challenge 12 (8,400 XP)

Swallow. A swallowed creature is blinded and restrained. It takes 1d10 + 6 bludgeoning damage plus 1d8 acid damage automatically at the start of each of the wallow-whale's turns. Any number of creatures can be inside the wallow-whale at one time. A swallowed creature is unaffected by anything happening outside the wallow-whale or by attacks from outside it. A swallowed creature can get out of the wallow-whale by using 5 feet of movement, but only after the wallow-whale is dead. When a creature gets out of the wallow-whale, it must make a successful DC 17 Constitution saving throw or contract filth fever.

Filth Fever. A creature with filth fever becomes sick 1d4 days after being infected. At that time, the creature gains 1 level of exhaustion. It also regains only half the usual number of hit points from spending Hit Dice and no hit points from resting. Once symptoms appear, the infected creature must make a DC 11 Constitution saving throw after every long rest. If it fails, the creature gains 1 level of exhaustion; if it succeeds, the creature loses 1 level of exhaustion. The disease is cured when the creature has no exhaustion.

ACTIONS

Multiattack. The wallow-whale bites once and makes one tail slap attack.
Bite. *Melee Weapon Attack:* +10 to hit (reach 5 ft.; one creature). *Hit:* 4d10 + 6 piercing damage plus 3d6 acid damage, and the creature must make a successful DC 17 Strength saving throw or be swallowed (see above).
Tail Slap. *Melee Weapon Attack:* +10 to hit (reach 15 ft.; one creature). *Hit:* 4d8 + 6 bludgeoning damage and the target is knocked prone.
Melee Atttack—Ram (recharge 6). automatic hit (one ship). *Hit:* the vessel makes a hull saving throw using the most appropriate DC from the table below, based on the ship's type. The vessel sinks when it has failed the indicated number of saving throws. The proficiency bonus of the ship's captain can be added to the saving throw.

Ship Type	Hull DC	Sinks after
Rowboat	20	1 failed save
Barge	19	1 failed save
Oared Galley, small	18	2 failed saves
Oared Galley, large	16	2 failed saves
Sailing Merchant, small	17	2 failed saves
Sailing Merchant, large	15	3 failed saves
Sailing Warship	13	3 failed saves

ECOLOGY
Environment sea (Between)
Organization solitary or mated pair

Originally found only in the Unsea of Between before some of these great cetaceans somehow escaped and began reproducing in the mundane world's oceans, wallow-whales are now the terror of the Fetid Sea and one of the primary threats for which the Castorhage Navy diligently patrols those waters. Wallow-whales are offal, carrion, husks, leavings, and scum given life. Stirges are frequently seen circling them when they surface to launch a spume of oily brine, purulence, and clotted fluids from their blowholes, and oozes capable of surviving in the acidic environment can sometimes be found infesting their cathedral-like stomachs. Wallow-whales aren't afraid to venture close to the city to feed upon the excrement, rot, and flotsam that seethes like a gyre around its foundations. Yet despite their foul body habitus, the ambergris of a wallow-whale is a thing both rare and highly valuable, selling for as much as 100 gp/pound. Daring or foolhardy whalers armed with cold-iron harpoons hunt these beasts upon the oceans, and in some cases upon the Unsea, with typical Gargantuan specimens typically yielding 1d6 x 10 pounds of the substance, and a Colossal beast yielding 3d6 x 10 pounds.

Appendix B: Templates

Alchymic-Undying Creature

More commonly referred to as the "reborn," alchymic-undying creatures are living creatures infused with the gifts of undeath through exposure to the mysterious *elixir of life*.

Any living creature can be transformed into an alchymic-undying creature when exposed to *elixir of life* (see **The Blight: Richard Pett's Crooked City** by **Frog God Games**). An alchymic-undying creature uses the base creature's stat block, with the following differences:

• Challenge increases by 1.

• Constitution declines by 2; adjust hit points accordingly.

• Always has proficiency on Strength and Dexterity saving throws, and on saves against disease (including ongoing effects of diseaases), paralysis, and poison.

• Is immune to exhaustion and unconsciousness

• Never ages or sleeps, and needs only 1/10 as much food, drink, and air as a normal creature of its kind.

• **Negative Energy Affinity: A**n alchymic-undying creature never has its maximum hit points reduced by attacks from undead creatures.

• **Regeneration:** An alchymic-undying creature heals 1 hit point per 2 HD at the start of its turn, unless it took acid or fire damage since its last turn.

Copyright Notice
Author Alistair Rigg, based on material by Richard Pett.

Alchymic-Unliving Creature

The alchymic-unliving are creatures tainted by the curse of undeath through exposure to *elixir of life*. Those who partake in the forbidden fruits of such alchymic experimentation face a dismal future. It is true that death, or at least mortal death by aging, is no longer a concern, but the life left is bleak and bereft of any of the joys of the living.

Any living creature can be transformed into an alchymic-unliving creature that is exposed to *elixir of life* (see **The Blight: Richard Pett's Crooked City** by **Frog God Games**). An alchymic-unliving creature uses the base creature's stat block, with the following differences:

- Challenge increases by 1.

- Strength increases by 2, Intelligence declines by 2.

- Type becomes undead.

- AC increases by 2.

- Uses Charisma rather than Constitution to determine bonus hit points per hit die; recalculate hit points accordingly.

- Immune to disease, exhaustion, paralysis, poison, stun, and unconsciousness.

- Immune to effects that reduce ability scores or maximum hit points.

- Gains darkvision 60 feet.

- **Legendary Fortitude (3/day):** When the creature makes an unsuccessful Constitution saving throw, it can choose to succeed instead.

- **Curse of Undeath:** The creature must make a successful DC 15 Wisdom saving throw every 30 days or its Intelligence is permanently reduced by 1. If its Intelligence declines to 3, it transforms into a zombie.

- **Regeneration:** An alchymic-unliving creature heals 1 hit point per 2 HD at the start of its turn, unless it took radiant damage since its last turn.

Between Creature

A Between creature is infused with the weirdness of Between and is shaped and changed by its environment and experiences. Some Between creatures are bizarre versions of existing creatures (such as gargoyles and wyverns), while others are new creatures that don't have a non-Between equivalent (such as caul cuckoos and hymes).

If you need (or just want) more Between creatures beyond those presented in this book and Blight adventures, you can create them three ways.

1. Apply a Between simple template to an existing monster stat block. This is quick and simple, and is perfectly adequate for most encounters.

2. Convert an existing creature to the Between subtype using the guidelines presented here. This involves more effort and is better suited to major foes, such as creatures that command groups of lesser, Between minions (which can be converted quickly with the simple templates).

3. Create a wholly new Between creature from scratch, following the guidelines below. This is ideal for a powerful villain or recurring foe.

Between Creature Simple Templates

Although all life in Between is unique, some creatures (wolves, for example) are common to the normal world and Between. The following simple templates can be used to turn any creature that does not have the Between subtype into a Between creature. A creature given one of these templates counts as a Between creature for the purposes of spells, abilities, and magical items but it does not gain the Between subtype or the many benefits of having the Between subtype — it gains only those benefits specifically described in the simple template.

Larval Between

1. Increase Strength and Dexterity by +1.
2. Increase hit points by 1 Hit Die + Constitution modifier.
3. Gains darkvision 30 feet if it doesn't already have darkvision.
4. Gains resistance to damage from monmagical weapons.
5. Gains Dislocated trait (attacks against it have disadvantage unless the attacker has blindsight, truesight, or their equivalent).
6. Increase CR by +1.

Naiadic Between

1. Increase Strength and Constitution by +1, Dexterity by +2.
2. Increase hit points by 2 Hit Dice + (Constitution modifier ×2).
3. Gains darkvision 60 feet if it doesn't already have darkvision.
4. Gains resistance to damage from nonmagical weapons.
5. Gains Dislocated trait (attacks against it have disadvantage unless the attacker has blindsight, truesight, or their equivalent).
6. Gains proficiency in Dexterity saving throws.
7. Increase speed by +10 feet.
8. Increase CR by +2.

Adult Between

1. Increase Dexterity by +3; increase Strength, Constitution, and Intelligence by +1 each.

2. Increase hit points by 3 Hit Dice + (Constitution modifier ×3).
3. Gains superior darkvision.
4. Gains resistance to cold, force, and poison damage, and to damage from nonmagical weapons.
5. Gains Dislocated trait (attacks against it have disadvantage unless the attacker has blindsight, truesight, or their equivalent).
6. Gains proficiency in Dexterity and Constitution saving throws.
7. Gains Innate Spellcasting (save DC 15): 1/day each—*invisibility* (self only, duration 1 minute), *spider climb*.
8. Gains Magic Resistance (1/day, when it fails a saving throw, it can succeed instead).
9. Increase speed by +10 feet.
10. Increase CR by +3.

Elder Between

1. Increase Dexterity by +4; increase Intelligence by +2; increase Strength and Constitution by 1 each.
2. Increase hit points by 4 Hit Dice + (Constitution modifier ×4).
3. Gains superior darkvision and blindsight 30 feet.
4. Gains resistance to acid, cold, fire, force, lightning, and poison damage,

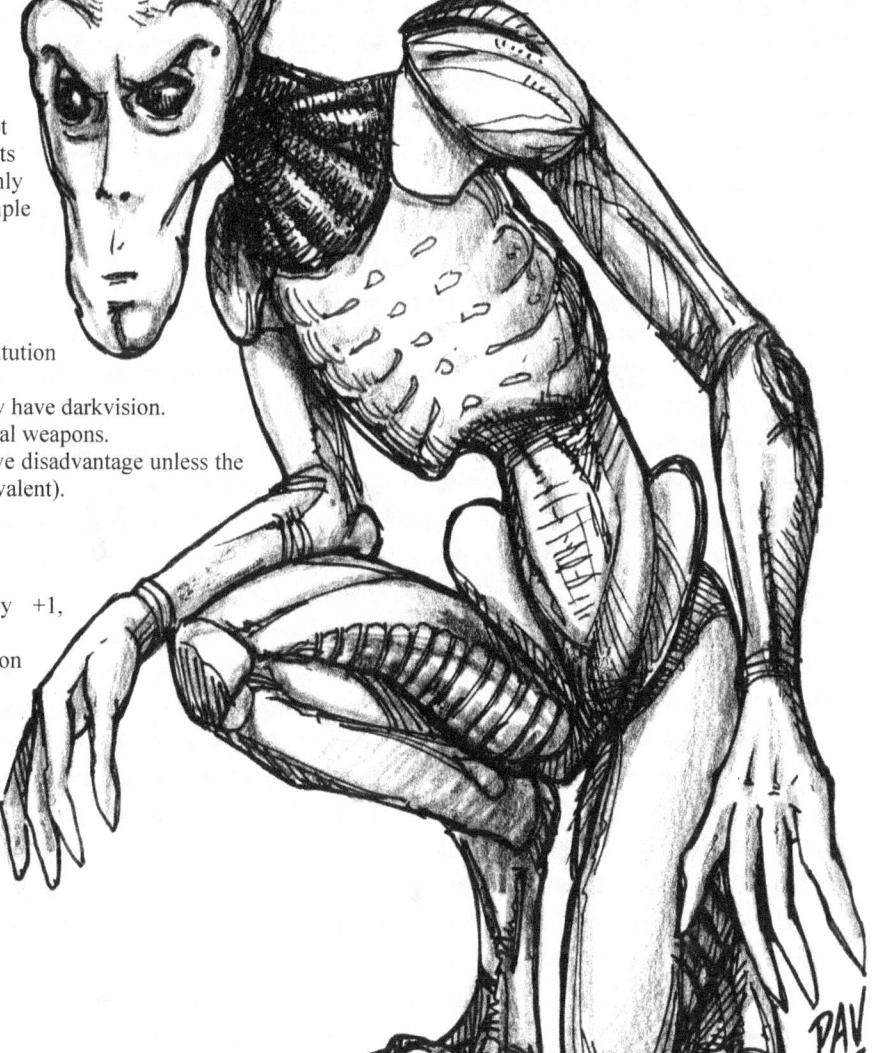

and to damage from nonmagical weapons.

5. Gains Dislocated trait (attacks against it have disadvantage unless the attacker has blindsight, truesight, or their equivalent).

6. Gains proficiency in Dexterity, Constitution, and Wisdom saving throws.

7. Gains Innate Spellcasting (save DC 16): 3/day each—*invisibility* (self only, duration 1 minute), *spider climb; 1/day each—blink, mirror image.*

8. Gains Magic Resistance (1/day, when it fails a saving throw, it can succeed instead).

9. Increase speed by +20 feet.

10. Increase CR by +4.

Ancient Between

1. Increase Dexterity by +5; increase Intelligence by +3; increase Strength and Constitution by 1 each.

2. Increase hit points by 5 Hit Dice + (Constitution modifier ×5).

3. Gains superior darkvision and blindsight 60 feet.

4. Gains resistance to all damage except radiant and bludgeoning, piercing, and slashing damage from nonmagical weapons.

5. Gains Dislocated trait (attacks against it have disadvantage unless the attacker has blindsight, truesight, or their equivalent).

6. Gains proficiency in all saving throws.

7. Gains Innate Spellcasting (save DC 17): 3/day each—*invisibility* (self only, duration 1 minute), *spider climb; 1/day each—blink, dimension door.*

8. Gains Magic Resistance (2/day, when it fails a saving throw, it can succeed instead).

9. Increase speed by +20 feet.

10. Increase CR by +5.

Converting an Existing Creature

Most Between creatures have the following abilities. (These are already included in the Between creature stat blocks presented in this book). Between creatures are highly varied, however, so it's not a hard-and-fast rule that every Between creature must have these traits or can't have others.

Between Age (BA). Many of a creature's statistics improve with the length of its exposure to Between. Because a Between creature can't die of old age, even normally short-lived creatures can become quite powerful through centuries of exposure. These increases are divided into five age categories, according to how long the creature has been exposed to Between: larval, naiadic (15+ years), adult (50+ years), elder (150+ years), and ancient (600+ years). At each age category, a Between creature gains the following cumulative benefits:

- +1 to its Dexterity score;

- +1 to one other ability score besides Dexterity;

- +1 Hit Die (added to its hit points, + its Constitution modifier, as usual)

- one feat (if feats are being used in your campaign) or proficiency in one type of saving throw.

Senses. A larval creature gains darkvision (30 feet) if it doesn't already have darkvision. The range increases to 60 feet at naiadic age and to 120 feet at adult. An elder creature gains blindsense (30 feet), and an ancient Between creature has blindsight (60 feet).

Damage Resistance. A naiadic creature gains resistance to damage from nonmagical weapons. An adult creature gains resistance to cold, force, and poison damage. An elder creature gains resistance to acid, fire, and lightning damage. An ancient creature gains resistance to necrotic, psychic, and thunder damage. All of these gains are cumulative, so an ancient Between creature has resistance to all but radiant damage and bludgeoning, piercing, and slashing damage from magical weapons.

Magic Resistance. An adult Between creature has Magic Resistance (1/day, when it fails a saving throw, it can choose to succeed instead). This increases to 2/day for ancient creatures.

Intelligence. If an animal's Intelligence score is increased above 2, it gains the ability to understand and speak Deep Speech.

Additional Abilities. Between creatures can have abilities that reflect their habitat, history, environment, and supernatural nature. Adding one such ability per age category is a good benchmark, but it's not a hard-and-fast rule. These abilities can be adapted from other monsters, drawn from spell-like abilities, or can be new abilities you create. These abilities should be thematically appropriate to the Between and to the creature's origin. Two new abilities that are especially suited to Between creatures are Dislocated and Distorted.

- *Dislocated.* The creature's form is made up of its memories, which shift and change. The creature is continually under the effect of a *blur spell (attacks against it are made with disadvantage unless the attacker has blindsight, truesight, or an equivalent).* The creature can suppress or reactivate this ability at will as a bonus action.

- *Distorted.* A distorted creature's internal anatomy varies from individual to individual and seldom makes any biological sense. Critical hits against the creature do a flat +1 damage but don't roll damage dice twice.

Challenge. After making all these changes, the creature's CR should be reevaluated from scratch. As a simpler alternative, just increase the creature's CR by +1 per Between age category. This will be close enough in most cases, unless the creature gained especially powerful attacks.

Create a New Creature

Creating a new Between creature is no different from creating any other creature, as described in the GM's rulebook. It's easiest if you start by choosing its age category and proceed from there, but do what you're most comfortable with.

Copyright Notice

Broken Creature

A broken creature is not born. Instead, cruel techniques of coercive persuasion applied over time systematically strip away its will until it unquestioningly accepts the instruction of a master. These techniques are taught only to high-ranking members of one of the guilds that specialize in breaking creatures, such as the Grand Society of Obedience and the Sisters of Bestial Discipline. These groups have created a considerable industry of breaking creatures and selling broken creatures as reliable-yet-docile servitors within the City-State of Castorhage.

Any living creature with Intelligence 1 or higher can be broken, with the exception of familiars and animal companions. A broken creature uses the base creature's stat blocks, with the following differences:

• Constitution increases by 2, Wisdom declines by 2.

• Has proficiency and advantage on Constitution saving throws.

• Dominated: A broken creature responds to its controller as if under the effect of a *dominate monster* spell that can't be dispelled or broken. There is no telepathic link; commands must be issued verbally, visually (hand signals), or aurally (whistle, drums, etc.). The creature never makes a saving throw to end the effect, even when it takes damage or is given a self-destructive command.

Copyright Notice
Author Alistair Rigg, based on material by Richard Pett.

Conjoined Creature

While there are many ways in which twins can be conjoined, this template assumes that one is a parasitic twin and fully dependent on the other. The parasitic twin emerges only from the waist up, is smaller than the base creature, and is completely under the base creature's control.

Any living humanoid and many beasts can become the basis for creating a conjoined creature. A conjoined creature uses the base creature's stat block, with the follosing differences:

• Challenge increases by 2.

• Constitution increases by 4.

• Has proficiency on Perception checks, or double proficiency if it already had proficiency.

• Has proficiency on Wisdom saving throws.

• Dual Mind (1/day): When the conjoined creature fails a saving throw against a mind-affecting effect, it can choose to succeed instead.

• Multiattack: The conjoined creature can make its basic attack twice. If it already has Multiattack, its number of attacks doubles. All extra attacks do half damage. Instead of making these extra attacks, the conjoined creature can instead cast a cantrip, search, or use an object as a bonus action.

Copyright Notice
Author Alistair Rigg, based on material by Richard Pett.

Nimbated Creature

A humanoid creature that becomes host to a nimb (see **Nimb**) is transformed into a nimbated creature. A nimbated creature uses the base creature's stat block, with the following differences:

• **Incorporeal Double.** A nimbated creature gains an incorporeal double of itself. The double behaves much like a *mirror image*, copying the original's movements exactly. It is not an illusion and is not automatically destroyed if hit, but is incorporeal (can move through gaps as small as 1 square inch without penalty; can move through solid objects and other creatures as if they were difficult terrain; takes 1d10 force damage if it is still inside something solid at the end of its turn). The double has the same defensive characteristics (AC, saving throws, etc.) as its original, but any damage done to it is applied against the temporary hit points (only) of the bonded nimb instead. When the bonded nimb has 0 temporary hit points, the double is destroyed. The bonded nimb can choose to retain its last temporary hit point and lose normal hit points instead, to preserve the double. If the double is destroyed, a new one can be activated as soon as the bonded nimb gains more temporary hit points. While the bonded nimb has 0 or 1 temporary hit point, it can be seen on the nimbated creature as a vague, subtle outline, similar to a heat haze.

• Parasitic Bond: An attached nimb reduces its host's Charisma by 1 each day, and the nimb gains 1d6 + 2 temporary hit points at the same time.

Copyright Notice
Author Alistair Rigg.

Appendix C: Hazards

Hazards

This appendix lists hazards that can be encountered in The Blight. Some of these can also be found in other areas, especially those with overflowing filth, rampant disease, or insidious Between influence.

Blight

This peculiar lichen is ubiquitous to the city of Castorhage. Reports of large infestations of it occur in the earliest city records, and it is from this constant presence that the city has obtained its nickname. It is a leafy foliose lichen with a dull gray coloring that is darker on the underside. Its drab coloration makes it difficult to see from distances greater than 10 feet in any conditions other than bright light; it's noticed with a successful DC 12 Wisdom (Perception) check.

Blight grows slowly except in total darkness, where it grows so rapidly it can cover hundreds of feet in only a few hours. Infestations of the lichen tend to pop up in the darkest of alleys or on heavily overcast or moonless nights. The dwarves of the Underneath warn of caverns where the stuff grows unchecked, forming drifts dozens of feet deep. Blight grows no more rapidly in bright light than normal lichen, but it isn't harmed by bright light.

Furthermore, some scholars speculate that the lichen might possess some form of intelligence. They base this on the fact that when options for growth exist toward and away from some living victim that the blight can grow on, it always grows toward the living victim.

Each 5-foot-square of blight has AC 5 and 16 (3d8) hit points. It is resistant to nonmagical bludgeoning and slashing damage, immune to piercing and psychic damage, and vulnerable to fire damage.

Blight is generally harmless to creatures that are aware of it, but its dense, rapid growth in darkness makes it very dangerous to a helpless creature. If a helpless creature (asleep, drunk, paralyzed, etc.) is in an area of total darkness that blight has access to, a thick, impervious layer of lichen can grow completely over the creature in 1d6 rounds. This causes no physical injury, but the creature is restrained and cut off from air; when its breath runs out, it begins suffocating. The creature can break free by using an action to make a successful DC 15 Strength (Athletics) or Dexterity (Acrobatics) check. An adjacent ally can free the trapped character with a Strength (Athletics) check, or by inflicting 15 slashing damage to the blight.

If a victim is slain by blight or if it grows over the corpse of a living creature, a truly remarkable quality of the growth is revealed. Whereas most surfaces that the lichen uses as a substrate are unharmed by its growth, the corpse of a living creature is absorbed in short order and will be completely gone within hours, leaving nothing behind but inorganic remnants such as belt buckles, swords and armor, gold fillings, etc. A Tiny or smaller creature is totally obliterated in 15 minutes; a Small creature disappears in 30 minutes, and a Medium creature in 1 hour. Large creatures will be completely absorbed in 4 hours, and Huge creatures in 9 hours. Gargantuan and Colossal creatures will be absorbed only if the blight is able to completely cover it. If so, the corpses are absorbed in 16 and 36 hours, respectively. A creature absorbed by blight cannot be returned from the dead by anything less powerful than *true resurrection*.

Derange

Derange is blamed for much of the unsavory behavior to be found in The Blight, or at least folk find it convenient to believe it to be the source.

Derange is a condition brought on when the tiny earwig spider lays its egg in the ear of a sleeping victim. The warmth of the victim's body causes the egg to hatch and the tiny earwig larva to burrow through the eardrum and inner ear into motor control centers in the victim's brain. Once the larva has nested in this area, it creates a small cyst and begins to draw nourishment from the hormones and chemical interactions within while bathing these centers with chemicals of its own. The result is that the victim's personality changes, his alignment randomly shifting each morning when he awakes (see table). The victim is still in control of his actions, but these actions reflect the priorities and methods subscribed to by this new alignment. At night, the victim often awakes in the midst of sleep with a return to his original alignment and a full and sickening awareness of the things he has been doing.

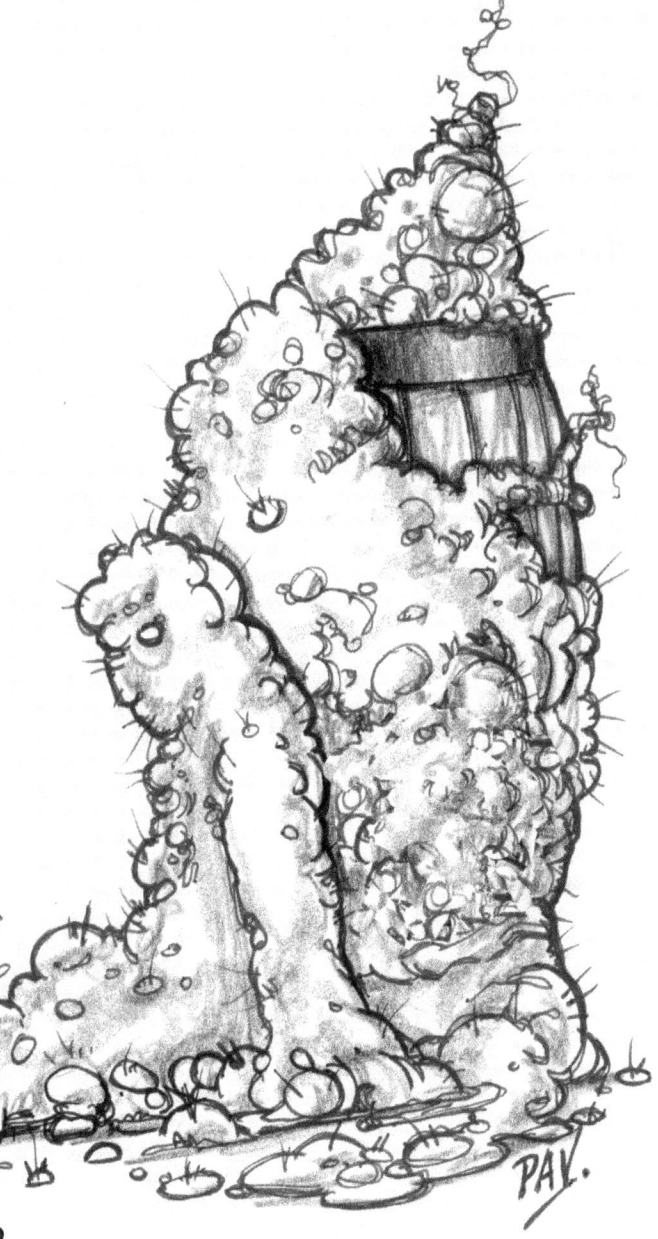

This condition can be removed with *lesser restoration or comparable* magic. Likewise, each morning upon awakening, the victim makes a DC 13 Wisdom saving throw to resist the alignment-altering effect and to function with normal alignment. After 1–3 weeks, the derange larva matures into an earwig spider and exits the victim to begin the next stage of its lifecycle. When this occurs, the victim must make a DC 8 Constitution saving throw. If it succeeds, the victim recovers fully (though there may be lasting repercussions from deeds done under different alignments; being under the influence of derange is not recognized as a legal defense before the Courts of Castorhage). If the saving throw fails, then the departing earwig spider ruptures an artery in the victim's skull as it crawls out of the victim's head; the victim bleeds to death internally in 2d4 rounds unless magical healing halts the bleeding before then.

1d10	Alignment Shifts To
1	Lawful good
2	Neutral good
3	Chaotic good
4	Lawful neutral
5	Neutral
6	Chaotic neutral
7	Lawful evil
8	Neutral evil
9	Chaotic evil
10	Same as previous day

Dislocating Larvae

These tiny green larvae resemble tadpoles no larger than a pinhead, but they can spawn in sufficient numbers in small pools of stagnant water to give it a greenish tint. A full-grown dislocating larva resembles a green hair 2 or 3 inches long.

When ingested, the larvae colonize the stomach of the victim, where they begin reproducing within 1d6 hours in the digestive tract. As they reach maturity, they feed on the surrounding tissue and migrate on to nearby organs as they lay thousands of eggs. These hatch into even more larvae, which continue the colonization. The pain causes terrible convulsions in the victim that can be forceful enough to dislocate joints.

The victim of a dislocating larvae infestation loses 1d4 points from Constitution every day. When the victim's Constitution has dropped to half or less of its starting value, the victim is stunned by pain, unable to do anything but writhe spasmodically. When the victim's Constitution drops to 4 or lower, the victim is incapacitated instead of stunned, and it feels an overpowering need to seek out a body of stagnant water and drown in it (so the larvae colony in the body can survive instead of dying with the host).

Any magic that cures diseases, kills all the larvae and eggs in the victim. Lost Constitution points don't recover normally but can be restored with magic.

Second-Head Fluke

This dreaded microscopic parasite is relatively common in the Lyme River, and many fishermen have caught the sickness after accidentally swallowing Lyme water. It can also be spread by physical contact with those already afflicted.

This foul sickness manifests as a large, swollen tumor on the victim's shoulder that, over a period of 4–6 days, grows into a second, cankerous head. This head is most horrible to look upon, consisting of disfigured and distorted features, random tufts of hair, misplaced teeth, and dark patches of melanoma. Despite its obvious disease origin, this head-like growth uncannily resembles the victim, even in its distorted and horrifying state.

Once a case of second-head fluke is contracted, madness and physical decline are sure to follow. After the second head fully manifests, the victim must make a successful DC 13 Wisdom saving throw each day or lose 1d3 points of Wisdom. In addition, each day there is a 10% chance that the victim loses 1 point of Constitution from the cancerous disease.

When the victim's Wisdom drops to half or less of its starting value, the second-head fluke begins having more pronounced effects. The pseudo-head utters nonsensical vocal sounds as if trying to talk, and the head flops about spasmodically at random times. In close quarters, the head tends to flop toward nearby creatures, and anyone who comes in contact with it or the host must make a successful DC 13 Constitution saving throw or contract a second-head fluke infestation of their own.

Second-head fluke is notoriously difficult to cure.

- Stage 1: Before the pseudo-head has grown, *lesser restoration* or comparable magic reverses the growth and cures the victim completely.

- Stage 2: Once the pseudo-head has fully formed, the disease can be cured by removing the head surgically, then casting *lesser restoration*. The patient takes 2d6 slashing damage, and the surgeon must make a DC 15 Wisdom (Medicine) check; only someone with proficiency in Medicine can even attempt the procedure. Whether the operation succeeded won't be known until six days later; if a new, cancerous head doesn't grow, then the surgery succeeded.

- Stage 3: Once the victim's Wisdom score is reduced to half or less of its starting value, the disease can be cured only with surgery (as above) and *greater restoration* or comparable magic. This casting of *greater restoration* doesn't restore lost Wisdom points, but a subsequent casting does. The target dies if this reduces its Intelligence or Wisdom to 0. Otherwise, the reduction lasts until the target finishes a short or long rest.

Lost Wisdom and Constitution points don't recover normally but can be restored with magic.

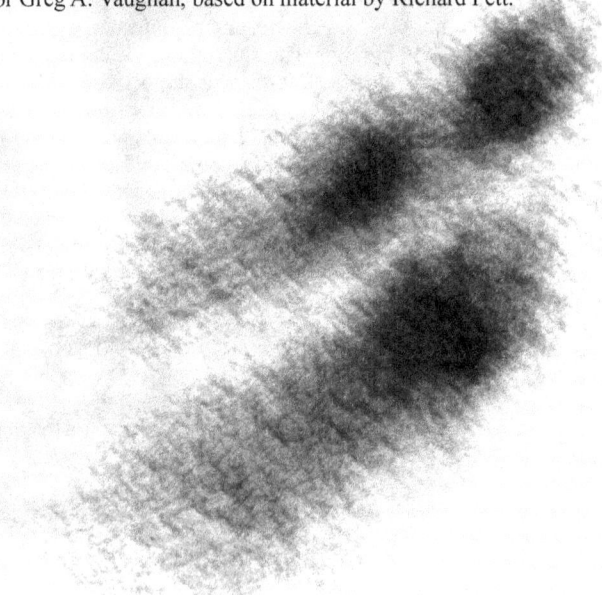

91

Appendix D:

Monsters by Type, CR, and Terrain

Monsters by Type

Aberration

Between Dream, Between-cat, Caul Cuckoo, Caul Cuckoo Syre, Chymic Spider, Crathog, Gloam, Herald at the Threshold, Hyme, Mantis-thing, Mockingbeast, Naga, Blight, Nightmare Choir, Nimb, Protyugh, Satyrmouther, Spiboleth, Spite-waif, Squarpy, Stircatrice, Wallow-whale, Woerm

Beast

Blight Albatross, Blight-bull, Blight Cockerel, Canary, Gable Spider, Great Canal Python, Hooded Raven, Lyme Angler, Pit Mastiff, Sough-Eel, Terrier

Construct

Fleshgine (Dungier's Buggy, Hobbreth's Pump, Macabre Lift), Lesser Flesh Golem, Scrimshaw Gargoyle

Elemental

Ragefire Elemental

Fey

Moon Angel

Humanoid

Lyme Walrus, Night-Slug Burglar

Monstrosity

Blight Ape, Blight Monkey, Blindingcrow, Blindingcrow Swarm, Bloody Flux (living disease), BookTown Panther, Festering Lyme Rat, Gable Hate-owl, Giant Rat of Shabbis, Hollow and Broken Hills Crocodile, Hydra-Hag, Larva Horde, Skulking Manticore, Slithering Bulette, Stegocentroper

Plant

Body Snatcher, Slithering Tangle

Undead

Bileborn, Bog Lantern, Gravid Ghoul

Monsters by Challenge Rating

0

Blight Cockerel, Canary, Hooded Raven, Terrier

1/8

Caul Cuckoo Syre, Blight Albatross, Blight Ape, Blight-bull, Blight Monkey, Blindingcrow

1/4

Festering Lyme Rat, Gable Spider (tiny)

1/2

Gable Hate-Owl, Gable Spider (small), Night-Slug Burglar, Pit Mastiff

1

Between Dream, Bloody Flux, Blindingcrow Swarm, Ragefire Elemental (tiny), Stircatrice, Woerm

2

Blight Naga, Gable Spider (medium), Hyme, Nimb, Ragefire Elemental (small)

3

Between-cat, Chymic Spider, Dungier's Buggy, Gravid Ghoul, Lesser Flesh Golem, Lyme Angler, Macabre Lift, Ragefire Elemental (medium), Satyrmouther, Scrimshaw Gargoyle, Spite-waif

4

BookTown Panther, Gable Spider (large), Giant Rat of Shabbis, Lyme Walrus

5

Bog Lantern, Caul Cuckoo, Great Canal Python, Moon Angel, Ragefire Elemental (large), Skulking Manticore, Sough-Eel

6

Bileborn, Mantis-thing, Slithering Bulette, Spiboleth

7

Protyugh

8

Crathog, Hydra-Hag, Larva Horde, Mockingbeast, Ragefire Elemental (huge), Slithering Tangle

9

Hollow and Broken Hills Crocodile, Stegocentroper

10

Squarpy

11

Gloam, Ragefire Elemental (gargantuan)

12

Hobbreth's Pump, Wallow-whale

13

Nightmare Choir

14

Body Snatcher, Herald at the Threshold

Monsters by Terrain

Abyss

Larva Horde; + Any

Any

Between Dream, Larva Horde, Nimb, Mockingbeast, Herald at the Threshold

Any Land

Between-cat, Bileborn, Blight Cockerel, Caul Cuckoo, Caul Cuckoo Syre, Gravid Ghoul, Hooded Raven, Lesser Flesh Golem, Mantis-thing, Nightmare Choir, Ragefire Elemental, Spite-waif, Terrier; + Any

Arctic

+ Any Land, + Any

Between

Between Dream, Between-cat, Caul Cuckoo, Caul Cuckoo Syre, Gloam, Herald at the Threshold, Hyme, Mantis-thing, Mockingbeast, Nightmare Choir, Nimb, Spiboleth, Spite-waif, Wallow-whale

Blight

Bileborn, Blight Ape, Blight Cockerel, Blight Monkey, Blight Naga, Bloody Flux, Body Snatcher, BookTown Panther, Chymic Spider, Dungier's Buggy, Festering Lyme Rat, Gable, Hate-owl, Gable Spider, Giant Rat of Shabbis, Great Canal Python, Hobbreth's Pump, Hollow and Broken Hills Crocodile, Hooded Raven, Hydra-Hag, Macabre Lift, Protyugh, Satyrmouther, Scrimshaw Gargoyle, Skulking Manticore, Slithering Bulette, Slithering Tangle, Stegocentroper, Stircatrice; + Any Land, + Any

Coast

Blight Albatross, Crathog, Lyme Walrus, Spiboleth; + Any Land, + Any

Desert

+ Any Land, +Any

Forest

Canary; + Any Land, + Any

Hills

+ Any Land, + Any

Mountains

+ Any Land, + Any

Non-arctic Land

Blindingcrow, Blindingcrow Swarm, Skulking Manticore; + Any Land, + Any

Plains

Hyme, Stircatrice; + Any Land, + Any

Sea

Lyme Angler, Hollow and Broken Hills Crocodile, Moon Angel, Sough-eel, Spiboleth, Squarpy, Wallow-whales + Any

Swamp

Bog Lantern, Hollow and Broken Hills Crocodile, Hyme, Slithering Tangle; + Any Land, + Any

Underground

Body Snatcher, Protyugh, Satyrmouther, Slithering Bulette, Stegocentroper, Woerm; + Any

Urban

Blight Ape, Blight-bull, Blight Monkey, Blight Naga, Bloody Flux, BookTown Panther, Chymic Spider, Dungier's Buggy, Festering Lyme Rat, Gable Hate-owl, Gable Spider, Giant Rat, of Shabbis, Gloam, Hobbreth's Pump, Hydra-Hag, Macabre Lift, Night-Slug Burglar, Pit Mastiff, Scrimshaw Gargoyle; + Any Land, + Any

Urban Waterway

Great Canal Python; + Any